Anythi

Sophie McKenzie is the Richard & Judy selected author of psychological thriller *Close My Eyes* and *Sunday Times* bestseller *Trust In Me*. An author of over thirty titles, Sophie lives in London and has worked as a journalist, editor and creative writing tutor. Her many teen thrillers include the best-selling, multi-award-winning *Girl, Missing*.

ANYTHING FOR YOU

SOPHIE McKENZIE

1O CANELO

First published in the United Kingdom in 2025 by

Canelo
Unit 9, 5th Floor
Cargo Works, 1–2 Hatfields
London SE1 9PG
United Kingdom

A CIP catalogue record for this book is available from the British Library.

Print ISBN 978 1 83598 024 8
Ebook ISBN 978 1 83598 025 5

Look for more great books at www.canelo.co

Printed and bound in Great Britain by Clays Ltd, Elcograf S.p.A.

1

For Susie

PROLOGUE

The expression registers shock, then fear. A hoarse gasp, then a slump to the floor. There's nothing in those eyes now, but they are still open. Still staring.

Blood pools on the ground, gleaming scarlet in the overhead light.

Somewhere nearby a phone rings.

The red creeps closer. The figure standing over it steps out of the way. It's a small movement suggesting calm, but inside their feelings crash and tumble like waves.

They stare at the body on the ground, frantically trying to understand what they've done.

Killer.

As the word sinks deep inside them, a single thought rises, quiet but insistent:

She must never know.

ONE

My client meeting in Muswell Hill ends early – when it comes to face-to-face contact, I'm well aware that Pepper is the company's star as well as its owner; I'm only ever a slightly disappointing substitute. Relieved that I'm done – and that the contract I took with me is at least signed – I hurry back to my car. The rain, which was a soft drizzle when I went indoors, is now building. I just get inside before a relentless downpour begins, drumming violently on the roof and bonnet.

I wipe a damp strand of hair off my cheek and check the time. Almost three p.m. Pepper told me not to bother coming back into work, which gives me some free time I wasn't expecting. Lola will be finishing school in just over fifteen minutes. It's Tuesday so there's no drama or art club, and she said nothing about going to Maisie's for one of their regular homework sessions. I smile to myself. I'm going to surprise her by picking her up from sixth form. Maybe we'll even get tea and cake somewhere on the way home, then curl up with a romcom. We've got the house to ourselves tonight; Seb is away on a business trip, while Michael – my ex and the kids' dad – is taking Josh to a football match.

The windows are starting to steam, so I open the one next to me a crack. I breathe in the sliver of damp, cold air, then set off. Lola has been working so hard recently, trying to keep up her across-the-board A★ grades *and* fulfil all her extracurricular projects and commitments on top. It will be brilliant to have a special mum-and-daughter evening, just like we used to when she was little. And good for her to take a break and enjoy herself.

Preoccupied with thoughts of the treat I'm going to give Lola, I find myself driving down a school street I'd forgotten about, crossing the invisible line in the road that means a certain fine at this time of day. Damn, Seb will be annoyed when the letter comes; he's always telling me to check the route before setting off.

I carry on, driving more slowly to make sure I double check before taking any more turns. The traffic is heavy all the way to Archway and, by the time I reach Lola's school, the pavement is already teeming with teenagers. I park and get out, looking around for Lola. The sixth formers here are allowed to wear their own clothes and, as I make my way through the throng, I'm struck by how alike they all look in their informal uniform of prairie dresses and trainers or wide-leg trousers and clumpy boots.

The rain has stopped but the wind has picked up, carrying with it a distinctly wintry chill. I shiver, tugging my jacket around me as the crowd momentarily thins out. *There.* At last, I spot the custard yellow of Lola's coat about thirty metres up ahead. She's with a group, chatting away.

'Lola!' I shout, but she doesn't hear me over all the noise.

I hurry towards her. Several girls in her group peel off and cross the road, giving me a better view of Lola herself. God, she looks tiny next to her peers, not just shorter than the rest, but slight and fragile looking too, her delicate hands gesturing as she speaks, her fair hair fluttering in the breeze. I'm about to call her name again, when she gives a half-wave to the others, then turns and speeds away.

Where is she going? Most of the sixth formers are streaming along the main road towards the tube, but Lola walks in the opposite direction, then takes the first turning on the right. Head down so I don't get spotted and held up by her friends, I speed after her. By the time I reach the turning, the sun has come out and Lola is already halfway up the hilly street ahead. She stops beside a red sports car, then steps back, hoisting her bag over her shoulder. Before I can call out to her, the driver door opens and a man with grey hair curling over the collar of his leather jacket eases himself out.

I stare, my breath catching in my throat. Who on earth is that? I can only see him from behind, but he is tall and lean and – from the hair – definitely middle-aged. My jaw falls open as he pulls Lola into a hug, then tilts her face to his and proceeds to give her a full-on snog. I freeze, my heart pounding.

Is this one of Lola's teachers? There's certainly something familiar about him. I stare at that silver, shoulder-length hair. The tail of a crumpled orange shirt is visible beneath the jacket and his faded jeans are rolled to the ankle. Despite the chill in the air, his feet appear to be bare and in sandals.

My stomach churns. Still kissing, the man lifts Lola off her feet – he must be a foot taller than her. He spins her round, planting her back on the pavement and lifting her yellow coat to grope her bum. *Ugh.*

Fury rises inside me. I'm about to stride forward, up the hill, and demand to know who this man is and what on earth he thinks he's doing with my teenage daughter. And then he draws back and the fading daylight catches his lined face as he smiles and ushers Lola towards the car. And even though I'm still at the other end of the road, I realise I know exactly who he is.

My hand flies to my mouth. Memories that I thought I had tamped down forever rush like poison through my veins: his face leering over mine; his cruel laugh, his taunting voice, the pain and the shame of his touch.

The man with Lola is Brendan Zeno, a once successful musician who Michael, Pepper and I were at university with, back when his name was still Brendan Murphy.

The worst person I've ever known.

Bile rises, filling my guts. For a moment, I think I'm going to be sick. I force the memories away as, up ahead, Lola and Brendan get into his car and zoom away.

I'm left on the pavement, my head reeling. What is Lola doing with him?

How did they even meet?

I hurry back to my car, my mind in freefall. I can't make sense of what I've seen. All I know is that I *have* to get Lola away from that man. But how? I heard on the grapevine Brendan now lives in a big house in Hampstead, bought, presumably, with the royalties from his late Nineties hit single, but I have no idea of his exact address. Sixth formers are still swarming the pavement, but I barely notice them. My thoughts tumble over each other. As I reach my car, my phone pings. I glance, distracted, at the screen. The text is from Lola:

Going to Maisie's to do homework, save me sum dinner ta x

I'm almost sick again. Lola has *never* lied to me. Unless… A fresh and horrific thought grips me. She's been going to Maisie's to do her homework three times a week since half term. Suppose she lied about *all* of those times? Does that mean she's been seeing Brendan for over a month? No. It's inconceivable.

I scroll to Lola's number, then hesitate. If I call her and tell her to come straight home, she'll ask why. And this is not a conversation we can have over the phone. Instead, I send a text:

> please come home straight away, it's
> urgent! xx

As I start driving home, memories surge up again. Shards of fear and pain I have spent most of my life keeping wrapped up are poking through, sharp and fierce.

–

I knew of Brendan months before I actually met him – he was the insanely charismatic singer with Baby Tumble, a band formed at my uni by a group of older students, during my first term. Baby Tumble would go on to have massive, if short-lived, success in the charts over the next few years but, back then, it was *our* band, and Brendan was our hero. Michael, in particular adored him. He talked about him so often on our early dates that November, I even wondered if he might be gay. Brendan was older than we were, in his final year, and with his sights set firmly on a recording contract.

In our second term, Michael and I joined an indie band music appreciation group – mostly an excuse to drink a ridiculous number of cheap student union beers. Brendan was often present at the meetings, holding court in the centre of the room, while Michael and I snuck admiring glances from afar. I soon got bored of the group, and made excuses to avoid it, but Michael kept going – and quickly became good friends with Brendan. He introduced us a few weeks later, at a St Patrick's Day gig. As soon as those bright blue eyes locked onto mine, I felt the full force of Brendan's personality. I found him – though I hate to admit it now – incredibly sexy, with his dark, messy hair, his peacenik T-shirts and his laidback lack of concern for what anyone thought of him. I was a small-town girl who desperately wanted to be cool – and Brendan *oozed* cool.

I don't know why Michael never noticed that Brendan liked to flirt with me. Perhaps because, in his honourable way, he couldn't conceive that Brendan would take things any further. More likely because, as Pepper, who never really let herself get drawn into Brendan's orbit acerbically observed, Brendan flirted with everyone. Which is true, he did, but he took things further with me. He called me Angelface behind Michael's back and let his eyes linger on my lips just a few seconds longer than felt appropriate. He never did anything boorish or aggressive. Not then. But he unsettled me. Did he really like me? Or was he just being friendly? Even at the time I felt ashamed that, happy though I was with smart, intense Michael, it was Brendan who I secretly fantasised about making love to; Brendan whose attention I desperately craved.

Looking back, I can't believe I was so naïve. All those lingering looks, all those small, hidden connections he made with me when Michael's back was turned, all those signs that he thought I was special… they weren't signals that Brendan was genuinely interested in me.

They were him grooming me. Setting me up for that terrible June night, when everything changed for me, forever.

I have worked so hard to give my own daughter more confidence than I had at her age. The confidence to spot and avoid abusers like Brendan. And here, with my own eyes, is terrible proof that I've failed.

Arriving back at home, I check my phone. Lola hasn't replied. I text her again.

> Please come home right away, its urgent!

But Lola doesn't respond.

TWO

An hour has passed since I got home and the light is fading from the day. I am still waiting for Lola, my stomach churning with anxiety. I go up to her room. I don't know exactly what I'm looking for, something that might provide an answer to the questions swarming my head. How did she and Brendan meet? How long have they been seeing each other? How serious is their relationship?

I pace around the room, peering into drawers and burrowing into the piles of clothes liberally scattered across the carpet. What does Lola see in him, for goodness' sake? Obviously, she has no idea about what he did to me all those years ago. But surely his behaviour, his *manner*, must indicate the kind of person he is?

You didn't spot it, says the voice in my head. *And Brendan's had nearly thirty years since then to hone his manipulation skills.*

I shove these thoughts aside and keep looking for information about their relationship. It's stupid, of course; everything will be on her phone. I hate myself as I turn to the mess of her wardrobe and methodically reach to the back of each untidy shelf. At least she's unlikely to notice I've been here. I stride over to her desk and lift up the books and papers there. Nothing. The overflowing bin beside the desk catches my eye. A letter from Lola's school pokes out of the top, I recognise the headed paper.

I snatch the letter out. It's actually addressed to me, from her pastoral tutor Mrs Butler, and states that not only has Lola dropped out of all her extracurricular activities, but she's missed handing in her last three A level assignments. Her academic tutors, one line reads ominously, are 'concerned'.

So much for all her homework evenings at Maisie's.

I sink onto Lola's bed. Despite the mess of her room, Lola has always been organised when it comes to schoolwork. Organised and successful, achieving top marks in every subject, never showing much interest in boys, and – unlike some of her friends – not ground down by mental-health issues. She has never, ever fallen behind like this.

It must be Brendan's doing. It's not that he'll want her to fail, he just won't care either way. The same thing happened to me at uni, after that terrible night at the party; it took me most of the following academic year to get my own grades back on track.

The front door opens and shuts. My stomach gives a lurch and I hurry downstairs. Lola is on tiptoe, straining to place her yellow coat on the already cluttered coat stand. As I reach the hall, she glances sideways at me, frowning.

'Why all the calls and texts?' she demands. 'Is something wrong?'

'Did you have a good time with "Maisie"?' I ask, unable to keep the edge out of my voice.

Lola shrugs, kicking off her boots and shoving them towards the general mess of shoes under the coat stand.

'Lola?'

'What do you want, Mum?' She turns, a weary pleading look in her eye. 'I came home like you asked, so...?'

My stomach twists into a knot. 'We need to talk,' I say, trying to keep my voice steady. 'I need to understand what's… why you've been lying to me about going to Maisie's… What you've really been doing…'

Lola's eyes widen, her voice suddenly defensive. 'What are you talk—?'

'I— I was emptying your bin upstairs and I saw the letter from school which you were supposed to give me,' I say. 'Mrs Butler says you've been missing homework assignments. And you've dropped all your extra-curricular activities. That's not like you.'

'Are you sure you know what's "like me" anymore?' Lola raises her eyebrows. 'Anyway, I *did* do the homework. Mrs Butler got me confused with someone else. *That's* why I didn't give you the letter. There wasn't any point.'

She's lying. Again. I'm sure of it.

'Really? So, where've you been this afternoon?'

'With Maisie, like I said.' She looks away.

'That's not true,' I say, as evenly as I can. 'I saw you earlier when you left school. I— I finished work early and came to meet you so we could maybe go for tea somewhere.' Lola meets my gaze; I can't read her expression. 'I *saw* you with… with Brendan Zeno.'

Lola doesn't flinch. 'Okay,' she says.

'You looked… it seemed like the two of you…' I can't bring myself to say it.

'We're together,' she says matter-of-factly. She shakes her head. 'We didn't want to say anything because I knew how you'd react. But loads of couples have big age gaps, it's really not that big a deal.'

The knot in my stomach tightens. An expression of contented coupledom was the last thing I expected. 'How long has this thing between the two of you been going on?'

'A few weeks. He came up to me at Camden Market, during half term.'

Well, that explains loss of interest in schoolwork over the past month.

'He said I looked like someone he once knew, and of course it came out I was your daughter.' I grimace – Brendan isn't the first person to make the comparison. Lola laughs to herself, as if reliving the memory. 'He introduced himself, though I recognised him anyway from that old song he did. And then he said how he was an old friend of yours and Dad's from uni and I said that I vaguely remembered Dad mentioning him.' She shrugs. 'We went for a drink and… here we are.'

'Well, we need to talk about wherever that is, because I'm not *at all* okay about you seeing him.'

'Yeah?' Lola frowns.

'It's not just that he's too old for you. He's… he's not a nice person.'

'Who says?' Lola strides away from me, across the hall. 'You and Dad knew him for, like, five minutes a million years ago.' She reaches the stairs and starts climbing.

'Are you having sex?' I ask.

Lola stops halfway up the stairs, turning to look down at me. There's a weary contempt in her eyes that I've never seen before. 'Mum, there's only one thing you need to know,' she says. 'Brendan and I are happy.'

It's like a slap to my face. 'I'm sure *he's* happy,' I persist, 'but he's abusive and dangerous. Brendan *manipulates* people, Lola. He always has done.' I hesitate, hurrying up the stairs to where she is standing. I want to tell her everything, the whole story, but it's been buried so deep, for so long, that feels impossible. 'He's violent, too. Violent and cruel.' I take a deep breath. 'I knew one girl he basically raped.'

'Those were just rumours, Mum.' Lola rolls her eyes. 'Brendan told me people said horrible things about him back in the day because he was so successful. He's already admitted to me that he took advantage of a few groupies at the time and he regrets that now. But it wasn't rape; they *consented*.' She pauses. 'Anyway, he's changed since then. He doesn't do drugs anymore, doesn't even drink that much.'

'Lola, *listen*.' I clench my fists. 'It wasn't a groupie. I *knew* the girl he attacked. I knew her *well*. It happened long before he was a pop star. They were friends and he led her on, but when she said "no" and tried to get away from him, he raped her.'

'So why isn't he in prison?' Lola demands. 'Did that girl even go to the police?'

'No, she didn't tell… I… she was ashamed.' My mind whirls. What can I say to make Lola believe me? 'You're not safe, Lola. Brendan will get violent. It's only a matter of time.'

'That's ridiculous,' Lola scoffs. 'That girl you knew, she must have made it up.'

'It was me.' The words shoot out of me.

The air around us seems to thicken. Lola blinks, clearly shocked.

'I never told anyone because I was with your dad at the time and I didn't want him to find ou— look that doesn't matter. All that matters is you understand what an evil person Brendan really is.'

My heart thuds painfully as Lola looks deep into my eyes. She shakes her head.

'Mum, I get that you're upset,' she says gently, 'but you can't go around making stuff up like this.'

I recoil as if she's slapped me. 'I don't—'

'First you say he raped your "friend", then it's *you*.' Lola sighs. 'You'd say anything to make me stop seeing him.'

'No, I—'

'Listen.' Lola cuts across me. 'Maybe for whatever reason you didn't like Brendan back in the day; and maybe he *wasn't* the nicest person back then. He's told me how ruthless and ambitious he was, but he's different now.'

'That's not—'

'And maybe you don't like there being a big age difference, but that's just a number.'

'For goodness' sake, Lola, you don't understand.'

'*You're* the one who doesn't understand,' Lola says impatiently. 'Brendan loves me and I love him. And there isn't anything anyone can do about it.'

THREE

I leave Lola in her bedroom and make my way down to the kitchen. I sit, feeling numb, staring at the chair where Lola did up her Doc Martens this morning, a few hours and an eternity ago. Josh races in from school, shouting 'Hiya!' from the hall. I just about rouse myself to call back, then slump back into my chair, my mind running in wild circles.

Memories poke at me: it was June. Swelteringly hot. Michael and I were invited to an end of year party. Some third years' house share. I remember everyone pouring into the back garden, loud music, a group of guys I didn't know snorting cocaine off a patio table. I wore a short blue dress with thin straps that kept falling off my shoulder. Brendan stared at me when I arrived, unable to hide the lust in his eyes. Michael was oblivious. He'd started working for the student newspaper that term and someone at the party knew someone who could get us into an underground gig across town. Michael was desperate to go but I didn't fancy the trek, so I said I'd stay at the party, then go back to our halls and meet up again the next day. Michael hesitated, but Brendan clapped him on the back, telling him not to worry, that he would make sure none of his friends hassled me.

The irony of that.

I knew, as soon as Michael left, that something would happen with Brendan. Every time I looked up, he was watching me, sending shivers of anticipation down my spine.

The doorbell rings, making me jump and forcing me out of my reverie. It's six thirty already. How did that happen?

Michael stands on the step outside. Nearly thirty years older than the Michael in my memory. For a few seconds I'm thrown. Then I remember. Of course. It's Tuesday night. He's here to take Josh to watch Arsenal play at the Emirates.

'Hi, Ali.' He rubs his high forehead, back to where the close shave of his hair begins. 'Hi.' I step back to let him in.

We don't touch each other. It's been an unwritten rule of our relationship since we divorced four years ago.

'Josh!' Michael calls up the stairs.

'Coming!' Josh yells back.

Michael raises an eyebrow at me. 'How's everything?'

'Fine,' I say. Insofar as I'd thought about Michael at all, I'd imagined I'd tell him about Lola and Brendan at the first opportunity. After all, he is Lola's dad. But now he's here, right in front of me, I can't bring myself to do it. It's partly the past; Michael has no idea what happened with me and Brendan – term ended soon after the party and Brendan quickly disappeared out of our lives forever, dropping all his old friends. Michael was angry at first, then grew resigned. He kept tabs on Brendan's career, but never tried to reconnect, which of course made it easy for me to keep my dark secret.

But it's not just my history with Brendan that I don't want Michael to know about. If he were to find out Lola

16

has been with *anyone* middle-aged, he'd explode. And his rage isn't going to help resolve this situation. Better I try talking to Lola again, before bringing her dad into it.

We stand, slightly awkwardly, in the doorway. Michael clears his throat. 'Interesting development at work,' he says. 'I'm doing a thing on high-level hackers. There's this one guy, you wouldn't believe the firewalls he can get through.'

'Really?'

'And he showed me how easy it is to hack a phone remotely too. It just takes a bit of proprietary soft—'

'Mum, where's my Arsenal scarf?' Josh thunders down the stairs.

'Taking a wild guess I'd say the coat stand,' I call back.

Michael rolls his eyes sympathetically at me.

'This is all Lola's stuff,' Josh grumbles, rummaging through the many jackets and coats crammed onto the stand.

'Are you sure everything's okay, Ali? Seb behaving himself?' Michael fixes me with his steel grey eyes and that same combination of insistence and impatience from when we first met. A world apart from Brendan's lanky charm. What was it Pepper said once? That when they stood next to each other, Michael looked like a tensed thumb.

'I told you,' I say. 'Everything's fine.'

Michael grunts, clearly unconvinced. He's never said as much, but I've always had the impression that he doesn't like the fact that Seb moved in here this spring, soon after his mother died, and when we'd been dating less than a year.

'That's a lot for the kids to deal with,' he'd muttered at the time.

He wasn't wrong of course, but neither Josh nor Lola have ever seemed as bothered by Seb's presence in the house as he does.

Josh appears beside me, his red-and-white scarf in his hand and a backpack slung over his shoulder. 'Bye, Mum!' He leans down – at sixteen he's a good two inches taller than me now – and pecks me on the cheek.

'Have you got everything?'

Josh nods. 'Hey, son,' Michael beams. 'Good to go?'

Seconds later they have left the house. I stare after them as they disappear along the road.

I *have* to find a way to make Lola end this relationship – if that's what it is – before she gets too sucked in. Assuming she isn't too sucked in already. Assuming Brendan isn't already hurting or abusing her. Oh, God, how can this have happened? She may only be just eighteen, but Lola is poised and accomplished and self-assured. At that age I was easy prey, my low self-esteem seeded by my own pushy, critical mother – the very opposite of the mother I have tried to be.

I go to her bedroom to try talking again, but Lola refuses to engage, jamming her headphones over her ears. All that happens is that I miss Seb ringing from his conference in New York. Too frazzled to call back, I text him good night, then go to bed, falling into a troubled sleep.

What on earth can I do to make Lola see sense?

–

I wake up the next morning – and the answer, as so often happens after sleep, is there: clear and simple and obvious.

If Lola won't listen to reason, I'm going to have to confront Brendan myself.

The thought makes me feel sick, but I can't see another option.

I decide to go to work and tell Pepper everything – along with the fact that I need some time off this morning in order to track Brendan down. Unsurprisingly, my head is not on the time, and it's past nine when my bus deposits me just past Kentish Town underground station.

Clutching my reusable mug of coffee, I make my way past the estate agents on the ground floor of our brick, terraced building and open the front door that leads up the rickety stairs to the businesses and flats above. I reach the bright orange sign next to our first-floor office: *Hot Pepper PR*, and open the door. Sunlight is streaming in through the windows that run along the side of the open-plan room. I notice the smears on the glass and – even in the midst of my emotional turmoil – make a mental note to book the window cleaner. Our PA, Hamish, is the only one in. He looks up from his desk – a tidy oasis in the midst of the general clutter.

'Hey Alison,' he drawls. 'Did you see *Fashion Victim* last night? That look on Buster's face when Charmain came out of the cake!' He chuckles.

I feign a grin. 'Sadly, I missed it.'

He rolls his eyes. 'Your loss.' Hamish is only in his mid-thirties, but dresses older, in a stylish-hipster-meets-1950s-businessman kind of way. Most days he turns up to work in a formal pinstripe three-piece suit softened by the addition of some flamboyant accessory attached. Today he's wearing a silver earring in the shape of a pirate's sword. It's a slightly eccentric look, but he gets away with it.

'Where's Pepper this morning?' I ask.

'Pitching for a new contract,' Hamish says. 'I'm inputting data for November accounts but mostly making coffee, want one?'

I hold up my cup. 'Thanks, I'm good.'

Hamish pushes himself up from his desk and lopes over to the kitchenette. We work in a small, open-plan room with a glass-walled meeting room in the middle that Pepper uses as a private office. There's a microwave, sink and cupboards in the corner and three desks set out near the entrance. Mine has the best position, beside the window that overlooks the street below. Hamish has the desk opposite, while the third is used by any one of the roster of writers and PR execs Pepper brings in ad hoc to work on specific campaigns.

I clear the papers off my desk and settle down to work. I try to push my anxieties about Lola out of my head until I can talk to Pepper, and busy myself sorting out a mix-up on a booking date for one of our regular clients – partyware supply company Go Chieftain.

Two phone calls later and a potentially embarrassing situation has been smoothed over. I sit back and take a sip of my coffee. It's gone cold while I've been talking. I set it down on my desk. I need to face facts: it would be naïve to think that Brendan and Lola's relationship isn't sexual.

It didn't sound as if there was any obvious physical coercion on his part. Not so far anyway. But I know what he's like. As soon as Lola does something he doesn't like, he'll find a way to make her pay.

I can't bear the thought that he might hurt her.

'Alison?' Hamish stretches back in his seat, stroking the dark stubble on his chin. 'Are you okay?' he asks. On the surface he sounds as casual as before, but underneath I can hear genuine curiosity and concern in his voice.

Over the two years he's worked here, I've come to realise that Hamish is often complicated like this: superficial, yet intense; aloof but nosey; super camp but insistently heterosexual.

Before I can answer, footsteps echo outside – the unmistakable stomp of Pepper in a bad mood, marching up the stairs.

'Nightmare meeting!' She explodes through the door, the fringing on her orange jacket flying up as she tosses it onto the nearest chair and storms into her partitioned office.

I stand up, breaking eye contact with Hamish. I can just hear him muttering 'Incoming' under his breath as I hurry after Pepper.

'What's up?' I poke my head around her glass door.

'Oh, the usual.' Pepper gives an irritated sigh. 'Patronising idiot who wants three months' work for the price of one. I sometimes wonder why I bother.'

'Because you like running a successful business?' I tilt my head to one side and cock an eyebrow at her.

She grins back. 'You know it.'

We both laugh. Handling Pepper's moods has always been part of the job though, if I'm honest, she's rarely truly difficult. Mostly she just needs a bit of ego stroking – which I've been giving her since we met at uni. It's how our friendship works: I soothe her and ground her, while she keeps me on my toes. She's not everyone's cup of tea, but when people click with Pepper, they generally end up adoring her. I certainly do.

Pepper must hear something forced in my laugh because she frowns. 'What's wrong, Alison?' she asks.

'Nothing.'

Pepper's eyebrows arch so high they're lost under her bright red curls. I met her dad a few times before he died and he confirmed her claim that she was named for her hair. It's faded a lot since our late teens and now comes out of a bottle, but once it was, quite naturally, the most extraordinary shade of paprika.

'I'm not buying "nothing",' she says.

Of course she isn't. Pepper has always had a sixth sense about my moods. We met on our first day at uni, in the student flat we found ourselves sharing, and have been friends ever since. Pepper runs her public relations business – Hot Pepper PR – in the same way she's always approached everything, with a combination of ruthless efficiency and easy, good-humoured charm. She works ferociously hard, bringing in the vast majority of new clients by herself as well as working on the most high-profile campaigns. I keep everything running smoothly; looking after a handful of our less important – and less glamorous – clients myself, while also managing the freelancers, overseeing the admin and generally dealing with whatever the day throws up. If I'm not checking in with journalists or managing freelancers, I'm likely to be handling enquiries and calming down truculent, worried and sometimes panic-stricken clients.

'Come on, Alison,' Pepper says impatiently. 'Sit down and spill.'

She nods to the chair in front of her desk. I take the seat, slumping as I do.

'Is it "Loverboy"? Is he home already?' She grins.

'No,' I say. 'Seb's still in the air. He won't be home until later.'

Outside the glass wall of Pepper's office, Hamish is slowly loading paper into the photocopier. I'm certain he is trying to earwig our conversation.

'What's the matter then?' Pepper's tone hardens.

I hesitate, then meet her cool, grey-eyed gaze.

'It's Lola,' I say quietly, glancing through the glass wall at Hamish. I don't want him to hear this – especially since he knows Lola; she spent a month here last summer doing work experience. 'She's… she's seeing someone.'

Pepper frowns. 'So? That's a good thing, isn't it? What's he like? Or is it a girl? I've had a hunch Lola might be fluid, but you've always been so over-protective you won't even see her as sexual, despite her now being eighteen which I still can't quite—'

'Lola's only *just* eighteen,' I protest, still keeping my voice down. 'And she's an innocent.'

'Please.' Pepper makes a face at me. 'She's not as sweet and innocent as you think she is. Anyway, why is age relevant?'

I stare at her. Hamish is now fiddling with the paper tray, pulling it out of the machine. I know that if I say Brendan's name Pepper will shriek, loudly, so instead I just mutter: 'The man she's seeing is *older. Much* older.'

'Ah.' Pepper flexes her fingers and places them behind her head, then leans back in her chair. She's always taken up space, Pepper. It's the force she charges the air with, the way she expands into everything around her. 'So *that's* why you're looking so worried. You need to loosen up, Alison, let go or she'll properly rebel.'

Hamish is still standing there, but I can't hold back any longer. 'You don't understand, Peps, it's *Brendan*.'

Pepper draws her breath in a sharp gasp, sitting bolt upright in her chair. 'Brendan *Zeno*?' As anticipated, her

23

voice rises. 'Fuck!' Our eyes meet. Pepper is the only person who knows what Brendan did to me that night at the party. It took me six months to tell her the truth. Six months when my life nearly spiralled out of control: I broke up with Michael, I stopped going to lectures and seminars, I drank too much, every night, trying to block out the pain. Telling Pepper, in the end, was what saved me, the start of my struggle back to a manageable life.

Outside, Hamish looks up.

'Lola thinks she loves him,' I mutter. 'Worse, she's convinced he loves her. Which we both know he's not capable of.'

'Fuck,' Pepper says again.

'Exactly.'

'How did this happen?'

'He bumped into her in Camden Market, apparently, then once he realised who she was, got his claws in fast.' My hands ball into fists. 'Never mind how we got here. What matters now is getting her away from him. Trouble is, Lola won't listen to me.'

'Did you tell her about… you know?' Pepper fixes me with her gaze.

'Yes.' I look down at my lap. 'She's so infatuated she won't believe a word of it.'

'Fuck,' Pepper says for the third time.

I take a deep breath. 'I'm going to talk to Brendan now,' I say, trying to control the shake in my voice. 'I just need to track down his number, then I'm going to call him and meet him. Make him see reason.'

'Right.' Pepper reaches for her phone. 'I bet I can get hold of his mobile. And wherever you arrange to meet him, I'll come too. Okay?'

I smile my thanks at her, filling with relief. 'Thanks, I was hoping you would.'

'Course.' Pepper taps at her screen, then presses send. 'But I don't think there's any point trying to get Brendan to "see reason" as you put it. We need to go in hot. Lay down the law. Tell him he *has to* end things with Lola.'

I frown. Laying down the law doesn't sound like a good approach to take with Brendan. If he's anything like he used to be, he'll hate anyone telling him what to do. 'But suppose he just says "no"?'

Pepper waves this away. 'Brendan's a child. Musicians like him always are – all ego and bluster. He'll crumble once someone stands up to him.'

I purse my lips. I'm certain Pepper is wrong. Brendan may have a big ego, but he's slippery. He and Pepper never got on – what did Michael once say? That they were two planets, orbiting the same solar system but entirely independently.

'I think we should feel our way a bit more than that,' I suggest. 'If we just tell Brendan what to do, we'll get his back up.'

'Well, I think we need a clear strategy before we start.' Pepper puts her hands on her hips. 'Look, Alison, I'm not being funny, but your history with him…' She makes a face. 'Maybe *I* should do the talking?'

Before I can reply to this, Pepper's phone pings. She looks at the screen, then makes a face. 'I was trying to get his mobile, but this is the next best thing,' she says, holding the phone towards me. 'Brendan's address.'

'How did you—?'

'I know a guy who used to do his PR,' Pepper explains. 'He owes me a favour.'

'Thank you.' I stand up, glancing outside. Hamish is, at last, wandering back to his desk.

'I just need to make one call, then I'll be ready to go,' Pepper says. She offers me a reassuring smile. 'Don't worry, Alison. I'll find a way to make him leave her, even if it means burning down his house with him in it.'

By the time I slip out of her glass-walled office, Pepper is already booming down the phone. I go to my desk and pick up my vegan leather tote, sliding my jacket inside it.

I glance back at Pepper. She's gesticulating with her free arm as she speaks. My heart thuds. I was wrong to want her to come with me. If we see Brendan together, Pepper won't be able to stop herself laying down the law and Brendan will never back down.

No. The best chance for getting him to do what I want, is to deal with him directly, by myself.

I whisper 'Back soon' to Hamish and, before he has a chance to ask where I'm going, I hurry outside, looking for a cab to take me to Hampstead.

FOUR

…even if it means burning down his house with him in it…

Pepper's words echo in my head as I arrive at Brendan's house on Edge Avenue, right by Hampstead Heath. It's huge – three times the size of my own terraced rental – and detached, with two storeys of ivy-covered brick set back from the road and faded blue silk curtains at the windows. Brendan must have bought this place with royalties from 'Come on! (You know you wanna!)', his mega-hit single back in the Nineties. I'd imagined him in something properly state of the art – all steel curves and glass walls. This is far more conventional. Elegant, even. I peer in through the nearest window. Has Lola been here recently? Surely, she must have?

And in Brendan's bed.

The thought makes me shudder.

Pepper sends a text as I walk up the gravel drive.

> You've gone to see him by yourself, haven't you?

Her message is accompanied by a series of shocked face emojis.

I reply quickly.

> Yes, sorry, but I think it's best to do this
> one-to-one xx

I ring on the doorbell.

The security camera positioned on the wall just above the panel is by Shine Security — a company we represent. How ironic. I gaze up at it, wondering if Brendan is looking at me right now. Pepper sends another text:

> Okay, but don't let him bully you or dictate
> the narrative, you know what he's like.

I put my phone away. My hands are trembling, so I shove them in my pockets.

And then the door swings open and Brendan appears. It's so weird; he's the same, yet not. His hair, once a swept back mane of lush, chestnut-brown waves, might be a little thinner and streaked with silver now, but his eyes still sparkle, lighting up his face. He'd looked all smiley and excited like that just after Michael left the party, taking me by the hand and silently leading me upstairs.

His mouth falls open in shocked delight as he peers at my face. 'It *is* you.' He grins at me. 'How long has it been, Angelface? Thirty years, give or take?'

My stomach twists into knots. I wasn't expecting him to use that old nickname. 'You're looking good, Angelface,' Brendan says, his voice swelling. '*Really* good.'

I gulp, feeling sick. Brendan was always full of complimentary words and admiring glances. How I'd loved that.

My head fills with the memory of that party again: me stumbling up the stairs after him, part excited, part trepidatious – every bit of me thrilled that someone so special had singled me out.

'Serenely silent as ever, I see.' His voice is slightly croaky. Is that because he's just woken up, or a result of too many joints. 'Lola called me earlier, so I wondered if I'd be getting a visit. I guess you're taking a bit of time off from that PR job you do with old Pepper. I'm honoured. Come on in.'

He opens the door wider, ushering me inside. I hesitate. The last time Brendan and I were alone together… I push down the memory. That was a long time ago. He can't hurt me now. Even so, now I'm here, I wish I'd brought Pepper with me after all. The nausea comes in waves, as I follow him along the gloomy hallway, into an open-plan kitchen area at the back of the house. The room is a confusing mix of styles, with an old-fashioned dresser in the corner and a set of fluorescent pink plastic stools spaced around the kitchen island. There's no trace of either cigarette smoke or spliff. In fact, the whole place is surprisingly clean and tidy; exactly what you'd expect to find in a middle-class Hampstead kitchen, from the shiny espresso machine next to the wall to the designer knife block by the sink. Brendan pulls out a stool and sits at the island. He motions me into the one opposite. I sit, taking a deep breath. I focus on the gleaming knives poking out of the block. Each one has a 'Z' carved on the handle. When exactly did anarchic Brendan become a person who monograms his knife collection? He indicates his mug, half full of coffee.

'Want a cup?' he asks.

I shake my head.

'Something stronger?' He grins again. And there's the hint of flirtation in his eyes.

Suddenly, the sick feeling in my stomach morphs into a hard, cold fury. He can't seduce me any longer. And he certainly can't intimidate me.

'No,' I snap. 'I don't want anything.'

'You know you've hardly aged at all.' He sits back and gives me an appraising smile. It's the same expression I remember from the party when, all handsome in the lamplight, he led me into the bedroom with the coats. Even at that point, I didn't realise what he was doing. What a fool I was. I could have walked away then. If I'd wanted to.

'I hear you've been spying on me and Lola.' He chuckles. 'Feeling jealous, Angelface?'

'You're unbelievable,' I snarl. 'And don't call me that.'

'Whoa, okay, okay.' Brendan holds his arms out in a gesture of appeasement. His fingers are long and elegant. Perfect guitarist hands, Michael always said. And quite out of sync with the rest of his scruffy, wild appearance. 'I get it, she's your kid and you're worried about her.' He pauses, smirking. 'It's very conventional of you.'

'She's not just *my* child,' I snap. 'She's *a* child. You've got no right to mess with her head.'

'She's not a child, she's eighteen. An adult. And I'm not messing with her head.' Brendan leans on the counter, suddenly serious. 'Don't you get it? I see Lola far more clearly than you do. She's not as vulnerable as you think. In fact, she came on to me. Did she tell you we met at Camden Market while she was on half term?'

I give a curt nod.

'I saw her standing by a stall,' he says, 'and for a second I thought it was you.' He laughs. 'She looks *so* like you did at that age.'

I look down.

'Anyway, she saw me staring and batted her eyelashes, so—'

'For God's sake,' I mutter.

'So, I introduced myself, not seriously thinking she might actually *be* your daughter and, well, we discovered we had you in common and got chatting from there.' He raises an eyebrow. 'Lola made it clear she was interested from the outset. Which, again,' he smirks, 'reminded me of you.'

'Shut up!' My heart hammers against my ribs. How dare he? I stare at the tangle of trees out in the back garden, trying to make myself focus. Memories surge up again. Brendan sprawled across the bed at the party, me hesitating, flushed with drink and guilt over Michael, but letting him pull me down beside him. Bile rises again as I remember him running his finger down my cheek and me suddenly feeling stone-cold sober, knowing I needed to leave, struggling to sit up, Brendan's hands already reaching under my dress.

I shake back the memory. I mustn't let Brendan manipulate my feelings, suck me into his pathetic drama. Pepper's earlier words come into my head: *Don't let him bully you or dictate the narrative.*

I take a deep breath. 'Can't you see how disgusting it is, you being with my daughter?' I demand. 'You're old enough to be her... her *grandfather*.'

'Lucky me.' Brendan gives a low, salacious laugh. 'She's one hell of a woman.'

I won't let him wind me up. 'You have to end it with her,' I say.

There's a short pause, then Brendan folds his arms.

'No.'

'You *must.*' Snatched images of the fear Brendan plunged me into that night almost thirty years ago flash into my mind's eye. Me trying to leave that bedroom; him accusing me of leading him on. Me crying; him hissing in my ear that I was a slut, playing hard to get.

And then the pain. As he held me down. Ripped off my knickers and forced himself into me.

It takes everything I've got to face him now.

'If you don't leave Lola—' I clench my fists. 'If you don't end things with her tonight, I will tell everyone what you did to me at that end of year party.'

Brendan frowns. A look of bemusement crosses his face. 'What I *did*?' He makes a face. 'In that bedroom? With all the coats? I seem to remember that was fairly consensual, you'd been leading me on for weeks.'

My mouth falls open as the words I couldn't find at the time pass my lips. 'You… attacked me. You *raped* me. You know you did.'

A beat passes, then Brendan wrinkles his nose. 'I think recollections may vary on that one, Angelface.' He leans forward. 'Are you sure you haven't reframed the entire thing because you felt guilty over Michael?' He pauses. 'Such a shame you guys didn't make it.'

I stare at him, too shocked for a second to speak. Then I draw myself up.

'This has nothing to do with Michael,' I say, keeping my voice low and steady. 'I'm giving you one last chance. Break things off with Lola or… or…'

'Or what?' Brendan tilts his head to one side. 'Come on, Angelface,' he goes on more gently. 'I really do understand why it's a big deal for you to see your daughter all grown up, but *you* need to understand that you've got everything out of proportion. Lola and I are good together.'

I shake my head, my lips pressed tightly together.

Brendan sighs. 'Try and look at things from my point of view for a moment. I've changed from when you knew me.' He grins. 'Back then I was Mr Sex, Drugs and Rock'n'Roll. Now it's a few beers in the kitchen while I listen to Spotify and twice-weekly calls to my mum in her care home.'

I stare at him. He can say what he likes, but I know who he is.

'I still make music, but I'd be a fool to think my career can get back to where it was in the late Nineties.' He sighs. 'I just made a new album, but I don't have the wherewithal to tour or promote it properly. Before I met Lola, things were pretty stale. But now...' His smile deepens, lighting up his face. 'I can't tell you what a buzz it gives me to walk around with such a young, beautiful girl on my arm.'

'You make her sound like a designer handbag,' I snap.

Brendan's smile falls. 'You're missing the point. I like being around her for all sorts of reasons: her curiosity, her energy... plus, of course, the fact that she's crazy about me.' He raises an eyebrow in an expression of fake modesty.

Fury surges up again. He's so entitled. So arrogant.

'Lola has her whole future ahead of her,' I spit. 'I won't let you mess it up.'

'Well, that's not fair, is it?' Brendan sounds injured. 'What makes you so certain I'm going to mess her up?

Way Lola talks, it sounds like the whole sixth form experience isn't really doing it for her.'

'I'm serious. You're not going to reel her deeper and deeper in, then dump her like a piece of rubbish.'

Brendan raises his eyebrows. 'Are we still talking about me and Lola?'

I look down.

Brendan sighs. 'Is that what this is *really* about? As if I'd hurt that sweet girl.'

My mind races. 'What would it take for you to leave her?' I stand up, hands on hips. 'What would you swap her for? What would make your life better?'

'Not much.' He runs his fingers through his silver-streaked waves. 'I guess… my career back, though that's impossible of course. I've got all these new songs from the album. It would be great to take them on tour.' He pauses, as if thinking it through. 'Yeah, a big tour. At least a year. I know for a fact there are people who'd be interested – mostly from the old hotspots where I'm still a bit of a name, like Holland and Germany.' He pauses. 'Trouble is, you have to spend money to make money. Unless I look like a success, I'm not going to get the sponsorship I need.' He sighs. 'I've looked into renting out this place but it's not enough…' He trails off, fixing me with a meaningful stare.

Money. He needs money.

'So, if you had the money, you'd be able to go on tour and you'd be willing to break all ties with Lola?'

Brendan looks at me thoughtfully. 'I guess I would, but unless I knew someone with a fifty grand inheritance just sitting in a bank account, it doesn't seem likely.' He takes another gulp of coffee. 'Know anyone who fits the bill,

Angelface? Someone whose mother died earlier this year, perhaps?'

I gasp. He's talking about Seb. Fifty thousand pounds is exactly the amount Seb inherited from his mother. The money came through a couple of weeks ago and is currently in Seb's instant access savings account, waiting to be dealt with.

Brendan chuckles at my shocked expression. 'Yeah, Lola told me about your boyfriend and his windfall the day we met. I think she was trying to impress me. Like most people, she assumed that because I was once successful, I must be rich, and she wanted me to know her family had money too.' He winks at me.

I stare at him, feeling uneasy.

'Of course, I think Lola was hoping she might get a clothes allowance or a new phone off old Seb, but apparently he recently let slip that, now the money has landed, he's thinking of proposing to you – and blowing some of the dosh on a big wedding.'

My jaw drops. Did Seb really say that?

'Sounds like he's fallen hard, Angelface. Though from that look on your face, I'm betting you're not quite as keen, eh? Still, I imagine the thought of that money helps.' He raises his eyebrows suggestively. 'It would certainly help me.'

I reach for the countertop, feeling again the horribly familiar sensation of being out of balance that I always used to have around Brendan. Is it possible that Brendan has planned his entire seduction of Lola in order to get his hands on Seb's inheritance?

'Here.' Brendan scribbles his number on a piece of paper and pushes it towards me. 'Have a think about it.'

Numbly, I take the paper and shove it in my pocket.

'You're still beautiful, you know?' Before I can stop him, Brendan reaches out his hand and strokes a finger down my cheek. Just like he did on that terrible night.

I leap off my stool and scuttle back, across the kitchen.

'Get off me!' I shriek.

'Jesus, Angelface.' Brendan curls his lip in a sneer, the softness on his face evaporating entirely. 'Don't flatter yourself.'

I turn away, all composure deserting me. I hurry away along the corridor, my stomach churning.

'You know when I saw Lola at the market,' Brendan calls after me, 'all I could think was that I had to have her. Just like I did when I first saw you. Remember? At that nerdy music appreciation group Michael brought you to?'

I pause in the hall for a second, hate surging like poison through my veins, then I storm outside, slamming Brendan's front door as hard as I can behind me.

FIVE

I stumble onto the pavement, half-blinded by fury. Who the hell does Brendan think he is?

'Alison?'

I turn. To my surprise, Pepper is parked a couple of car-lengths along the road.

'What happened?' she asks, leaning out of the window as I stomp over.

'He says he's changed,' I snap. 'And he *so* hasn't.'

Pepper nods. As I slide into the passenger seat, the fury I'm feeling twists into fear.

My mission to make Brendan leave Lola has failed. How am I going to keep her safe now? I turn to Pepper, suddenly overwhelmed that she's here, that she's in my corner. 'Thank you for being here,' I say.

She gives me an impatient nod. 'So what happened?'

I blow out my breath, trying to calm my rising sense of panic, then say: 'He point blank refused to leave her, Peps. He was like he *always* was, vain and entitled and... and manipulative.'

'He didn't hurt you, did he?' she asks, giving me a sideways glance, as she revs the engine.

'No, but...' I frown. 'He's not backing down. We need to *force* him to end things, but...' I hesitate. 'Hey, how about we do a PR campaign exposing how he attacked me. Maybe ask other women to come forward if he did something similar to them. You know, like a #MeToo thing?'

Pepper rounds the bend of the road. The sun appears from behind a cloud and she dips the sun visor over the steering wheel down a fraction.

'Pepper?'

'Are you really prepared for that?' she asks, keeping her eyes on the traffic ahead. 'Quite apart from the risk that Brendan sues us for libel, speaking out in public means *everyone* knowing what happened.' She glances at me. 'And that will have a knock-on effect on Lola.'

'Shit,' I sigh, slumping down into my seat. Pepper is right. 'Lola thinks I'm making it up anyway, so going public would probably just drive her deeper into Brendan's arms.' I sit back, feeling humiliated.

Pepper clears her throat. 'You should tell Michael, see what he thinks.'

I say nothing. I can't imagine what Lola's dad might say that will make any difference. Plus he'll be furious, which is why I didn't tell him yesterday. No, confiding in Michael would be like chucking a hand grenade into a ceasefire. Anyway, Brendan made it clear that money to set up a tour and revitalise his career was the only thing that might push him to leave Lola.

Seb's money.

I look out of the window and am surprised to find that we're already past the turning for the office and zooming up Junction Road.

'Where are we going?' I ask.

'I'm dropping you at home,' Pepper says firmly. 'Take the rest of the day. Talk to Michael. Talk to Lola again.' She hesitates, then adds darkly. 'And think about everything

Brendan said – there has to be something you can use to make him do the right thing.'

–

I haven't been home long, when Seb texts to say he's in the taxi from the airport, signing off:

> Can't wait to see you x

What if I ask Seb to borrow his inheritance? What if I explain how important it is to get Lola away from Brendan before he hurts her?

I try to imagine how I might frame the request and am so full of nervous anticipation that as soon as I hear his key in the door, I hurry into the hall. I find Seb stepping over the pile of Lola's shoes under the bulging coat stand, struggling to find a peg that isn't too overloaded for his wool Crombie. Unaware I'm standing there, he casts an irritated glance at the mess.

'Seb?'

He turns to face me and the irritation falls away. There is real tenderness in his smile, though he looks tired, too, a greyness about his handsome face – all sharp cheekbones and square jaw.

'Missed you,' he says gruffly.

'Me too.' I hurry over and let him wrap his arms around me. I breathe in the sour scent of his travel sweatshirt, then tip my face up. The familiar sight of his furrowed forehead actually brings tears to my eyes. 'It's so good you're home.'

'I didn't expect you to be here.' He plants a soft kiss on my lips. Seb is nearly six years younger than me. And, though the lines on his brow definitely age him up, especially now he is pale with exhaustion, there's an earnest openness about his face that is almost childlike.

The first time Pepper met him she nicknamed him Clark Kent. Seb had no idea how to take that, glancing anxiously at me as if trying to work out whether she was joking or not. Pepper, I'm sure, thinks he's dull, and he's certainly not as smart or as exciting as Michael. But he's also not as selfish.

Seb pulls me to him again, his breathe warm against my ear. At six foot one, he's a good two inches taller than Michael – which I know irritates my ex-husband no end.

'How's everything been?' Seb runs his hands along the tops of my shoulders. 'You feel kind of tense.'

'Er, well… there is something.' I draw away. 'I found out yesterday that Lola is seeing someone…'

Seb raises his eyebrows. '*Someone?* That sounds ominous.'

'It is, I'm afraid. It's Brendan Zeno.' I look at him, confident he'll know exactly who I'm talking about. Anyone remotely our generation would know. 'Come on! (You know you wanna!)' was a big hit.

'The Nineties musician?' Seb makes a face. 'Ugh, he's far too old for her.'

'Yes,' I say, 'but it's more than that.' I hurry on, the words tumbling out of me. 'I've been really worried since I found out. Lola's so vulnerable and Brendan is… he's not a nice person. That is… I don't think I ever mentioned it but… but I knew him briefly when we were at uni. He—' I stop, tamping down the memories that rise, unbidden, once again.

Like Michael, Seb has no idea what happened to me all those years ago.

40

'Well, I grant you Brendan's far too old for her and I'm sure he's a bit of a player, or at least tries to be, but Lola's a sensible girl. In fact, technically, she's an adult, so I'm afraid there's not an awful lot you can do.' Seb gives me an encouraging smile. 'I'm sure it'll burn itself out before too long.'

It's like he's chucked a bucket of ice over me. I take a step away from him. 'You don't understand. Brendan is… he's much worse than a player. He's— He…' I can't quite bring myself to tell Seb the whole truth. 'He raped a girl I knew well. Led her on, then raped her.'

Seb raises his eyes. 'Are you sure? All sorts of stuff gets said about people like him. Was he actually convicted?'

'No, but that doesn't prove anything.' I frown. 'And it *definitely* happened. Brendan's evil. He's capable of anything.'

'Then Lola will work that out.' Seb makes a face.

'I can't wait for that; I can't wait 'til he hurts her.' My voice rises. How can Seb not understand this?

He puts his muscular arm around my shoulders and gives me a squeeze. 'Come on, love, the worst thing you can do is interfere, that'll just get her back up.' He picks up his suitcase.

'I'm going to take a shower, then maybe something to eat?' He looks at me hopefully. 'I want to try and keep myself awake, not give in to the jet lag, but I'm knackered. I've had less than four hours' sleep in the last twenty-four hours.'

He lugs his case over to the stairs. I wander into the living room, the truth settling like a shroud. No way is Seb going to accept me giving his inheritance to Brendan.

Not even if I tell him the truth, that Brendan raped *me*. In fact, he'd probably be so angry with Brendan if he knew, he'd be even less willing to hand over any money to him.

If only I had the cash myself, but I live from hand to mouth every month. Have done since Michael and I split up and I started renting this house. Michael himself has no savings and has poured everything he has into his new flat – not that I can imagine him agreeing to pay off Brendan either.

What about Pepper? She's hardly super wealthy, but she runs a successful business – which surely means that if she doesn't have the savings to lend me, she'd be able to borrow the money. And I know she'll want to help Lola, whom she has always adored.

I should have mentioned that Brendan wanted money earlier, Pepper might even have suggested paying him off herself. Maybe she will if I talk to her again now? I check the time. It's almost one. Pepper will be heading out to buy a salad in the next ten minutes.

I snatch up my phone and call her.

'Alison?' she sounds slightly surprised to hear from me so soon. 'Is everything okay?'

'I can't stop thinking about Brendan and what I'm going to do.' My voice breaks a little, my emotions surging up.

'I know,' Pepper says sympathetically. 'He's a total—'

'I have an idea,' I rush on. 'And I really need to talk to you about it. I know you only just dropped me, but can we do lunch?'

A slight hesitation on the other end of the line, then Pepper sighs. 'Fine. Actually, I've had an idea too. I was going to tell you tomorrow, but… Look, lets meet at Bella Bacio, yeah? Just get there as soon as you can, I have a meeting at three.'

She rings off and I rush upstairs to tell Seb I'm heading out. He's already fast asleep on the bed, so I check his phone is on silent, then message him to say I'm heading back to work for something urgent.

A minute later and I'm flying out of the house, my heart thudding and my hopes high. Pepper knows Brendan – and how materialistic he can be – and she's also the most intuitive person I know. I'm certain she'll have already worked out that money will be the only way to get him to do what we want and is about to suggest that she lends me the cash herself. Which means, surely, that Lola will soon be free.

SIX

I fly into Bella Bacio just before half past one. Pepper is already ensconced in our favourite booth, tucked away at the back of the room. She is studying her phone with a frown as she sips at a glass of sparkling water.

I hurry over and sit down opposite her. Pepper pours me water from the big bottle on the table, then pushes the glass towards me. She watches me intently as I take a sip. Classic Pepper, waiting to gauge the other person present before she says what's on her mind.

Well, two can play at that game. There's no need for me to ask her for money if she's about to offer it.

'You said you had an idea for dealing with Brendan?' I raise my eyebrows.

Pepper nods. Her face takes on that intense, serious look she deploys with certain clients – the ones who need to know that there's substance beneath the flamboyant manner.

'It was something you said,' she says, her voice low and intent, 'about exposing Brendan for the evil rapist he is by telling your story in public.'

I frown. 'Right, but—'

'But we both agreed that Lola probably wouldn't believe you, anyway.'

'Exactly.' My frown deepens. 'So…?'

'So, we expose Brendan for who he is *anonymously*. Not through mainstream media of course; they wouldn't touch an anonymous, unsubstantiated claim they couldn't stand up – but we don't need them. We put your experience with Brendan out there on all the socials, keeping your name out of it, then—'

'Wait.' My head is spinning. Clearly Pepper's mind hasn't been running along the same lines as mine at all. 'I don't see why Lola is likely to believe an anonymous accuser any more than if it were me.'

'Fair enough,' Pepper acknowledges. 'But once the truth is out there, more women will come forward and accuse Brendan themselves. I'm *sure* of it. You can't be the only one. Then Lola will *have* to believe in what they're saying – what you're *all* saying.'

I sit back, feeling perplexed. Pepper's idea has merit. I can't deny that. But it's a risk.

'How long do you think it would take for people to come forward?' I ask.

'After the *New Yorker* article about Weinstein, the ball got rolling within days. And that included a bunch of A-listers.' Pepper's eyes light up. 'It might take a bit longer with Brendan as he's hardly a big celebrity anymore, maybe it would take the next few weeks to build a head of steam, but I really think it would work.'

The next few weeks? I can't bear the thought of Lola under Brendan's spell for the next few *hours*.

'I guess it's one option,' I say, slowly, 'but there's something else I've been thinking about that might work faster and is far more guaranteed.' Pepper looks at me expectantly and I clear my throat. 'Brendan made it obvious he would leave Lola if I gave him money. He's looking for about fifty grand I reckon. But...' I force myself to look directly at Pepper, 'but I don't have that kind of money.' I hold her gaze, watching as the realisation of what I'm asking for dawns in her eyes.

'Oh,' she says. 'I see.' She takes a sip of water, as the waitress comes over to take our order.

Salads requested, I reach for Pepper's hand and give it a brief squeeze. 'Well?'

Pepper's expressive face clouds. 'I don't have it,' she mutters, so quietly I can barely hear her. I sit, waiting for her to continue as Bella Bacio hums around us. She looks up and I can see the embarrassment in her eyes. 'The business has been struggling since Covid,' she says quietly. 'Our profit was down by fifty-six percent for two years running.'

I wrinkle my nose. 'I know things were tricky for a bit, but I thought we'd come out of that now?'

'We have,' Pepper says with a sigh. 'But I had to take out a loan and remortgage to get through, so—'

My hands fly to my mouth. 'Oh Peps.'

She makes a face.

'I had no idea things were that bad.'

'Why would you?' She shrugs. 'You've never been involved in the financial side of the business. Hamish doesn't know either. At least, he hasn't asked. He does all the admin on the accounts so he *could* know if he wanted to, but I don't think—'

'But why didn't you *tell* me?' I demand. 'Not from a work point of view, but because we're friends.'

'I didn't see the point in worrying you,' Pepper says, folding her arms. 'Look, Alison, even if I had the money to pay off Brendan, I'm not sure I would – it just feels like letting him win. But the truth is that I don't have it. Every penny I make goes on paying back my loans and trying to keep the business afloat.'

'I get it,' I say quickly. 'I'm sorry I asked.'

Pepper waves her hand airily, looking suddenly far more like her normal self. 'Puh-lease, darling. But if you really think money's the answer with Brendan, what about Michael?'

'He has a massive mortgage too,' I say gloomily. 'He doesn't even have a pension, so—'

'What about Seb?' Pepper's eyes widen. 'Didn't he get all that money from his mum recently?'

I open my mouth to explain that not only do I think Brendan has been targeting Seb's money since he met Lola, but that, if asked, Seb would refuse to hand it over to him. Then I change my mind; I don't have the energy to discuss the merits of my partner – and our relationship – with Pepper right now.

'It's not fair to drag Seb into it.'

'Hmm.' Pepper purses her lips. 'Then we're back to my idea, aren't we? Exposing Brendan as a serial, abusive, rapist bastard, but without you being named.'

'I don't know, Peps, let me think about it.' I look away. Truth is that though Pepper's plan might bring results in the long run, it won't work anywhere near quickly enough.

I need Lola away from Brendan right now.

Thankfully, she changes the subject to discuss how best she should handle her upcoming meeting. We eat our salads as we talk, then Pepper heads back to the office and I make my way home, feeling troubled. Nobody I know has any significant money, apart from Seb – and I'm certain he won't lend me his precious savings.

What on earth am I going to do?

As I wait for my bus, a fresh and startling idea unfurls in my brain.

What if I were to take Seb's money without asking him first?

My mind goes back and forth the entire journey home. I'd be taking the cash for a really good reason, not to benefit myself, and I'd pay Seb back – though I have no idea how or when. So, it wouldn't really be stealing, would it?

As I walk into the house, I can hear the shower running, which means Seb must be awake after his jet lag induced nap; it's too early for the kids to be back from school. I wander across the hall and into the living room, where I stand, staring out of the window. The rain which was threatening all the way home starts to fall, shrouding the grass in a light, delicate mist.

Who am I kidding? Taking someone's money without permission is the *definition* of theft. Which makes it impossible, doesn't it? I've never stolen anything in my life. Even as a teenager, I never wanted to rebel; when the cool girls in year nine said they were planning to shoplift chocolate from the corner store, I made an excuse and ran away.

I place my hands on the cold glass of the window, my guts knotted with anxiety.

Maybe I haven't stolen before, but that's because I haven't ever had a good reason. What I'm contemplating now isn't like nicking a bar of chocolate for kicks. It's more akin to stealing a loaf of bread to feed a starving family. I have to do whatever is necessary to get Lola away from the man who raped me. She is in danger – and I couldn't live with myself if I didn't keep her safe, even if that means committing a crime far worse than stealing. Because I'm fully aware that taking Seb's money wouldn't just be an act of theft, it would be a total betrayal of his trust.

It would devastate him.

I lean forward, closer to the window and press my nose against the glass. An ugly new thought crawls, unbidden, through my veins: *Seb won't feel devastated by my betrayal if he never finds out it was me who stole his money.*

I turn away from the window and glance up at the ceiling. The sound of running water has stopped; Seb must be out of the shower now. I imagine him combing his hair in front of our bedroom mirror in that way he does – a stroke for the parting, then two brisk strokes on either side – totally unaware of what I'm contemplating.

It comes down to this: I need Seb's money.

He needs to believe a genuine fraud was committed on his account, so he can get the bank to refund him.

So... how about I take the money and somehow make it look like a stranger took it?

That way I won't have stolen from my partner; I'll just have stolen from the bank, who will have to refund Seb his savings.

I let out a sigh. I'm getting way ahead of myself. No way should I do anything until I've confirmed Brendan will leave Lola for the money – and he's produced proof that he's actually done it.

My fingers tremble as I fish Brendan's number out of my pocket and call him.

He answers straight away.

'I'll get you the fifty grand,' I say, quietly. 'I'll pay you.'

I hear his short intake of breath. 'Are you serious?'

'Deadly,' I say. 'But there are two conditions.'

'Which are?'

'You have to give Lola up *tonight*. No delay. Be firm, but don't humiliate her.'

A short pause. 'And what's the second condition?' Brendan asks.

'You have to leave the country this weekend.'

'But it's already Wednesday,' Brendan protests. 'Come on, it's going to take months of schmoozing to get sponsors on board and—'

'So what? You can schmooze them from anywhere. Look, I don't care where you go, but it needs to be abroad. Somewhere you can put together that music tour and be completely out of Lola's life.' My throat feels dry.

A long pause, then Brendan asks: 'What bank is Seb's money with?'

'Why?' I clutch my phone.

'I need an account at the same bank so the transfer will go through in hours, not days. If you're setting deadlines like the weekend, I need to make sure I can get my hands on the funds as fast as possible.'

'Right.' I give Brendan the name of the bank.

'Good,' he mutters, 'that's going to work. I already have access to an account there.'

'So, do we have a deal?' I ask.

'I guess I could consider it.' Brendan's voice is light and mocking.

Jesus. He's enjoying toying with me; an aloof cat to my desperate mouse.

'Yes or no?' I persist.

'God, you used to be a lot more fun,' he grumbles. 'Well, I don't know why you've got such a poker up your arse about all this but, okay, it's a deal.' He hesitates. 'But if I do everything you ask and you don't pay up…'

My throat tightens. 'What?'

'Instead of going abroad this weekend, I'll have Lola dropping out of school and living with me here by Monday morning.' The airy quality vanishes from his voice. 'Same if you repeat any of this conversation, which I will of course deny.'

'Okay, I've got it. Just tell her tonight.' I hang up, my heart racing.

What the hell have I done?

I'm not a thief, and yet I've promised away money that doesn't belong to me. Even worse, I don't regret it. In fact, far from thinking I've made a mistake, all I can focus on is how on earth I'm going to get my hands on Seb's savings without him realising, before Brendan's had a chance to cash it out. I head upstairs, to find Seb on his way down, his phone in his hand.

I'm barely listening as he we sit in the kitchen and he chats about his trip. I keep glancing at the mobile on the table beside him. I know the backup code he uses when Face ID doesn't work: *1608* for the date we met, 16 August, a year and a half ago. I know the icon for the bank app where he keeps his inheritance.

I just need to know that Lola is free from Brendan, then I'll work out how and when to access and transfer the money.

SEVEN

Seb finally stops talking and gets out his laptop to check his emails. I try to focus on dinner, making chicken empanadas for our supper.

Will Brendan really fulfil his side of the bargain and leave Lola?

Or will he hurt her just to spite me?

'Anything need doing?' Seb asks, rubbing his eyes and looking up from the kitchen table. He's wearing a loose jumper that shows off the breadth of his shoulders and the muscular cut of his upper arms.

'Would you make some dressing?' I ask.

Seb nods and starts finely chopping some garlic.

We work companionably in silence for a little while as the light fades outside. A few minutes after five p.m., Josh arrives home, asking immediately if he can have his supper in his room, so he can get straight into his homework. I suspect he's more interested in playing some computer game, but I'm too distracted to argue. Lola is, of course, out with Brendan, so Seb and I sit down on our own at the kitchen table. I keep imagining Brendan and Lola together. What is Brendan doing and saying? Is he keeping his promise to break up with her? How is she reacting?

I pick at my food, unable to summon up much appetite. The conversations I picture Brendan and Lola having coalesce around a single question. It darts around my head like a demented fly: *Has Brendan ended things yet?*

After we've eaten, Seb pours himself a second glass of wine and regales me with a long, dull tale about a man he met at his conference in New York.

'…he was telling me about his wedding in Bali. I've never been a fan of destination weddings, but it did sound really cool. Expensive of course.' He pauses, clearly trying to inject a casualness into his voice but instead sounding hopelessly self-conscious. 'What do you think? About, you know, the idea of getting married abroad?'

Oh, God.

Thankfully, the doorbell rings at that moment. 'I'll get it,' I say, leaping out of my seat. I feel sick as I cross the hall, certain I'm going to see a hurt, angry Lola on the doorstep.

I open the door, bracing myself.

But it isn't Lola on the doorstep.

It's Michael. He's got that harassed look in his eyes that usually means he feels overwhelmed or out of his depth.

'What the hell, Ali?' he mutters, pushing past me and coming inside. It's at this point I notice Lola is there too, halfway down the front path behind him, her head bowed and her shoulders shaking with sobs.

'What's happened?' I try to act as if I have no idea why Lola might be crying.

'Lola turned up at my place half an hour ago,' Michael snaps. He lowers his voice, drawing closer so his breath is hot on my ear. 'She says she's been seeing Brendan – *our* Brendan who is, may I remind you, older than *I* am!' He pulls back, glaring at me. 'Did you know about this?'

I hesitate, then nod.

'Jesus, Ali, why didn't you tell me?' Michael demands. 'Apparently he's just dumped her. Wait till I get my hands on that bastard, I'll—'

'But he's ended it,' I say quickly. 'You don't need to do anything.'

Michael's eyes narrow. 'Did you *know* he was going to do that?' He glances back at Lola. 'She's insisting you did, that you warned him off her or something.'

'What?'

'That's why she came to me, because she thinks you must have *interfered*, as she sees it,' Michael mutters. 'What happened?'

I follow his gaze to where Lola is stumbling along the front path. She looks up at me as she makes her way inside. Her eyes are red-rimmed and there are mascara streaks down her cheeks. I thought I'd feel nothing but relief once I knew Brendan had left her. Instead, I'm overwhelmed with the desire to hold her and soothe away her pain. I take a step towards her, but she shrinks away.

'What's going on?' Seb emerges, blinking into the hall.

'Everything's fine,' I say. 'Lola's upset… about some-thing.' I'm hoping Seb will wander away, not wanting to get in the middle of a mother–daughter moment. But he stays, his eyes on Michael.

'Did you tell Brendan to split up with me?' Lola can barely get the words out, her chest heaving with jagged breathes. 'You did, didn't you?'

'*What?*' I sidestep the question. 'Why on earth would you ask that?' I throw Seb a quick glance, trying to convey that he mustn't let on he knows about the relationship.

'Because he just dumped me. Oh, how *could* you Mum?' Lola dissolves into fresh sobs. Beside her, Michael rolls his eyes at me, then pulls Lola towards him sideways.

I watch them hug, feeling both glad she's letting him comfort her and annoyed that Michael should be the good guy while I am clearly being painted as Queen Bitch.

'Apparently Brendan's decided to leave the country to organise a music tour,' Michael says, releasing Lola. He pats her awkwardly on the back and attempts a smile. 'Which, as I've been saying, is a lucky escape for her.'

In response, Lola grimaces, shrinking away from him. She's wearing her yellow coat again. I have a sudden memory of Pepper giving her that same coat a couple of months ago for her eighteenth birthday. I can see Lola in my mind's eye, unwrapping it with a delighted squeal. A vintage Gucci with shiny black buttons that Pepper had found in a designer sale, it was, by far, Lola's favourite birthday gift. That memory, along with the cheerful yellow of the coat, contrasts horribly with the miserable expression on Lola's face right now.

I can feel Seb's eyes boring into the back of my head. I glance round at him and he frowns, clearly wondering what on earth I've been up to.

'Oh, sweetheart.' I clasp my hands together and turn to Lola again. 'I'm so sorry.'

'Are you?' Her head jerks up, a flash of anger in her eyes that makes her look just like Michael. 'Brendan said it didn't have anything to do with you, but it's such a coincidence after you... you got so angry yesterday...' She swallows hard, wiping her eyes. 'Did you tell him to leave me, Mum?'

We stare at each other. For a second, I hesitate, then I take a deep breath.

'No,' I lie. 'No, I didn't say a thing.' I glance swiftly at Seb, then at Michael, who is standing next to Lola, his eyebrows raised. I drop my gaze. My heart thumps against my ribs, the weight of my lie pressing down on me.

'But it doesn't make sense he would just end things,' Lola mumbles, tears bubbling up in her voice. 'Dad, what do you think?'

I bite my lip. She's asking Michael if he thinks I'm telling the truth.

It's obvious from the frantic look on Michael's face that he has no idea what to say. 'Er, I don't know what Mum's done, but I do know all she wants is to protect you,' he says at last.

Jesus. I glare at him.

'Alison has just made it clear she hasn't "done" anything,' Seb interjects, clearly as irritated as I am. I smile gratefully at him, and he squeezes my arm.

'Okay.' Michael holds up his hands, then turns to Lola. 'Look, this isn't about Mum, it's about Brendan. *He's* the one who hurt you.'

Lola nods. She slumps against the hall wall, all the hot fury seeping out of her. 'Brendan said he couldn't miss the opportunity to get a tour together,' she says quietly, 'and that he didn't even want me to *visit* him while he was away.' Her lips tremble. 'Oh… oh, Mum.' Suddenly it's like she's ten years old again with flu or a stomach bug, sick and fragile. She moves towards me and I hold her, feeling her tears damp through my top.

Beside me, Seb shuffles awkwardly. Michael is staring at me, his gaze curious and intense. Lola pulls away, wiping her face again.

'Why don't you run a bath, darling?' I suggest. 'Have a soak – unless you want to go back to Dad's of course?'

Lola shakes her head. 'No, I'd like to stay here.'

We both look at Michael. He blows out his breath. 'Of course,' he says, then turns to me. 'I need to go anyway.' He glances upstairs. 'Say hi to Josh.'

I nod.

'Bye, Dad.' Lola wipes her face and offers him a weak smile.

Michael smiles back and kisses the side of her head. 'Bye, Babycakes.'

Lola hesitates. 'Go on, Lo,' I urge. 'Get that bath running. I'll bring you up some hot chocolate, yeah?'

'Okay.' Head bowed, Lola takes off her coat and trudges to the stairs. My heart lodges in my mouth. I've never seen her so devastated. She plods slowly upstairs. Seconds later, the sound of the bathroom door shutting echoes down to us.

Michael walks across the hall to the front door. Seb and I follow.

'She's really upset,' I say, my throat tight.

'She'll be fine,' Seb says reassuringly. He puts his arm around my shoulder.

I nod, though I don't feel so sure. I'd hoped Brendan emphasising his passion for touring, would stop Lola feeling so personally rejected.

'Of course Lola will be fine,' Michael casts Seb a withering glance.

'Bye then, Michael,' Seb says, his voice tight with irritation.

Ignoring him, Michael glances upstairs, to where the bath is now running loudly. He lowers his voice. 'So tell me the truth, Ali. How did you do it? What did it take to make Brendan back off?'

'Alison has already informed you that she hasn't spoken to Brendan,' Seb says, sounding more than a little pompous.

I wince.

'Bollocks to that,' Michael snaps. 'Come on Ali, what happened?'

'Er…' I glance at Seb, who looks uncertainly back at me. He takes his hand off my shoulder.

'*Did* you talk to him?' he asks.

Shit. Why didn't I tell him everything earlier?

Upstairs the bath taps are still thundering away. I take a deep breath. 'No,' I say.

Michael snorts. 'Yeah, right.'

Beside me I feel Seb bristle. 'You need to leave,' he snaps.

Michael shakes his head. Trust him and his journalist instincts to start sniffing out the truth. He could always bloody see through me. I brace myself for him to carry on arguing, but instead he turns and leaves without a word.

'What an arsehole,' Seb mutters, stalking off to the kitchen.

I stand, suddenly alone in the hallway.

A text pings onto my phone. Dread washes over me as I gaze at the screen. The message is from Brendan:

> Done, honey. Now, money?

Upstairs, the bath taps have been turned off, meaning Lola must now be soaking in the tub. I close Brendan's message and wander into the kitchen. Seb is sitting stiffly at the table, an empty tumbler and a bottle of Glenfiddich in front of him. He pours a glug of whisky into the glass.

'Michael was totally out of order,' he says sullenly.

'I know,' I say, hoping he can't see the heat that flushes my cheeks.

'When are the kids next going to be out?' he goes on. 'I'd really like a proper evening together.' He takes a sip of his drink. 'There's something I want to talk to you about. A question I'd like to ask…'

Oh, God. Is he hinting at proposing? Has he really discussed this with Lola, like Brendan said?

'I… er, I don't know,' I stammer. 'Maybe at the weekend.'

'Okay.' Seb sits up, looking a little brighter. 'Let's go into town. Make a day of it.'

'I'll let you know tomorrow,' I say, desperate for the second time this evening to change the topic of conversation. 'I need to make sure Lola's definitely okay before I start making plans to go out for the day.'

'You know you're far too overprotective of that girl.' Seb sighs, then picks up his whisky and walks out of the kitchen.

I stare after his departing back, then put some milk on the hob to make Lola's hot chocolate and look at Brendan's message again. I'm not sending him any money until I am sure he's definitely leaving the country.

My fingers tremble over the screen.

Need proof that you are going away asap, then will sort funds.

I press send, then busy myself making Lola's hot chocolate. As I'm pouring hot milk into a mug, Brendan texts me with a screen grab of his ticket to Amsterdam this Saturday and a link to his Facebook page where he hints that he may be playing a pop-up gig for Dutch fans soon. He also writes me a short message, bookended by heart emojis:

♥ taken the plunge, remember what will happen if you don't keep up your end ♥

I shiver.

Account details for a Mrs Roisin Murphy – Brendan's mum – are underneath the message.

My heart thuds as I finish making the hot chocolate, then take it upstairs to Lola, now wrapped in a towel and draped across her bed. She offers me a weak smile as I set the mug down on her bedside table. I peek inside Josh's room, next door. Sure enough, he's playing *Call of Duty*, his physics workbook open in front of him. Normally I would tell him to turn his PC off, but tonight I just withdraw quietly and head downstairs.

I sit beside Seb on the living room couch, gazing with uncomprehending eyes at a TV documentary on the Brazilian rainforest. Tonight is make or break. I either steal Seb's money, or Brendan will take out my failure to pay him on Lola.

I work through a plan. It sounds crazy in my head, but I can't see another way.

Seb always leaves his phone charging on silent on the hall table overnight – he insists it's better for our mental health if we keep devices out of the bedroom.

I watch him plug it in, then follow him up to bed. He's yawning, clearly sleepy already. I'm too wired to imagine sleep, but I go through the motions, getting into my pyjamas and brushing my teeth.

'God, I'm all over the place,' Seb grumbles as I get into bed beside him. 'I barely slept on that red eye but after that nap earlier it feels like the middle of the day now.'

'So take a siesta.' I smile at him.

He grunts and yawns again.

'I'm really tired,' I say, just in case his mind drifts from his sleep schedule to other activities he might want to do to help him wind down.

'I know.' He folds his arm over mine, caressing the skin. 'I am too. The conference was exhaust—' The end of the word is swallowed by yet another yawn.

A few minutes later he's asleep.

I lie, my heart beating hard in my chest, waiting for his breath to become slow and deep and regular. It's just gone eleven p.m. I glance at the clock on his side of the bed, willing the time to tick on to midnight.

As the digital numbers line up to 00:00 I ease myself out from under the covers and tiptoe downstairs. Silently, I curl my fingers over the cool metal of Seb's phone and unplug it from its charger. I creep into the kitchen and close the door, then hold the device up in front of me. It gives a judder, not recognising my face. I input Seb's pin code and the home screen comes into view.

I take a deep breath and search for Seb's instant access bank app. There. Typing in the code a second time, I wait for the verification text, then open the app. I slip into the hall for a second, ears straining to make sure everyone is still asleep. The house is silent.

My heart is in my mouth as I set up the transfer to the Roisin Murphy account. I press send on the transaction, then wait for another verification text and input another code. I have to answer several security questions – the town where he grew up, the name of his first pet, etc. –

and all the while I'm waiting to be caught out by a request I can't respond to, or by the creak of a floorboard and Seb's shocked face at the door.

But it doesn't happen. I have all the answers and, ridiculously quickly, I'm able to make the transfer. Of course I have to go through the process twice, as £25,000 is the maximum the bank will let me move in one go. But in less than ten minutes it's done.

I've stolen Seb's money.

A surge of guilt rises inside me. I push it away. There'll be time for my feelings later, right now I need to turn off the locator app on Seb's mobile, then hide the phone itself. If everything works out as I've planned, Seb won't find the device until this evening, or notice his cash is missing until well after Brendan has withdrawn it. Transferring even large amounts of money within the one organisation only takes a few hours to clear.

All I need to do is find a hiding place that Seb won't think of before he goes to work. Then it can miraculously turn up by the evening. Obviously, it's going to seem like a weird coincidence that Seb misplaces his phone the same night that it gets hacked – but I know from what Michael said the other day about the story he's currently working on, that remote phone hacking is perfectly possible. So hopefully Seb will accept that weird coincidence, assume a fraudster has hacked him and report the theft to the bank.

Then the bank will refund him the cash.

And I will be in the clear.

I burrow into the pile of coats in the hallway, shoving Seb's phone deep inside one of my winter boots, then covering it over between two of Lola's jackets, another wave of guilt washes over me. I'm a terrible person for doing this.

It's for Lola, I tell myself, but the thought doesn't help. As I creep back upstairs to bed, three words circle my head on a loop.

Coward. Liar. Thief.

I reach for my own phone and text Brendan a single word:

Done.

EIGHT

I'm woken the next morning by the sound of Seb's voice on the landing: 'Shit!'

'What's the matter?' I call out, as innocently as I can.

'My phone's gone,' he says, striding into the bedroom.

'Are you sure?' I make a confused face at him. 'When did you last use it? The living room was the last place I saw you with it.'

'I set it to charge in the usual place, like always. I'm *sure* I did.' Seb turns and hurries away. As the rapid thud of his footsteps on the stairs rises through the silence, I feel sick.

How come I never realised before how awful lying makes you feel?

I'm basically gaslighting the man I love.

To save Lola.

Prompted by this thought, I hurry next door to her room. To my surprise she's already up and getting dressed, selecting a top from the mess of clothes on the floor.

'Did you sleep okay?' I ask.

Lola shrugs, reaching for her school bag.

I head next door, to check on Josh. He's still fast asleep and, by the time I've chivvied him out of bed and gone back to my own room to dress, Lola is shouting a curt 'Goodbye'. As the front door shuts behind her, I hurry downstairs.

Seb is pacing from room to room. 'I've looked every-where,' he says. 'Find My Phone isn't working for some reason, but I *know* it's in the house somewhere.'

My guts twist uncomfortably. 'At least you know it can't have been stolen,' I point out.

'Damn it, I need to go, I'm already late,' he says, letting out a frustrated sigh.

'Don't stress.' I put my hand on his arm. 'We can look for it tonight.'

Seb nods and, a few minutes later, he goes, still grumbling as he leaves the house.

I make toast for me and Josh then, once he's gone too, I retrieve the phone from its hiding place and put it under a cushion on the sofa, next to the spot where Seb was sitting last night.

My heart is pounding as I make my way to the office. Suppose Seb realises it was me that took the money?

I tell myself that he can't, that he won't. That I've done what I needed to do. Lola is free and Brendan is leaving the country this weekend.

The whole, terrible situation is over and, though I may have put myself in an entirely new and terrible situation, at least I know Lola will soon be safe.

–

At work that morning, I try to concentrate, but I'm so preoccupied with what I've done that poor Hamish has to repeat his offer to make me a coffee three times before I hear him. Pepper is on a long call when I arrive, but as soon as she finishes, she beckons me into her office. I'm expecting her to ask how Lola is – or whether I've found a way to deal with Brendan. Instead, she waves me towards the seat opposite her desk, then leans forward, her hands clasped excitedly and her eyes sparkling.

'I did it!' she announces.

'Did what?' I frown.

'Created a series of anonymous social media accounts and posted your story about Brendan. Look!'

She hands me her phone. Too stunned to speak, I take it and peer at the screen. It's open on a post on 'X' from @AvengingAngel.

> Brendan Zeno is an abusive monster. He groomed me, manipulated me and then raped me. I have been silent but now it's time for the truth to come out – for this evil predator to pay for what he did. #MeToo #YesAllWomen #BelieveSurvivors #WhyIDidn'tReport

My jaw drops. 'What is this?'

'I've left the same post on all the main socials. Hopefully if there are other women Brendan abused, they'll see and respond.' Pepper grins. 'I thought the "angel" reference in the username was good; remember how he used to call you Angelface?'

I stare at her aghast. 'But… but what if Brendan finds out it was you? He could sue you?'

'He can't, the accounts aren't connected to me at all – I used fake everything to set them up. And posted from an internet cafe. Anyway, he's hardly likely to draw *more* attention to this kind of accusation by trying to sue over it, especially since he knows that its true.'

My head spins. I can't believe Pepper has gone so far without speaking to me first.

'I thought we were going to talk about this?' I protest.

66

Pepper shrugs, the smile fading from her face. 'We did talk, yesterday. And you yourself pointed out we needed to move fast. I'm just trying to help here, Alison.'

'I know,' I say, still feeling uncomfortable. 'It's just there's no need, as it happens. Brendan decided to break things off with Lola last night.'

'He did?' Pepper looks sceptical. She peers intently at me. 'What made him do that?'

I shrug. 'Perhaps something I said got to him after all.' I force myself to meet Pepper's gaze. 'Lola was in floods last night, of course, but I do think it's really over. And she will move on.'

Pepper opens her mouth to say something else, but luckily, her phone rings at that exact moment, leaving me free to scurry back to my desk. I sit down, relieved to have got away without Pepper interrogating me further. If I'm not going to tell Seb the truth about taking his money, I'm certainly not going to talk to anyone else about it.

I can't stop imagining the moment when Seb gets home tonight, finds his phone and discovers his money is gone. He'll be upset, naturally, but he'll tell the bank and they will refund the money.

Everything will be all right.

I don't have to think about any of it until this evening.

–

At quarter past three that afternoon, Seb rings me.

'Someone's hacked my savings account!' he exclaims, without preamble. 'All the money Mum left me, it's gone!'

I can hear the panic in his voice, and all my guilt rises up again, swamping me.

I'm a terrible person. The *worst*.

'Oh, no!' I don't have to try to sound concerned. 'I'm so sorry, Seb. What happened?'

'I came home early to look for my phone and it was on the bloody sofa, which I'm sure I checked this morning and… and God, Alison I have no idea how it was taken. I've been on to the bank. They can't work it out either. The theft happened during the night apparently. We think maybe someone hacked in remotely; maybe I clicked on a dodgy link at some point without realising.'

Oh, God.

'That's awful.' I hesitate, waves of guilt washing over me. 'Can the bank recover the money?'

'It's already been cashed out,' Seb says. He sounds close to tears.

'But the bank will refund it, won't they?' I can hear the desperation in my voice.

Poor Seb.

'They haven't guaranteed they will yet, but they've opened a case.' He pauses. 'I can't believe it.'

'I'm so, so sorry, I…' I stop talking, my mind whirring. I feel a huge impulse to confess. I swallow it down. 'Try not to worry,' I say. 'You'll get your money back.'

'Thanks.' He heaves a sigh. 'See you soon.'

I can't tamp down the sick, remorseful feeling that rises through my body as I end the call. What was I thinking? I should never have taken Seb's money. It's not just illegal, and a total betrayal, it was cruel, too. Hating myself, I try to turn my attention to a press release Hamish has just drafted.

Half an hour later, my phone pings with a message from Lola.

> School is too shit, I feel sick, have come home early.

Two minutes after that, Michael texts to say he'll be round later to talk to her.

I make an excuse to Pepper and leave work straight away.

–

Seb is on his phone when I get home. He raises his hand and points to the mobile. I nod, sympathetically, to show him I understand, then head up to Lola's bedroom. The door is shut, so I knock lightly, then peer inside.

'Lola?' She's on the bed, bent over with her head in her hands. Oh, God, she must be wracked with misery. I hurry over. 'Come on love,' I say, 'I know break-ups are hard, but you've got so much going for you. On course for top grades in everything, you just need to get back on track, focus on your uni applications. Are you still thinking Law? Or History, then the conversion course?' I gaze at her, eager for some sign of the former enthusiasm about her future that used to bubble out of her. Instead she just heaves a huge sigh. I stare helplessly as her shoulders start to shake with sobs. I perch on the edge of the bed and put out my hand to touch Lola's shoulder. Her frame is so slight, the start of her collarbone so fragile.

I'm trying to work out what to say to her, when there's a knock at the front door, then the sound of people talking. Who on earth is that, now? Lola doesn't seem to notice any of this. I listen harder to the two voices downstairs. Oh, God, that's Michael. With Seb. I should go down; referee between them.

69

I sit back. 'Sweetheart, I'm just going downstairs for a moment, then I'll make us some tea and we can talk.'

Lola slowly takes her hands from her face. She looks up at me, dry-eyed. Her mouth curves into a mocking smile.

'You,' she says drily, 'are the last person I want to talk to.'

I stare at her, utterly thrown. 'Please, Lola, I'm just trying to be here for you… To help you—'

'I think you've helped enough.' Lola's eyes harden. She sucks in her breath. 'I know that you gave Brendan the money for his tour.'

My guts twist into a painful knot. 'No,' I say, stupidly trying to deny it.

'Oh, shut *up*.' A fleck of spit flies out of her mouth and onto the crumpled duvet. I gasp. Lola has *never* talked to me like this before. 'Stop lying to me. I know everything you've done, how you tried to manipulate Brendan… to split us up in return for *money*. It's… it's *pathetic*.' She stops, her breath jagged. 'He told me the whole thing.'

'Oh, Lola.' The air around us stretches with tense silence. 'I'm so sorry that Brendan said all that but even if it doesn't feel like it now, Brendan leaving is a *good* thing.'

'I already know that,' she says flatly.

I shake my head, lost again, my head spinning. My mind vaguely registers footsteps on the landing, but all I can see is Lola in front of me, a look of triumph on her face.

'What… I don't—' I frown. 'What do you mean?'

Lola gives me a cold smile. 'Brendan is leaving the country to start planning his tour on Saturday,' she says. 'And I'm going with him.'

It's like all the air has been sucked out of my body.

'What did you say?' Michael appears in the doorway, eyes wide.

'You can't, Lola,' I gasp.

'You're *not*,' Michael adds, marching into the room.

Lola glares at us. 'You can't stop me.'

'Oh yes we can.' Michael draws a furious breath.

I jump up and put a hand on his arm. 'Lola, *please*,' I say. 'This doesn't make sense. You and Brendan just split up, you—'

'We were pretending,' Lola says icily.

'You… you lied?' I clutch my forehead.

'Why the hell did you do that?' Michael demands.

Lola stares silently at us both. I'm suddenly aware that Seb is now in the doorway of her room, frowning as he looks inside. A moment later Josh appears, school blazer slung over his shoulder. He stands next to Seb, following his gaze and, clearly, wondering what we're all doing in here.

'Please *think*, Lola,' I plead. 'You can't just *leave*. What about your A levels? University? Your whole *life*? You can't give it all up for *Brendan*. For a *tour*.'

Lola unfurls herself from her bed and stands up to face us.

'What's going on?' Josh asks uncertainly. 'Who's Brendan? What kind of tour?'

'Josh, please go to your—' I start.

'A music tour. With Brendan Zeno,' Lola explains, her voice light and scornful. 'I'm going along to help him with planning and promotion, do his social media, that sort of thing. Mum's invested fifty grand in it.'

Oh no.

'What?' Seb strides into the room, his forehead wreathed in a frown. 'What are you talking about?'

71

My heart sinks.

'No way, Lo.' Josh laughs. 'You're making it up.'

'I'm not,' Lola insists.

'Seriously?' Josh's eyes widen. 'Can I come too, then?'

'No.' Lola, Michael and I speak together.

'Alison?' Seb's bewildered voice cuts in. 'Please will you explain to Lola that she has misunderstood the situation regarding the money?'

The three of them look at me, the atmosphere tensing. Lola raises her eyebrows. 'Ooh, Mum,' she teases, 'doesn't Seb *know* about the money?'

I stare at Seb, unable to speak. His jaw drops.

'What money?' Josh asks.

Michael throws me a sardonic look. 'Yeah, Ali, what money?'

'I already said.' Lola rolls her eyes. 'Mum has invested £50,000 in Brendan's tour. She got it off Seb, apparently.'

I can't meet Seb's eyes anymore. I stare at the carpet.

'*Fifty grand!*' Josh exclaims. 'Couldn't you have invested in me instead? I'd like a holiday in Thailand and to go to some festiv—'

'Is this true, Alison?' Seb's voice is hard as stone.

'Oh dear, oh dear,' Michael murmurs.

'I don't get it,' Josh moans. 'Why would Seb give Mum money for—?'

'Alison,' Seb interrupts, touching my arm. 'We need to talk. Right now.'

Michael sighs. 'Come on, Josh, let's play *Call of Duty*.' He puts his hand on Josh's shoulder, then glances at Lola. 'I'll be back to talk to *you* in a moment,' he adds.

Josh rolls his eyes, then lets his dad steer him onto the landing.

Seb shuts the door behind them, then turns to me. 'Alison, we really—'

'Wait,' I say, then turn to Lola. 'I don't know what Brendan told you, but he's manipulated us both, he—'

'No, Mum,' Lola drawls, her voice dripping with venom, 'you're the manipulator. As well as a liar, a thief and a total bitch.'

I stagger back as if she's punched me. Normally Seb would leap on Lola – on anyone – for talking to me like that but right now he's just watching me in silence, repressed rage emanating from his entire body. I shake my head. 'Please, Lola, that's not true.'

Lola sinks onto her bed. The duvet is a crumpled heap beside her, a scattering of fruit-flavoured lip balms lie beside a half-empty perfume bottle and a BB cream tube on the exposed stretch of white sheet. She looks sulkily up at me. 'You went to *Brendan*. He didn't come to you. You lied to me and stole from Seb, so—'

'Please listen, I'm sorry for lying, but—'

'When you started telling Brendan he had to leave me and even offering him money, he realised there was a way for us – him and me – to play you at your own game.' A look of self-satisfaction creeps across her face. 'So Brendan pretended to accept your offer, then later we talked, and I agreed I'd make out he dumped me so you'd pay him all the money you'd promised.'

'Jesus,' Seb mutters.

I gaze at Lola, pierced to my core. 'But you were so upset when you came home afterwards.' My voice shakes as I speak.

'Of *course* I was upset,' Lola says, her own voice trembling too. 'My own mother had gone behind my back

73

and tried to ruin my life, then lied to me about it. I was devastated.'

I stare at her.

'Alison?' Seb's voice is edged with iron. 'Let's talk. *Now*, please.'

I ignore him. 'Lola, you have to understand that everything I did – all I've *ever* done – it's to protect you.'

Lola shakes her head. 'Try to protect your *image* of me, that's what Brendan says.'

'Brendan doesn't know me.'

'Doesn't he? He says you're neurotic and controlling.' Lola folds her arms, jutting out her chin. 'But you can't control me. It won't work.' She turns away, jamming on her headphones. 'Now leave me alone.'

'Alison.' Seb's voice is like steel. '*Now!*'

'Okay!' Tears prick at my eyes as I follow him out of Lola's room. What the hell has Brendan done? Half-blinded by tears, I let Seb lead me into our bedroom. He shuts the door.

'You need to get my money back,' he snaps.

And make Brendan leave Lola. 'I know, I'm calling him.' I take out my phone and scroll to Brendan's number.

The call goes straight to voicemail. I look up, feeling helpless. 'He's not answering.'

'What a surprise,' Seb says coldly.

'I can't believe this…' I say, my voice hoarse.

'What the hell, Alison?' Seb glares at me. 'You stole all my money? Then let me think my phone had been hacked?'

'I'm so sorry.' I sit down on the bed, feeling winded. Shame floods my face with heat. 'I was sure the bank would cover it.'

'So you planned to defraud a high street bank as well as betray me and our relationship?' Seb's voice is like ice.

'I'm so sorry,' I plead. 'I swear I'll get the money back. I'll make Brendan repay every penny.'

'We'll talk about restitution in a minute.'

I frown. *Restitution?* 'Seb, it's not a war crime, I was *desperate.* I swear I didn't do any of this deliberately to hurt you.'

'And yet that's *exactly* what you've done.' Seb shakes his head in disbelief. 'Don't make things worse by belittling my reaction. It's not just the money, it's that you *lied.*' He hesitates. 'Do you know what an idiot I feel like right now? I had *plans* for that money. Plans for *us.*' He hesitates, and I'm suddenly horribly certain he's about to mention getting married.

'Seb, you're right,' I hurry on, before he can speak. 'Of course, you're right. And *I'm* the idiot here, not you. I'm so, so sorry I didn't tell you everything before. I just *had* to get Lola away from—'

'You need to stop focusing on Lola,' Seb interrupts.

I stare at him. 'What?'

'I know she's your daughter and Brendan isn't who you'd choose for her, but this isn't about who Lola is involved with.'

'Of course it is, I—'

'This is about *power,*' Seb interrupts again. 'Who has it. Who doesn't. You took a gamble and lost. Brendan cheated you and now Lola is understandably furious that you tried to manipulate her, which means getting her away from him will be even more impossible than it was in the first place. Brendan and Lola have all the power here.'

'But I *have* to do something.'

'You can't do *anything* about *any* of that, Alison,' Seb goes on. 'All you *can* do is focus on getting my money back. That's if you care about our relationship at all.' He pauses. 'I'm going to call my bank now and explain what's happened. We can talk later about options.' He pauses again. 'I'll be sleeping next door until it's sorted.' He stomps away.

Left alone, I walk over to the window and stare out at the lamplit street and the houses opposite. It seems bizarre that there are homes just metres away containing other people with other problems.

Other lies.

A light rap on the door and I spin around. Michael is standing in the doorway, eyebrows raised. I explain quickly how paying off Brendan seemed like my only option.

'What an arsehole,' Michael mutters.

I groan. 'Me or Brendan?'

'Him,' Michael says. 'I don't blame you, you just got caught up in one of his manipulations.'

'I don't think Seb sees it like that.' I hesitate. 'I'm wondering now if Brendan's main motive was even the money. Or not *just* the money. I think he wanted to humiliate me as much as anything.'

'He is a piece of work,' Michael growls. 'I'm going to track him down right now. Demand that he leaves Lola *and* pays you back.'

I frown. 'I don't kn—' But Michael has already disappeared, his heavy tread sounding on the stairs.

I follow quickly. Michael is putting on his coat in the hall. Seb appears as I reach the bottom step. He strides over, lowering his voice so Michael can't hear.

'I've told the bank what you did,' he mutters. 'They won't refund me unless I press charges.'

'Against *me*?' I draw back.

Seb nods. I gulp, then glance over at Michael who is watching us both intensely.

'Listen, Seb,' I say. 'I'm going over to Brendan's right now. I'm going to demand he gives you your money back.'

'And I'm going to knock some sense into the man over Lola,' Michael adds, darkly.

'If Michael's going, I'm coming too.' Seb reaches for his overcoat.

'No,' I say. 'I *really* don't think—'

'Don't try and stop me,' Seb snaps, casting a scornful glance at Michael. 'It's my money that's at stake.'

'And it's my daughter.' Michael bristles.

'Okay. Okay,' I say. 'We'll all go.'

NINE

Half an hour later, Michael pulls up outside Brendan's house. As he switches off the engine, Seb – who is sitting in the front passenger seat – starts to open the door next to him.

'Wait!' I order.

Both men turn and look at me. Seb looks mutinous, his mouth set in a grim line. Michael raises his eyes sardonically. 'What, Ali?'

'Let me try talking to Brendan on my own first,' I say. 'He's not going to respond well if we turn up mob handed. Our best chance of getting the money *and* making him keep his promise over Lola is if I can persuade him, one-to-one.'

Michael purses his lips doubtfully. 'I don't think that'll work. Look what happened the last time you talked to him.'

'Quite.' Seb pushes the passenger door fully open.

'Just give me two minutes before you both wade in,' I plead. 'I got us all into this mess. At least let me try and get us out of it, please?'

'Okay,' Michael says with a sigh, sitting back.

'Fine.' Seb folds his arms and pulls his door shut again. 'You've got two minutes.'

I hurry out of the car and across the road. The security light comes on as I scurry up the brick path to the front door. I press the front doorbell, turning my face to the camera above it to make sure Brendan sees that it's me. I step back and wait. No one comes.

I ring again, keeping my finger pressed on the buzzer. Still no reply. I hammer my fist against the wood.

'Excuse me?'

I spin around. Brendan's white-haired neighbour is peering over the hedge that separates their front gardens. 'He's away,' she says. 'Visiting his mother.'

I nod, slowly. That makes sense. The account Brendan asked me to pay the money into was his mother's, so he probably needed her signature to get his hands on the cash.

'Do you know when he'll be back?' I ask. 'I know he's planning on leaving the country this weekend.'

I'm expecting the neighbour to look surprised at this, but instead she nods. 'That's right. He's off abroad Saturday, but he'll be back tomorrow night to sort out a few last things, he said. He's going to pop his keys through my letterbox to hand to the letting agents.'

'Right.' I glance over at the car. I can see Michael and Seb watching us through the windscreen.

'He's doing some sort of music tour apparently.' The woman rolls her eyes, then indicates Brendan's house behind me. 'Subletting that, he says. I'm just praying the place doesn't go to hooligans.' She looks at me with naked curiosity. 'Are you a friend of his?'

'Sort of,' I say, then, before she can ask my name, 'I'll see if I can reach him some other way. Thanks.' I scuttle away, back to the car.

–

That night I dream of Brendan, shadowy images from the past. I wake with a jerk, sun flooding in through the window, memories crawling over my skin like ants. The house is silent. I scramble out of bed and check the time. Almost nine a.m. Normally, I'm woken by Seb's alarm but, of course, he slept next door last night and will now be long gone to work. I hurry onto the landing. The house is silent. Empty. I fetch my phone and peer at the screen. Lola has sent a text:

> Meeting Maisie to shop ALL DAY for
> CLOTHES FOR BRENDAN'S TOUR!!!!!!!!
> So FUCK YOU!

I lie back on the bed, feeling sick. How am I ever going to mend things with my furious daughter?

I'm more certain than ever that Brendan won't help. Even if I had managed to talk to him last night, I don't believe it would have made any difference. Seb was right about me having no power here. I can't imagine a bribe – or a threat – that would make Brendan either give up Lola or give back the money.

Which means I'm going to have to find another way to keep Lola away from him, another way to pay Seb back. My phone rings.

'Not coming to work today?' Pepper asks drily.

I frown. Why does she sound so waspish? I'm not even technically late yet.

'Michael just rang,' she goes on. 'Told me everything.' She pauses. 'Why on earth didn't you tell me you paid off Brendan?'

'I didn't want to involve you,' I mumble.

'Make me an accessory to your theft, you mean?' Pepper chuckles. 'I guess I ought to thank you for that. Hey, I bet Seb is mad as hell?'

'He is.'

'Ah.' I can hear her voice softening. 'Well, he'll get over it and in the meantime @AvengingAngel has already had loads of likes and reposts. Some horrible rape threats too, unfortunately, and nobody coming forward yet, still its early days.' She pauses. 'At least the truth is out there.'

She's right, I guess, but I don't want to talk about that right now, so I turn the conversation to Michael and ask how he sounded when they spoke.

'He was all set to wait for Brendan when he gets home tonight and beat him to a pulp, but I think I talked him out of it.' Pepper sighs. 'I tried calling Lola just now but when I started explaining what an arsehole Brendan is, she hung up on me.'

'Oh, God.' I pause. 'You know you told me to burn down Brendan's house?'

'Uh-huh.'

'I think I may have burned down my own instead.'

'Oh, Alison.' Pepper sighs again. 'Is there anything I can do?'

'No,' I say. 'I'm coming in now. There's no point me staying at home. Lola's going to be out all day. I'll try talking to her again later.'

–

As I reach the office, Seb sends a text.

> Talked to a solicitor. He says I can't legally
> go after Brendan as you weren't coerced
> into giving him the money and that the
> bank isn't liable. Serious talk tonight.

Oh, great.

In the office, Hamish is particularly attentive, offering me a series of sympathetic smiles and making me an unsolicited cuppa. He sets it down in front of me. 'Are you okay?' he asks, softly. 'About what's happening with… with Lola? Pepper explained the latest.'

'Did she?' Annoyed at Pepper's lack of discretion, I glance up at him. Today he's dressed in a crisply ironed blue shirt and velvet waistcoat. I catch the light scent of what smells like a very expensive cologne. His eyes are as bright as his shirt and intent on my face, but his expression couldn't be more concerned. My irritation fades. He might be as nosey as Pepper is gossipy, but he's kind. They both are. The very opposite of Brendan.

'Don't be nice to me,' I say, my eyes pricking with tears.

'Sorry… sorry…' An anxious frown knots Hamish's brows. 'I know it's none of my business, it's just Lola's a sweet kid.' He offers me another sad smile.

I nod. Of course, Hamish knows Lola quite well, after she spent most of the summer holiday helping out in the office. He's bound to be affected by what's happening to her.

'It's fine, thank you for caring.' The tears are threatening to bubble up now, so I turn my attention pointedly to the letter about local business rates that's open on my screen. Hamish creeps away.

As morning turns to afternoon, I message both children asking whether or not they'll be in for food. Josh replies straight away to say he'll be back after football practice.

Lola doesn't reply at all.

–

Seb is already home when I get there, sitting at the kitchen table and rigid with tension.

'What really gets me,' he says before I even set my bag down, 'is the arrogance of you thinking you can just help yourself to my money. You obviously don't care about me or my feelings.'

I shake my head. It's understandable Seb should be angry, but I'm already so ground down. In twenty-four hours, my only daughter – who hates me – is due to drop out of school, abandon her family and leave the country and the future she has spent years working for. Worse than all that, when she goes, she'll be totally at the mercy of the cruellest man I've ever met.

'I *do* care about you, Seb,' I protest.

'You care about Lola more,' Seb snaps.

My breath catches in my throat. 'I know I've messed up, Seb, but don't ask me to choose between you and my children.'

'That's not what I'm doing.' He pushes himself up off the table, so fast his chair clatters back across the floor. 'And how dare you make out *I'm* the monster here. *Brendan's* the monster. And *you*! *You're* the one who's taken my money and thrown everything I've given you back in my face.' He stalks out of the kitchen and stomps upstairs.

I'm still sitting at the table, wondering what to say to him, when he reappears in the hall five minutes later, dressed for a run. He leaves without saying goodbye and I'm left alone in the house.

83

It's almost eight when he returns and he, Josh and I sit down for the lasagne I've heated up from the freezer. Seb is clearly still seething, but makes a pointed effort to be pleasant in front of Josh, asking about his earlier football practice. Josh replies politely enough, shovelling in his food in the same methodical way he approaches all vital tasks. Unlike Lola, who got on with Seb from the start, Josh initially acted out, but then quickly calmed down and now basically treats Seb like a large piece of furniture: a neutral – if cumbersome – presence, that Josh must manoeuvre around every day but can otherwise ignore.

We are just clearing the plates from dinner when Lola bursts into the house. She slams the front door behind her, hurrying across the hall.

'Hiya!' I call out.

No response, just the sound of her stomping up the stairs.

I meet Seb's gaze. He shakes his head. 'Leave her,' he mutters, in a tone that clearly indicates I am, once again, fussing.

Irritation at him surges inside me. The desire for Lola to be little again, when a cuddle and a plaster on a scraped knee would set the world to rights, grips me as I stride to the bottom of the stairs and call up. 'Lola?' The shower in the bathroom starts. Clearly she's not in any better mood than she was earlier. I return to the now empty kitchen and finish clearing away. Maybe she'll be calmer in the morning. Surely by then I'll have worked out a way to stop her from leaving with Brendan.

But, in the end, when it comes to it, there's no need for that conversation at all.

–

I'm still deep in pillow-y unconsciousness when the door-bell rings. Three sharp, metallic chimes wake me with a jolt. I sit up in bed, my hand flying to my chest. It's still dark outside.

I reach for my phone. It's just gone six a.m. I struggle onto my elbows as another insistent series of chimes echo through the house.

Seb appears in the doorway. 'Who the hell is that?' he mumbles grumpily.

'I'll go and see,' I say, flinging back the bedcovers. I'm running over the possibilities in my mind. It can't be the kids, they're both in bed. I grab my dressing gown and hurry downstairs.

Above me, I can hear Josh stumble, grumbling onto the landing. 'Whass goin' on?'

Seb's footsteps hit the creaky floorboard outside our bedroom door. 'No idea,' I hear him grunting back to Josh.

I cross the hall and peer through the spyhole. Two police officers: one man, one woman stand on the door-step. They are both dressed in navy uniforms, buttons sparkling in the porch light. The man is older with grey hair and red cheeks. The woman looks about my age, maybe younger. The serious expressions on their faces shoot an arrow of panic into my chest. I yank open the door.

'Hello,' I say. 'What's happened?'

The officers exchange a look I can't read. The man clears his throat. 'I'm Police Constable Stanley and this is PC Turnbull. May we come in?' Both officers flash their badges.

I step back to let them in. I'm vaguely aware of Seb and Josh hurrying down the stairs and into the hall. Lola hasn't appeared.

'Please tell me what's going on?' My voice catches in my throat.

'Are you Lola White's mother?' PC Stanley asks. I nod. 'We'd like to speak to her. Is she here?'

'Er, yes.' Confusion sweeps through me. I turn to Seb. He blinks at me, clearly as bewildered as I am.

The landing creaks. We all turn. Lola is standing at the top of the stairs, a jumper tugged on over her pyjamas, her hair hiding half her face. 'Hi,' she says shyly. 'I'm Lola.'

'We just need to ask you some questions, Lola,' PC Turnbull says crisply. 'Can you come down, please?'

Lola pads slowly downstairs. Josh is fidgeting beside Seb. His jaw hangs open, his eyes darting over the police officers. He's terrified, I realise. Anger rises inside me. I turn on PC Stanley. 'It's not even dawn yet. Why do you need to speak to Lola? What do you want to ask her about?'

The officer glances from me to Lola, appearing beside me. 'We're here in connection with a death,' he explains.

I stare at him, blankly. Lola huddles closer to me.

'*What?*' I ask. '*Whose?*'

PC Stanley draws in his breath. 'The death of Brendan Zeno.'

TEN

Lola's hand flies to her mouth, muffling a low moan.

The hall suddenly feels cold. I draw my dressing gown more tightly around me.

'Brendan's dead?' My throat is dry.

'That's right.' PC Stanley smiles sympathetically at me.

'Oh God.' Lola leans against me. I feel the press of her slender frame on my arm.

'But... *how*?' I stammer. 'What happened?'

'I'm afraid I'm not free to give details, but I can confirm that we are investigating the cause of death,' PC Stanley says.

What does that mean? That it was somehow suspicious? Or a suicide?

No. Not suicide. Not Brendan.

'May we sit down?' PC Turnbull asks. 'It's just you we need to speak to, Lola.' The officer glances at Josh, then raises her eyebrows at me.

'Yes, of course. Josh, please go back to bed,' I order.

'But—' Josh protests.

'Seb?' I meet Seb's eyes. He gives a curt nod. 'Come on, Josh,' he says. 'Let's give the police some space to talk to Lola.' He leads a grumbling Josh towards the stairs.

I usher the two officers into the living room.

'Can my mum stay?' Lola asks.

'Yes,' PC Turnbull says. 'We just want to get a few preliminary answers at this time.'

What does that mean?

Unsettled, I sit down on one sofa, Lola huddled against me. The two police constables take the couch opposite. PC Stanley removes his notebook from his pocket and taps a pen on the cover to click out the inked point. He leans forward, his pen poised over his pad, his eyes on Lola.

'When was the last time you saw Brendan, Lola?'

Fear drips like ice water down my spine. Why is he asking that?

Lola stares at PC Stanley. Her slender fingers reach for my hand and squeeze tight. She's trembling.

'We understand you were in a relationship with him, so—'

'No.' Lola squeezes my hand harder, panic in her eyes. 'Mum? No, I–I've changed my mind, I... I don't want to talk to them.' Her voice cracks, her breath coming in shallow, panicky gasps. 'This... can't... no... not Brendan... *can't* be...'

'Where were you between six and eight yesterday evening Lola?' PC Stanley persists. 'Did you go to Brendan's house?'

'No!' Lola's face is pale and horrified. 'No, I didn't.'

A protective anger rises inside me. 'What are you implying?' I demand. 'Lola doesn't have anything to do with Brendan being... being...'

'It's a suspicious death,' PC Turnbull says, again speaking in a tone that implies she's offering helpful information.

My heart lurches into my throat.

'I can't talk to you.' Lola sits up, blowing out her breath. I can see she's making a massive effort to control herself. 'I just can't. Not now.'

'Perhaps if you give us some time?' I suggest. 'Give Lola a chance to come to terms with the news… This is a terrible shock for her.'

The police officers exchange meaningful looks.

'You're definitely saying you didn't see Brendan last night, Lola?' PC Stanley asks.

Lola nods. Her hands are clasped together so tightly that the knuckles are white.

The officers look at each other again. PC Stanley clears his throat. 'Okay, then, Lola, we're going to have to take this down the station.'

'What?' I gulp. '*No.*'

Lola stares in front of her, her head held high. I have the strange sense of time slowing down.

And then Lola pulls away from me, wiping her eyes as she sits up.

'I don't want to talk to you,' she says to the officers. 'And I don't want to come to the station.'

There's a short pause, then PC Stanley says briskly: 'If you don't come, Lola, we'll have to arrest you.'

His words are like a slap. I gasp. 'But this is ridiculous, Lola and Brendan were a—' I hesitate, the word sticking in my throat. 'They'd been seeing each other. A… a couple.' I trail off, looking over at Lola.

Her lips are pressed defiantly together, but as she stares at the officers her mouth trembles slightly. 'I think you should answer the officers' questions, Lo,' I say, more gently.

Lola stares straight ahead of her, her expression glassy and dazed.

I turn to the police officers. 'She's overwhelmed,' I explain. 'She's—'

'Fine, I'll go to the station.' Lola stands up.

'Lola?' I frown.

Without looking at me, Lola reaches for her shoes on the floor beside the sofa.

PC Stanley rises to his feet, watching her. I can't tell what he's thinking.

I stand up too. 'Lola, just speak to the police here,' I urge.

Lola turns to me as she slides on her shoes. 'It's better that I do this now,' she says. 'Officially. Get it over and done with.'

'I'll come with you.' I turn to the police officers. 'If you're going to interview my daughter, I'd like to be with her.'

'I'm afraid not,' PC Stanley says. 'Lola is eighteen, not a minor. If we're conducting an official interview, then—'

'It's okay, Mum.' Lola draws herself up. Her face is sheet white, but there's a grim determination in her eyes. 'I'll be fine.'

We make our way out to the hall. For all the resolution on her face, I notice Lola's hands tremble as she takes her black jacket off the peg.

'We'll come to the police station and wait. We'll be right behind you.' I glance at Seb who has returned from ferrying Josh upstairs. He gives a curt nod.

I pull Lola to me in a swift, desperate hug.

'I didn't do anything, Mum,' she whispers in my ear.

'Of course you didn't,' I say, squeezing her tightly.

'I can't believe that Brendan… I didn't…' Her voice is a fragile whisper. 'Mum, oh, God, *Brendan*…' She breaks on that last word, swallowing the most pitiful sob I've ever heard in my life.

I want to cry too, but I have to be strong for her. I hold her close and breath what reassurance I can into her ear. 'They just want to ask some questions,' I whisper. 'There won't be anything more to it.'

I try to believe what I'm saying. Everything will be all right. Won't it?

–

Seb and I follow the police car to the station. The traffic is just starting to build, as a misty dawn struggles to appear through the gloom of night. Seb drives. I peer anxiously through the windscreen, trying to catch a glimpse of Lola in the back seat of the police car. Why on earth wouldn't she just talk to the officers in our house?

It doesn't make sense, but the combination of that calm, slightly glazed expression and the tell-tale trembling of her hands suggest that, when she left the house, she was in shock. I might not know much about it, but that's no state in which to be answering questions from the police.

After a few minutes, I lose sight of the car ahead and sit back, my chest knotted with an anxiety that won't unwind. A soft rain patters down outside, gleaming under the streetlamps. I can understand why the police would want to speak to Lola about when she last saw Brendan, about his state of mind, but why on earth do they want to know where she was yesterday evening? Could they seriously think she had something to do with Brendan's death?

Brendan's death. The words don't make sense.

I call Michael, my voice shaking as I go over what's happened. The words sound surreal as I say them –

Brendan is dead and Lola is being questioned by detectives. Predictably, Michael explodes down the phone at the police for dragging Lola to the station, at Brendan for being dead and at himself for being unable to prevent any of it. I'm explaining that the officers only took Lola away because she refused to talk to them in the house, when he interrupts to snap that he's going to call a lawyer at a firm he knows through his work as a journalist. Before I can ask who, he rings off.

I gaze at the streetlights that glow, blurrily, through the early morning drizzle. Neither Seb nor I speak much for the rest of the drive. Seb mumbles a few times that he can't quite take in what is happening. As he speaks, I realise that alongside my shock, I also feel massively relieved. Brendan is gone. Out of our lives forever.

'And then there's the money.' Something in Seb's voice pierces through the fog of my thoughts.

'What?' I turn my head to look at him.

We've stopped at the traffic lights before the station. Seb glances at me, his foot hovering over the pedals, ready to set off again. 'Look, I know this is really upsetting because… well, the police taking Lola and the suspicious death thing, but I'm sure that will get straightened out in the next few hours.' He hesitates. 'And there's still the issue of my money. Now Brendan's dead, I'm wondering if it makes it easier to get that back? And whether, well, maybe we should strike while the iron's hot?'

Is he serious? 'You want me to say – *today* – that our main concern is getting your cash back?'

'You make it sound like a bad thing,' Seb protests. 'Surely its important the police know what Brendan was like – what he did. Which means you're going to have to explain that he manipulated you. And if you're telling them how you let yourself get bullied into giving him money, you might as well add that you want that money returned.'

'Right.' I fold my arms. 'I get it, Seb, but first things first.'

The lights change and Seb presses on the accelerator pedal. There's a swish as we drive through a kerbside puddle, then Seb slows the car to turn left. He clears his throat.

'When you say "first things first", you mean Lola? You're worried about her talking to the police?'

'Of course, I am.' I can't keep the bitterness out of my voice. 'She's just had a terrible shock. Then this. A police interview is trauma on top of trauma.'

'I'm sure they don't suspect her of anything,' Seb says, missing my point. 'They'll be talking to everyone Brendan was involved with.' He glances at me. 'After all, she was his girlfriend.'

I fall silent as we drive the final stretch of road before the police station, then pull up outside. Seb parks, then switches off the engine.

'Listen,' he says. 'I get that tonight you're focused on Lola, but — and I'm just flagging this up — if we can't mention the money right now, maybe next week we could talk to the executor for Brendan's will?' He pauses. 'Who do you think that will be?'

'I don't know,' I say, gritting my teeth. 'Maybe this lawyer Michael's sorting out for Lola will be able to find out?'

'Right, okay, that's something.' Seb pats my hand. 'Come on, then, let's go and support Lola.' He gets out of the car and shuts the door with a careful click, then stands back, waiting for me.

The drizzle is easing but, as we make our way into the police station, a single, cold drop trickles down the back of my neck.

ELEVEN

Lola has already gone into the police interview room so I can't tell her that Michael's lawyer is on her way, though the duty sergeant reassures us he will pass on the message. Seb and I seat ourselves in the waiting room. It's almost empty and depressingly bleak, with plastic-backed chairs in rows and paint peeling off the grubby grey walls.

Fifteen long minutes pass, then a dishevelled Michael hurtles into the room, his coat collar crumpled and his hair all ruffled at the back. He must have driven fast to get here so quickly.

'The lawyer will be here soon,' he growls, sitting down beside us.

I'm well aware of how successful at making things happen he is, but even so I'm impressed when a solicitor arrives barely ten minutes later. Michael introduces her as Stacy Greening. I just have time to note how young she looks – twenty-seven or twenty-eight at most – in spite of her sober black suit and sleek red-haired bob, before she hurries off to the interview room to sit with Lola.

I can see Seb thinks the provision of a lawyer is overkill but, much to my relief, he says nothing. Nor, thankfully, does he repeat his desire to get his money back. The three of us retake our seats and I call Pepper, she's usually already awake around now. I tell her what's happened and ask her to go to the house to check Josh is okay. 'I think the police coming earlier really upset him,' I say.

Pepper agrees to pop by immediately. I can hear her down the line, crashing about in her bathroom, her voice echoing off the tiles as she talks, fast and breathless.

'They're hinting Brendan's dead on the radio – you know, "man found dead at his house" stuff. What the hell?' She sucks in her breath. 'Christ, and you only saw him – what, three days ago? What do the police think Lola can tell them?' Her voice drops to a horrified whisper. 'Do you think it could be someone who saw the @AvengingAngel post and decided he needed to die?'

'I don't know,' I say, feeling helpless.

'No, it's too soon for my post to be part of it,' Pepper says, sounding like she's trying to convince herself. 'Knowing Brendan of old it was probably an overdose.'

'He didn't look like he was on anything,' I mutter.

'You can never really tell,' Pepper says darkly.

Another forty minutes pass. While Seb scarcely says a word, Michael won't shut up.

'This is outrageous,' he rants. 'Ridiculous. I mean I get Lola was dating the man, but she was out with Maisie before she came home. Surely they'll have confirmed that by now. What on earth do they think she can tell them about Brendan's death?'

'I don't know, but—'

'I could kill Brendan for putting her through this,' Michael mutters without irony. 'Suspicious death, my arse. I bet it was drugs. I bet he overdosed on some bender.'

'That's what Pepper thinks,' I say.

'How much longer do you think this will take?' Seb murmurs. 'She's been in there for ages.'

Michael glares at him, but Seb doesn't notice. I roll my eyes and pointedly ignore the pair of them. Michael subsides into a twitchy silence. Every couple of minutes he gets up and paces around the waiting area. There are no other groups here, just a couple of weary-looking men and an anxious-faced woman. They are slumped and staring, as we are, at the muted TV screen on the wall.

Sky News which, when we arrived, featured ticker tape saying that the body of a middle-aged man had been found at the home of former pop star Brendan Zeno, now reaches the eight a.m. bulletin.

I gasp as Brendan's picture – a photo from his heyday in the Nineties showing him smiling outside a nightclub – flashes up alongside an announcement of his death. I nudge the others. According to the script at the bottom of the screen, the police have launched a full investigation.

'Oh, God.' Michael puts his head in his hands. 'That means it *wasn't* an accidental overdose.'

At last, the waiting room door opens. We're called outside by PC Turnbull. Stacy Greening is already standing in the foyer, speaking into her phone in a low voice. Seconds later, Lola appears, her face tear-stained and pale.

'Oh, sweetheart.' I hurry over. 'Are you okay?'

Lola nods, but refuses to meet my eyes. Tension tightens in my throat.

'Hey, Babycakes.' Michael puts his arm awkwardly around her shoulder. 'Stacy says you're free to go, let's get you home.'

Lola nods, leaning against her dad. Seb hovers awkwardly behind us.

I turn to Stacy, noticing for the first time that her suit might be sober, but it's also expensively cut, and that she is wearing a bright slash of crimson lipstick.

'What's going on?' I ask her. 'Why did the police spend so long talking to Lola?'

'Just gathering information,' Stacy says briskly, slipping her phone into her jacket pocket. 'They want to speak to you now Alison. I can stay if you'd like?'

'Me?' I frown. 'Why do they want to talk to me?'

Stacy glances at Lola, who looks up at last. 'I told them about the money you paid Brendan,' she says in a small voice. 'I'm sorry Mum, but they were asking about me and Brendan and… and…' Her voice cracks.

'It's fine,' I reassure her. 'It's good they know. We have nothing to hide.'

'Alison?' Seb nudges me, lowering his voice. 'If the police already know about the money, it's worth making your position *absolutely clear*.' He furrows his brow meaningfully, to make sure I've fully grasped his point.

'Right,' I say, my irritation rising. Can't he see now is not the time?

'Are you happy to talk to them this morning, Alison?' Stacy says. 'I'm sure we could rearrange for later in the day?'

'You should talk to them, Mum,' Lola urges. She leans across and whispers in my ear. 'They need to know how happy Brendan and I were, how excited I was about going away with him…' Her voice cracks and I squeeze her hand.

I nod, turning to Stacy. 'I'd rather get the interview over with. I'm sure it won't take too long.'

'So, just to be clear,' Michael interjects, 'Lola isn't under any suspicion? The detectives are simply trying to piece together Brendan's last movements?'

'Hopefully.' Stacy wrinkles her nose. 'I can't promise they won't want to speak to her again,' she says, 'but everything they have is circumstantial and Lola was great.' She offers Lola a smile, real kindness in her eyes. I like her immediately. 'She was very open with them, very clear, too, about when she was where and what she knew.'

'Of course she was,' Michael says gruffly, patting Lola on the back. 'Thanks, Stacy.'

The faintest of blushes creeps up Stacy's neck. Jesus, is she interested in Michael?

Unbidden, a sharp prick of jealousy punctures my anxiety about Lola.

'Can I go home now?' Lola asks.

'I could take you back to mine,' Michael offers.

Lola wrinkles her nose. 'I'd rather be in my proper room at Mum's.'

Michael nods.

I glance at Seb. 'I'll take you home, Lola,' he offers. 'I'll do a food shop later, too.'

'Thanks,' I say.

Lola nods but doesn't look up.

'Are you sure you're okay, sweetheart?' I ask.

'Oh, Mum.' Lola's voice cracks, as she fights back tears.

There's a brief flurry as we say our goodbyes. As Seb and Lola head outside, a young police officer calls Stacy and I into one of the interview rooms: bare walls, a single table with recording equipment and chairs on either side.

I sit, suddenly feeling guilty for no reason. What are they going to ask me?

Another few minutes pass, then two detectives walk in and introduce themselves: a man, DI Barnbury, and a woman, DS Strong, both about my age. I glance at Stacy, wondering if she'll feel in any way intimidated by being the youngest in the room.

She tucks her shiny hair behind her ears, all purposeful and serious. I glance down at my lap. My hands are shaking. Who am I kidding? I'm the one who feels intimidated.

'May I call you Alison?' DI Barnbury asks.

He has a long, thin face and narrow-set eyes that peer out, fox-like, from behind a bushy, greying fringe.

'Sure.' My voice sounds hoarse.

DS Strong sits back and looks at her boss. Clearly DI Barnbury is going to run the interview. He's studying my face carefully. The silence is unnerving. I glance at Stacy and she offers me a reassuring smile.

'Your daughter has told us—' DI Barnbury says at last, pausing to consult his notes '—that you gave money to Mr Zeno in the belief that he would agree to end his relationship with your daughter then leave the country. Is that correct?'

I nod, my throat dry.

'Were you aware that Mr Zeno had significant debts?' DI Barnbury asks.

'No,' I say, honestly, 'though I'm not surprised. Brendan was... was never exactly responsible... about anything.'

'We've already found out that he borrowed from other friends,' DS Strong interjects. 'Did he ever borrow from you?'

'No.'

'Okay, let's get back to the money you gave him, how much are we talking about?' DI Barnbury's tone is light. But I'm not fooled. He already knows the answer. Lola will have told him. Anyway, he'll have seen Brendan's bank accounts by now. Or soon will do. 'Alison?'

'I gave him £50,000.' I stop. Should I admit to stealing this from Seb? Has Lola already told them that's what I did?

'The idea being that Mr Zeno would leave Lola and go abroad?'

'That's right, but he double crossed me, he took the money but told Lola all about it and she pretended they'd split up but actually she knew all along he was going to take her on tour with him.' I'm speaking too fast, gabbling with nerves. I press my hands onto the tops of my thighs and my feet into the floor. A sudden memory of Brendan from soon after I met him, smiling as he shows me to ground myself this way before an exam, forces its way into my head.

'So initially you thought they'd split up, but then Lola told you that was a lie?' DI Barnbury asks.

'Yes.'

'That must have made you angry?' DS Strong interjects.

Barnbury glances at her, giving the tiniest shake of his head. DS Strong sits back.

'Lola already told us she was furious with you for trying to "buy Brendan off" – that's the phrase she used.' DI Barnbury raises his eyebrows.

'Yes, she was.' I look up. 'Don't you see? Lola had absolutely no reason to hurt Brendan. She loved him.'

'Your daughter's response must have been very upsetting.' There's real warmth to DI Barnbury's eyes, like he's trying to convey he feels my pain. 'When you were only trying to protect her…' There's the hint of a question in his voice.

I stiffen, immediately on guard. Is he trying to trick me in some way? Does he somehow know that Brendan raped me all those years ago?

No. There's no way he can know that. Unless he's seen the @AvengingAngel post and somehow connected the dots. I'm guessing he hasn't, or else he'd have asked already. Should I mention it? It might point him away from Lola. On the other hand, a claim that my daughter's boyfriend once raped me gives both of us a motive to kill him.

I decide to stay quiet.

'I was upset that Lola was involved with a much older man who I knew to be—' I hesitate. 'Brendan wasn't a nice man, at least he wasn't when I knew him at college. I wanted Lola away from him and though I knew it was a risk to interfere, I thought that she'd get over him leaving her. And *that* was the really important thing, more than anything else, that he should leave her, leave the country, but…' I trail off.

'Let's get back to Lola's movements last night.' DI Barnbury reaches for one of the sheets of paper in front of him.

I frown, feeling confused.

'What time did your daughter get home last night?'

'About eight twenty or eight thirty I think, we'd just finished eating.'

'Did you speak?'

'No, she went straight up to her room.'

'So you didn't see her?' DS Strong leans forward. 'Or notice what she was wearing?'

'No.' I frown again. 'But Lola had already texted earlier to say she was spending the day with her friend Maisie.' I pause. 'Why are you asking all this?'

DI Barnbury sighs, ignoring my question. 'Right, I'm going to need a full statement from you – the times and dates of all your conversations with the victim and details of the money transfer. Okay?'

I nod.

'Victim?' Stacy asks. 'Are you definitively ruling out suicide?'

DI Barnbury purses his lips. I watch his face intently. 'As I told you earlier, Ms Greening, we're waiting on forensics to confirm.' He pauses, his gaze flitting to meet mine. 'However, yes, we're treating the death as murder.'

I sit back in stunned silence.

Stacy nods. 'Okay, then. Well, Alison will get together all the information you want this afternoon,' she says briskly. 'But, right now, my client would like to get home to her daughter.' She pushes back her chair, indicating I should do the same.

'Before you go, there's just one more thing.' DI Barnbury leans forward, his arms on the table between us. I watch him. A few tense moments tick by.

'What?' I can't stop myself from asking. Is he going to ask about @AvengingAngel now?

Stacy lays a hand on my arm.

'It's just one thing, but its rather confusing to me.' DI Barnbury says slowly. 'Why do you think Lola went to visit Mr Zeno's house last night?'

'She *didn't*.' I stare at him. Is this another trick? 'She told the officers back at our house she didn't see Brendan last night.'

'She did indeed lie about her visit at that point,' DI Barnbury says carefully. 'But Lola is quite clearly recorded entering on the video camera at the front of the house at 7:03 p.m.'

My jaw drops.

DI Barnbury raises his eyebrows, watching my face keenly. 'That's not all, Alison. What *really* interests us is what took place during the following twenty or so minutes, when Lola was apparently shrieking at Mr Zeno at the top of her voice.'

My heart thuds. I can barely breathe.

'Would you like to know *what* your daughter was shouting, Alison?' the detective asks smoothly. 'I have it here on this witness statement.' He holds out a piece of paper, his hand covering the name of the witness. I peer closely, as the words Lola supposedly yelled sear themselves into my brain:

I'll kill you, you bastard, I'll kill you.

TWELVE

I stumble out of the interview room in a daze, the words that DI Barnbury claims Lola said ringing in my ears: *I'll kill you, you bastard, I'll kill you.*

It doesn't make sense. Lola *insisted* she didn't go to Brendan's last night. Why would she lie? And yet DI Barnbury says her image is captured on the front door video camera, which surely means she must have been there. And shouting her head off at Brendan. What on earth happened?

Could she have killed him? As soon as the thought rises in my head, I squash it. The idea is ridiculous. Lola doesn't have that kind of violence in her. And, even if she did, she'd never be able to hurt Brendan; she's barely five foot two and slightly built, while Brendan was broad, muscular and well over six foot.

Stacy is speaking, her voice low and soothing. I catch a word here and there: she's saying the police are just fishing for information, that I mustn't worry.

Michael materialises in front of us. I start, surprised.

'Hey, I thought you'd gone?' Stacy says, lightly.

I notice, as if it's happening on another, parallel plane, that there's something familiar, almost flirtatious, in her tone. She's definitely interested in him.

Michael doesn't respond. His eyes are fixed on me. 'You okay, Ali?' he asks.

I nod, too numb to speak.

Michael makes a sympathetic face. 'I thought I'd wait, give you both a lift home… if you'd like?'

Stacy and Michael speak in low voices as we walk across the small parking area to the pavement outside. Michael's second-hand Audi is three cars along. He whispers something to Stacy that I can't make out as he clicks open the doors. Without speaking to either of them, I crawl onto the back seat, leaving the front for the two of them.

Stacy carries on talking as we drive away. She fills Michael in on what the detectives just told us.

'So, the security cam caught her going inside and a male neighbour overheard a girl shouting.' Stacy pauses. 'I'm assuming the video footage doesn't show anyone else entering after her, which is why they're so convinced it was Lola doing the yelling.'

'No way that was Lola,' Michael insists. 'It *can't* have been.'

'Oh, God.' My guts twist painfully, as I think back to the glassy-eyed way Lola had stared at the officers this morning… her flat denials. 'Do you think Lola made things worse by initially denying she was there?'

'In the long run, probably not as much as you'd think,' Stacy says thoughtfully. 'She was clearly in shock about Brendan's death and she is only just eighteen. I think the police will take that into account. And once they showed her the video footage, she admitted she was there but insisted she just went to drop off a bag for Brendan to take to the airport the next day. She described the bag and its contents – new clothes apparently – so it should be easy enough for the police to verify.'

'So, she was only there a few minutes,' Michael says hopefully.

'Yes, she says she left out through the back garden, where there isn't a video camera.' Stacy sighs. 'I know her being there the night he died looks bad, but when the dust settles I don't think the situation is actually all that terrible.' Stacy puts a reassuring hand on his arm.

'What about her being overheard threatening to kill Brendan?' I ask tartly. 'That's pretty terrible, isn't it?'

'Lola denied that was her.' Stacy turns her head to meet my gaze. 'Anyway, witnesses are notoriously unreliable and this is an overheard conversation from a house several metres away. A good barrister should be able to pull it to pieces.'

'A *barrister*?' My voice fills with horror. 'You think this will go to court?'

'It *can't*,' Michael protests. 'This is ridiculous. The police just told you that Brendan had debts. I bet some mate of his lent him some cash, which he hadn't paid back, then went round to get the money off him and discovered he was running off to Amsterdam to organise a big concert tour. That's a motive for murder right there.'

'I'm just saying. Going to court is absolutely worst case,' Stacy says, now sounding flustered.

'It'd better be,' Michael mutters.

We drive on a little way in silence. The streets are far busier than earlier, sun glinting off the bonnets of the cars ahead. We slow at a set of traffic lights.

'Wait a minute,' Michael says, his voice rising as he speaks. 'If Lola says she left Brendan's straightaway, isn't there CCTV on a street nearby that proves it?'

'That's right.' I nod, eagerly. 'I read somewhere that London has more street cameras than any city in Europe.'

'I'm sure the police will look into that,' Stacy says.

'Right.' Michael inches the car forward. 'Do we know how Brendan was killed? Or who found the body?'

'Not yet,' Stacy admits. 'They're waiting on forensics before they confirm cause and time of death. I'm sure we'll hear in the next couple of days. Lola gave them her DNA, so that should help rule her out of… of any violence.'

'Oh, God,' I say.

Michael glances over his shoulder at me. 'Can you believe all this, Ali?'

I shake my head. Michael turns to face the road ahead. I glance out of the window. At least I'll be home in a few minutes, able to talk to Lola myself, hear from her own lips what happened.

'Lola also let the detectives take her jacket, she said it was the one she was wearing when she went to see Mr Zeno.' Stacy pauses. 'Apparently, thanks to her height, the video camera only shows her from the nose up, so it won't prove anything conclusively, but the fact that she's letting them test it for Brendan's blood speaks well for her.'

Somehow this detail upsets me more than the idea of her being swabbed for DNA.

'I keep wondering…' Michael says, darkly. 'Do you think Lola is being set up?'

I stare blankly at the back of his head. *Set up?* Is he serious?

'It's possible, I guess,' Stacy muses. 'Though unlikely, seeing as Lola didn't tell anyone she was going over there.'

I lean against the back seat while Stacy and Michael carry on their conversation. Stacy's explaining that the police will want to interview everyone who had dealings with Brendan, including anyone who ever knew him. That means Michael and Pepper will have to talk to them soon. The police might find out about Pepper's @AvengingAngel post and the fact that she published it anonymously is surely going to look bad, not just for her but maybe for me and Lola too? Or maybe it will take suspicion away from Lola? I can't work it out. I can barely focus, every fresh thought tangled up in the one before. All I want now is to get home as fast as possible and speak to Lola properly. I'm expecting Michael to drop me first, but instead, before I know it, he's pulled up outside a smart apartment block in Canonbury. I blink. I hadn't even noticed which direction we'd been driving in.

Stacy gets out and smiles at me. 'It's going to be okay, Alison,' she says, 'try and get some rest. I'll call you in the morning.'

I check my watch. It's nearly midday. It feels far later. And as if days have passed since Brendan died – weeks since I found out about his affair with Lola.

'Come and sit up front with me,' Michael grunts. 'You know I hate looking like a bloody taxi driver.'

Too wrung out to argue, I slip out of the back and take the front passenger seat. Michael zooms off.

'What did you make of Stacy?' he asks.

'Seemed efficient, reassuring. She was nice,' I say, then glance sideways at him, remembering the look she gave him earlier. 'Are you two, you know…?'

Michael grins. 'Christ, you know me too well. We *were* months ago, just a casual… well, that's how it was for me. Anyway, we're on good terms.'

'Right.' As if I'm watching myself through a fog, I note the twinge of jealousy at this admission and then the spark of pleasure at his dismissal of the relationship.

Michael glances sideways at me. 'Are you okay, Ali?' He pats my arm. 'I know this is horrible, but I'm sure in a couple of days we'll look back and – if not laugh – at least see it all in perspective.'

'Sure.' I turn and gaze out of the window. There's no sign of the earlier rain, though the morning sky is dark with heavy grey clouds. 'I just can't get my head around any of it.'

'I know.' Michael taps on the steering wheel. 'Of course, there is one possible explanation that makes sense of it all…' He hesitates.

'What?' I frown.

'Well…' He grimaces. 'I hate to say it, but was Seb at home yesterday evening? *Early* evening, I mean, when… what happened to Brendan?'

'No,' I say. 'He was out for a run. Which is normal for him. He often goes out then, after work.'

'Ah, and did he *shower* when he came back? Change all his clothes?'

I stare at him. 'Michael, for goodness' sake, of course he did. He'd been *running*.'

Michael purses his lips.

'Come on, Michael, Josh took a shower when he came back from football practice that evening. Does that make him a suspect too?'

'No, obviously not.' Michael makes a face, then falls quiet. He starts tapping on the steering wheel again. 'Though of course Josh doesn't have a motive, whereas Seb…'

'What does that mean?'

We turn into my street. Michael pulls up outside the house. I stare at the large potted rosemary that I brought from our old home when I moved here four years ago. It feels like a million years since we used to live together.

'Listen to me, Ali,' he says very seriously. 'The fact that you gave Brendan Seb's money *definitely* gives Seb a motive.'

'A motive to get the money back,' I protest. 'Not to kill Brendan. I'm sure lots of people who knew Brendan had that motive. The detective actually said in my interview that he had lots of debts.'

'Fair enough.' Michael switches off the car engine. 'But it still fits that Seb could have done it. Maybe he went over to Brendan's house, *after* Lola had been there, demanded his – your – money back and then, when Brendan laughed in his face…'

My jaw drops. 'Michael, that's crazy.'

'Less crazy than the idea Lola did it? Seb is easily as strong as Brendan. He could have snapped. I mean, the police haven't said how Brendan died, but Seb could have—'

'Michael, stop—'

'I'm not saying he meant to,' Michael persists. 'But in anger… the heat of the moment.'

'Seb's not like that.' I reach for the door handle, but Michael leans across and puts his hand over mine. His palm is heavy, his body too close. I smell the familiar scent of his neck, mingling with the soap powder smell from his collar. His arm presses against my side and for a brief second the old attraction flares, unbidden, deep inside me.

I shrink away, like he's an electric shock, and press the door handle. It doesn't give.

'You don't know what people are capable of,' Michael says softly, his breath is hot against my neck. For a single terrifying, thrilling moment I think he's about to kiss me, then he reaches over, flicks up the door lock, and sits back.

'You're being ridiculous,' I hiss, opening the car door. The rush of cool air is like a gentle slap against my cheek.

'Am I?' Michael asks. His voice is irritatingly calm.

'*Stop it*,' I snap, hauling myself out of the car.

Fury boils up inside me. This is typical Michael, getting his hooks into an idea as if it were one of his news stories, then worrying at it, making all the evidence fit his agenda. Not a thought for whose feelings he might be trampling all over.

'Just think about—'

I cut Michael off by slamming the car door shut. What an arsehole, trying to point the finger at Seb. How dare he? This self-serving, obsessive behaviour is exactly why our relationship was doomed from the start.

Without looking back, I stomp across the road and into the house.

It's silent. Seb must be at the shops, like he said earlier, while Pepper has left a note saying she's taken Josh out for lunch.

Still fuming over Michael's selfishness, I take off my coat and head upstairs. There's no sound coming from Lola's bedroom. I knock softly – no reply – so I turn the handle and slip into her room. She's sitting cross-legged on her bed, staring at her phone.

'Lola?'

She looks up, her elfin face creased with misery. Her lips wobble and in an instant I've forgotten the stress of the police interview and my exasperation with Michael. I hurry over and sit beside her on the bed. I want to fling my arms around her and soothe away her pain but, with Lola, it's always best to wait until she's ready to be held. Unlike Josh, she was never a particularly tactile child, mostly happy in her own company; smart, resourceful and self-sufficient. Even when she was ill, she rarely wanted cuddles.

A tear trickles down Lola's face. She wipes it roughly away.

'I can't stop crying,' she says.

I nod. 'It's… it's a lot to deal with,' I say. 'The police interview on top of…' I trail off.

'I can't seem to… Brendan just isn't here anymore,' she says, 'I… it doesn't feel real…' She trails off, her gaze drifting to the window. The sun is bright outside, showing up the smears on the glass.

'Oh, sweetheart.' I chew on my lip watching her. 'What happened last night, Lo?' I ask, softly. 'The police say you went over to Brendan's house. Why did you lie about that when they first asked?'

She shrugs. 'I panicked, I guess.'

'So why *did* you go there? Was it really just to drop off a suitcase?'

She meets my gaze, her eyes heavy with sorrow and – I realise with a jolt – more than a little shame. 'It was,' she says, 'but the truth is that I was having doubts about ditching my entire life and going away with him, too. I think I needed to see him before we set off, just to be sure.'

'And were you? Sure, I mean, after you saw him?'

Lola shrugs. 'I don't know, Mum, talking to him didn't really help. I think that was why I was in such a bad mood when I got home.'

'You were still having second thoughts?' I ask.

She nods. 'I wanted to talk to you about it, but I hadn't stopped being mad at you.' She gives me a wry smile and I pull her into a hug, relief flooding through me.

Downstairs, the doorbell goes, an insistent screech that pierces my head like a knife.

I release Lola. 'Who on earth is that now?' I mutter.

She frowns, wiping her eyes.

I wander to her bedroom door. Voices drift up from downstairs, Seb's among them. Then footsteps sound on the stairs. Lola and I hurry onto the landing. Seb storms towards us, a look of outraged fury on his face.

'What is it?' I ask. 'Who's here?'

'The police again,' Seb spits. 'With a bloody search warrant.'

THIRTEEN

I stare at Seb in horror. 'A search warrant? What on earth are they looking for?'

'Presumably something that might link Lola to Brendan's murder.' Seb pauses, then says accusingly: 'They want to interview me too. That bloody detective has seen Brendan's bank statements. He knows the money you paid him came from my account, a fact which apparently you neglected to mention to him yourself.' He glares at me. 'I explained that you took the money without my consent, but that I'm not pressing charges.'

I gulp. 'Oh, God, Seb, I'm so sorry.'

'I also made it clear that I'd be petitioning the executor of Brendan's will to get the money returned.' He shakes his head and disappears into our bedroom. I glance at Lola, who is standing in her own bedroom doorway, ashen faced.

'Did you say "search warrant"?' she gasps.

'Don't worry,' I say. 'I'm sure it's routine. The police know you were at Brendan's house and they know about the money. They're bound to want to dig a bit deeper.' I smile weakly at her.

'Do you think they'll look through everything?' Lola glances back at the floor of her bedroom, strewn with discarded clothes. 'All my stuff?'

'Let me find out.' I hurry downstairs to find DI Barnbury in the hall, muttering orders to a team of four – no, five – uniformed officers. I spot the two police constables who came for Lola yesterday morning, though I can't remember their names now.

As I walk over, the detective hands me a copy of the search warrant.

'What are you looking for?' I ask.

DI Barnbury raises an eyebrow. The dark rings under his eyes are more obvious here in the natural light of the hall than they were this morning, under the fluorescent glare of the police station interview room. 'I know this is disruptive,' he says, sidestepping my question, 'but the sooner we can conduct a thorough search, the sooner we can leave. One of my officers will take your full statement while we're here – save you making another trip to the station. Same with your partner.'

I nod. What else can I do? I call Stacy, who comes straight over. She demands to know why the police are searching the house, but DI Barnbury simply tells her that Lola's presence at Brendan's house last night justifies the intrusion. Stacy purses her lips and follows the officers from room to room, watching them root through all our things. The rest of us wait in the kitchen. After a barrage of angry questions from Seb that, of course, I can't answer, he retreats to his phone. Lola just sits and stares out of the window, her face streaked with tears.

I make some tea that nobody really wants to drink, then fetch a loaf of bread from the freezer and prise off slices for toast. Both Seb and I speak to the DI again; in my case, this just means going over the same questions as before, then explaining, shamefacedly, exactly when and how I took Seb's money and paid it to Brendan.

Pepper drops Josh off about an hour later; she hints that she'd like to come in, but I put her off. Dealing with Pepper is the last thing I feel up to right now.

Seb, Josh, Lola and I sit around the kitchen table, while the police carry on searching the house. Apart from the occasional bump and thump, they make very little noise.

'This is surreal,' Seb mutters at one point.

'How much longer will they be, Mum?' Josh asks.

'I don't know, love.' I put what I intend to be a comforting hand on his shoulder.

Josh pulls away with a sullen: 'I'm fine.'

Another hour passes. Stacy pops into the kitchen to inform us that she still has no idea what the police are looking for, 'though it must be something specific,' she adds, tapping her fingers on the kitchen table, 'for them to be doing such a thorough search.'

I glance across at Lola, who is now listening to music through a thick pair of Beats headphones.

'Do you think they're looking for a murder weapon?' I whisper.

Stacy meets my gaze. She gives me a single nod. I gulp.

'That means they're sure how he died, doesn't it?' I ask. 'They're just not telling us?'

Stacy nods again.

I wander over to Lola. She tugs down her headphones and leans against my side. I slide my arm around her shoulders.

'Oh, Mum,' Lola whispers, her voice heavy with despair.

'Please don't worry,' Stacy says, earnestly. 'I know this feels massive, but you have to remember that the police are almost certainly just fishing; if they had a clear idea about where a piece of evidence might be, they'd have gone straight to it.'

'How much longer do you think they'll be?' I ask.

'I'll go and see.' Stacy leaves the kitchen. She's back just five minutes later. 'Okay,' she says. 'There's good news and bad news.' She smiles. 'Good news is that the police are just finishing up, so you'll have your Saturday back in about fifteen minutes.'

'What's the *bad* news?' Seb asks, his voice tense.

The smile falls from Stacy's face. 'They're taking more of Lola's clothes to examine, plus...' she hesitates, 'they've asked for all your personal devices: phones, tablets, laptops. Every device that belongs to each member of the household.'

'What, even me?' Josh looks up, eyes full of outrage. 'Even *mine*?'

'I'm afraid so.' Stacy makes a face. 'They can't promise when it will all be returned... could be a while I'm afraid.'

'No way!' Josh spits.

'Work are going to be furious,' Seb moans.

Fifteen minutes later and the police are gone. Stacy takes her leave shortly afterwards, saying she'll be back in touch as soon as there is any further news.

Seb follows her to the door. 'I'd be grateful if you'd keep your ears open regarding Brendan's will,' I can hear him mutter. 'I'd like to know who the executor is.'

Once Stacy leaves, Seb vanishes upstairs. Josh has already gone to his room, which leaves me alone with Lola. After the tension of the search, I'm not surprised when she collapses into floods of tears again, vomiting up her pain on the crest of endless, heaving sobs.

'He's gone... Oh, Mum... So–so awful... How can anyone think I could... Hurts so much... I'm so scared...'

I hold her, whispering in her ear that she will be fine and that everything will be all right. But inside I'm wondering whether either of these things can possibly be true.

–

Somehow, we get through the rest of Saturday. Seb, thankfully, doesn't mention the money I took again, though he moves more of his things out of our bedroom. Meanwhile, Brendan's murder enquiry is still in the news, though only as a minor item, and without any mention of Lola's name. I make a brief trip to the shops and buy everyone new pay-as-you-go phones in case it's a while before we get our old ones returned. No one is particularly gracious about this. Josh and Seb accept theirs with resigned grunts, while Lola throws hers down on her bed with a sigh, saying: 'There's nothing I want to look at, Mum, no one I want to see.'

Michael calls that evening to let me know he's been interviewed by the police and that Lola's room at his flat has been searched thoroughly too.

'I don't know what they thought they'd find,' he mutters. 'They manage to twist *everything*. You know, Lola called me on her way back from Brendan's that night. Didn't tell me anything of course, I guess she just wanted to hear a reassuring voice. The police saw the call logged on her phone; they went on and on about it, asking what she was ringing me about, insinuating it had something to do with Brendan's death.'

'That's *crazy*,' I say.

'I know.' Michael sighs. 'At least no one in the media has connected her with the investigation. Apparently, there are no pictures of her on Brendan's social media, so they're not likely to find out either.'

'Do you really think so?' I ask, feeling anxious.

'Yeah, Brendan's not exactly A-list anymore,' Michael growls dismissively. 'One thing has come up, though. Someone calling themselves "Avenging Angel" posted two days ago that Brendan was an evil predator who raped them; made threats that he should pay.'

'Oh.' My heart beats faster.

'No details and it's all anonymous, but obviously that'd be a big coincidence if it *wasn't* connected to his murder, coming so soon beforehand.' Michael pauses. 'I've told Stacy. She says the police are aware.'

I nod. Should I fess up to Michael now? Tell him that Pepper wrote that post – and why? It will mean opening up about what Brendan did to me all those year ago.

Under the circumstances I have to, don't I?

'At least an anonymous, threatening post is good news for Lola,' he says. 'Whoever @AvengingAngel is, they have a clear and strong motive for killing Brendan.'

'Right.'

Maybe it's self-serving of me, but I decide to keep my mouth shut for now. The longer it takes for the police to realise @AvengingAngel is a dead end, the less time and energy they'll have to focus on Lola.

–

Sunday is wet and cold, as grey and miserable as my mood. I stay inside, watching the rain batter the windows while Lola spends most of the day shut up in her room, her eyes red raw from crying. She refuses to talk to anyone except her father and, to a lesser extent, me. Michael is brilliant with her, coming over in the afternoon and sitting with her for hours. It feels strangely normal for him to be here – or maybe the entire situation is just so weird that having him back in the house is the least strange thing about it. I bring them food on trays and endless cups of tea, knocking gently on Lola's bedroom door before entering. A couple of times I hover outside, wondering what they are talking about, but both of them are speaking in such subdued voices it's impossible to hear.

Michael is vague about it when I ask, simply saying that he's been trying to take her mind off both Brendan's loss and his betrayal. He clearly handles her better than I do – silent when I might speak, and finding the right moments for humour where I would hold back for fear of upsetting her all over again. Not that Lola is unwilling to let me in. She even asks me if I'll stay with her later, while she falls asleep, as if she's five years old again and scared of the monsters she used to be convinced were hiding in her wardrobe.

Seb leaves us to it, dedicating most of the day to getting work to give him a new laptop. He is barely speaking to me. In fact the only proper conversation we have takes place that evening, just after Stacy texts to say she will call the police tomorrow for an update.

I pass on this information to Seb who gives a grim nod.

'When you speak to her, please remind her to see if she can find out who the executor of Brendan's will is.'

'Sure.' I press my lips together.

'I know it's not a priority for *you*, Alison,' Seb's voice twists into a snarl. 'But I want to start taking steps to retrieve my money as soon as possible.'

–

An hour later and I'm cooking some pasta for dinner when Lola appears in the kitchen saying she's going to eat with us. It will be the first meal she hasn't carried up to her room since we got the news about Brendan's death. I don't know what Michael has been saying to her, but it's obvious his words have had a calming effect. I thank Michael for this as he leaves, after rejecting my offer to join us for dinner.

'Ah, well, I hope I'm helping.' He sighs, turning on the doorstep. A brisk wind breezes in from the street and I shiver, wrapping my cardigan more tightly around me. 'I wish it could make up for how selfishly I behaved when we split up.'

I stare at him, shocked. In all the years we've been apart, I've never heard Michael speak like this. We broke up after I discovered he'd had a brief affair with a PR contact. In the end, it wasn't the infidelity I really minded – a short, drunken fling at a press conference with a woman he didn't know and wasn't likely to cross paths with again. No, it was the dishonesty, all the stories Michael invented in a desperate attempt to cover his tracks along with his mocking insinuations that I was being ridiculous to get suspicious.

His lies nearly drove me crazy. They created stress points in our relationship that led to a fracture we were never able to repair. I was angry and bitter for a long time and it took everything I had not to bad-mouth him to our children.

But I managed, and Michael apologised for the affair – and so we have found a way forward. Even so, today is the first time he has ever apologised for putting himself first that entire time.

'I used to think it was Josh who suffered most from our break-up,' Michael continues, a frown knitting his forehead. 'After all, Lola was older and already had such a strong social life; plus, she had you. But looking back I can see that I didn't offer her enough time. I mean, I still did things with them and that was great for Josh. We kept on doing video games, all his sports stuff...' He makes a face. 'But Lola needed more of *me*... Conversations... Me just being there for her.' He sighs. 'I've been wondering if this whole business with Brendan is really my fault.' He looks at me sheepishly.

'What do you mean?'

'Just that... she didn't see enough of me when it mattered, so a part of her was looking for a father figure. Ergo, Brendan. What do you think?'

I stare at him. 'Honestly, I don't know whether it's as simple as that,' I say, leaning against the front door. 'Or maybe it's simple in a different way: Lola wasn't looking for a father figure; Brendan targeted her. She didn't stand a chance.'

'I guess.' Michael gazes at me, his eyes filling with regret. 'I'm sorry anyway, I was stupid, the way I handled everything.' He reaches forward, his fingers sliding under the loose sleeve of my cardigan. He strokes the inside of my wrist, drawing his finger along my arm.

I'm not expecting the light pressure of his touch – or the goose bumps that erupt on my skin in response. I pull my arm away, turning to check that Seb can't see us from the kitchen. He can't. The door is shut. I turn back to Michael, my cheeks flushing.

The faintest ghost of a smile curls around his lips.

'I really am sorry, Ali,' he says, lightly, holding my gaze for a few seconds, before striding away along the front path. I watch him walk out of sight, towards his car, feeling unsettled. I'm not exactly sure what he was apologising for that last time.

Nor why my body still seems to respond to his, even when I don't want it to.

FOURTEEN

Monday morning and, after the gloomy weekend, the sun is shining. Seb leaves early for work, having reminded me yet again to ask Lola's lawyer to see if she can find out the identity of Brendan's will's executor. Josh, who has spent most of the weekend on his friend Anil's borrowed Xbox, grumbles a little when I wake him but is soon off to school. Lola sleeps late – I've already called in sick for her, explaining the situation in confidence to the head of her sixth form, who has agreed to get her subject teachers to email some work for her to do at home this week.

I'm about to leave for the office, to pick up some things so I can work at home with her, when Michael calls to say he's bringing Stacy over.

'She says she's spoken to the police and has an update for Lola,' Michael says darkly. 'It doesn't sound good.'

An hour later, they appear. I usher them into the living room, where Lola is already perched on the sofa. Freshly showered, she looks drawn and pale in her sweatshirt and leggings. I sit down next to her and look expectantly at Stacy.

Stacy adjusts the hem of her smart, pink suit as she clears her throat. 'The police have just told me they are issuing a press release later,' she says. 'This will confirm Brendan was stabbed at some point between seven thirty and eight p.m.'

'Oh, God!' Lola's hands fly to her mouth.

'Well, that proves Lola couldn't have done it.' Michael leans forward in his armchair. 'There's no way she could knife someone.'

'Forensics aren't back yet, so there's no information on the murder weapon but my understanding is that it wasn't found at the scene.' Stacy pauses. 'The police have identified Lola's suitcase, which confirms why she was at Brendan's house, so that's good. They've also confirmed that Brendan's body was discovered by a neighbour. Not the man on the left-hand side, who claims to have heard a female voice shouting,' she clarifies. 'But the neighbour to the right, who was expecting Brendan to leave his keys with her, for the letting agent to pick up.'

I sit up. 'That's the woman I spoke to last Thursday.'

'Apparently this neighbour went round to his place at about ten, didn't get an answer at the front door, so tried the garden door at the back on the off chance.' Stacy pauses. 'It was open, so she went in. She found his body in the kitchen.'

Lola lets out a low, whimpering noise, like an animal in pain.

'It's okay.' I squeeze Lola's hand, then turn to Stacy. 'This surely helps Lola, doesn't it? Nobody looking at the physical difference between her and Brendan could possibly imagine she'd win in any kind of knife fight.'

'Quite,' Michael says with feeling.

'Ah, well, that's not all.' Stacy makes a face. 'There's something else.'

My guts twist into a knot. Lola withdraws her hand from mine and tucks her knees under her. It's like she's trying to take up as little space as possible.

'What is it?' she asks, in a tiny voice.

'I'm afraid,' Stacy says, 'that though the police have now searched through all Brendan's recent bank statements and phone records, they can't find any evidence that he was planning on taking Lola on tour with him.'

'What?' I sit up, glancing at Lola.

She's frowning. 'I don't understand.'

Stacy offers her a sympathetic smile. 'The detectives have gone over Brendan's spending, his emails, they found his ticket, details of accommodation in Amsterdam. Lola isn't mentioned. Not once. It strongly suggests that Brendan was leaving the country without you, Lola.'

'What?' Lola's tear-stained face crumples. 'But... but he never said that. No... he let me leave my suitcase. He said he'd give me my ticket at the airport and... Oh, God...' She dissolves into tears.

I draw her to me, gazing numbly at Stacy. Is it possible Brendan was going to go through with his promise to leave Lola after all? The more I think about it, the more it makes perfect sense; the ideal way to upset both me and her as much as possible. Classic Brendan.

'Wait, this is a good thing, isn't it?' Michael insists. 'I mean, how does it change anything if Lola didn't know what Brendan was really up to?'

'That's the problem,' Stacy says. 'There isn't any way to prove what Lola knew or didn't know. And if they think she knew he was going away without her, in spite of all his promises... that doesn't help her case.' She hesitates. 'There's something else.'

I raise my eyebrows. Michael groans. Lola shrinks further into her chair.

'The @AvengingAngel post...' Stacy glances at me. 'You've heard about that, Alison?'

I nod, heat rising up my neck.

'Michael and Lola have already seen this printout.' She passes me a piece of paper. Pepper's @AvengingAngel post is printed on it in small black type, the date and time of the post underneath it.

I pull it towards me, trying to control the trembling in my hands. Lola's hair falls across her face as she leans closer to me.

> Brendan Zeno is an abusive monster. He groomed me, manipulated me and then raped me. I have been silent but now it's time for the truth to come out – for this evil predator to pay for what he did.

'Have the police found out who @AvengingAngel is?' Michael asks eagerly. 'It's surely the strongest lead they have.'

'Not yet; that's what I wanted to explain.' Stacy shuffles uncomfortably in her chair. 'The combination of the post's anonymity and its timing, the morning of the day before Brendan's murder, seem to be reinforcing the police's belief that Lola herself created the content.'

I gasp, horrified.

'*What?*' Michael explodes.

'But it wasn't me!' Lola's voice bubbles with tears. She points to the printout on the table between us. 'I didn't write this – why would I? It isn't true and—' She stops abruptly and glances at me. I can see in her eyes that she's remembering how I told her Brendan raped me and is wondering if *I* wrote the post. Then she shakes her head and says, 'It wasn't me and it can't have been Mum or Dad either. At the point this was published, they both thought Brendan and I had split up. They didn't find out we hadn't until later. Why would any of us provoke him like that, if we all thought we were getting what we wanted from him?'

I cover my face with my hands. I have to tell the truth now, that Pepper was behind the post, that I'm its subject.

'Hey, everyone, calm down,' Stacy says. 'I'm not saying it's a *bad* thing the police think Lola wrote this.'

I look up.

'What do you mean?' Lola asks.

'They are currently trying to track down @AvengingAngel through the IP address that was used. That should provide an exact time and geographical location for the post, possibly even the identity of the author, which will give them a new prime suspect. Either way, it should count out Lola. And *that* will force the police to question their prejudices over the other clues that seem to implicate her. In the meantime, there's no evidence connecting the post to Lola. The police can't use it to arrest her. That's the point to hang onto: they don't have enough evidence to arrest her.'

I nod, slowly. Perhaps I've been right to say nothing after all. Provided Pepper really did cover her tracks when she put the @AvengingAngel post online, there'll be nothing, even remotely, to connect Lola with it. On top of which, once the police realise that Lola *couldn't* have written it, they'll carry on looking for whoever did.

Michael blows out a shaky breath.

'Are you sure, Stacy?' Lola asks in a tiny voice.

'Absolutely.' Stacy's smile broadens.

'Of course she's right,' I say, stoutly. 'There's nothing to worry about.'

–

Stacy leaves, promising more updates when she gets them. Michael says he'll stay with Lola while I pop to the office. I arrive just before midday, to find both Pepper and Hamish are out at separate meetings. I scurry around, gathering notes and files and hoping I'll make it out of here before either of them return. Five furious minutes later, I am so intent on gathering a final set of Go Chieftan reports that I don't hear the office door open.

'Could you be trying any harder to get out of here?' says a sardonic voice.

I look up with a start. Hamish is grinning at me from the doorway. He has trimmed his beard into a smart goatee which makes him look even older than usual.

'I just want to get back to Lola,' I say, pulling a box file from the shelf above my desk.

'Of course.' The smile slides off Hamish's face. 'Sorry, you just took me by surprise. I didn't expect you to be in at all today.' He slides off his blue velvet jacket as he walks over to his desk. He keeps his eyes fixed on me as he lays it carefully over the back of his chair.

'Do you have the new Shine Security press release?' I ask.

'Not yet.' Hamish makes an apologetic face. 'How's Lola doing?' he asks. 'Are the police going to speak to her again?'

I frown. How does he know they spoke to her already? *Of course.* Pepper.

'Lola's okay, thanks,' I say, sweeping over to the Shine shelf and snatching up the latest company brochure. I'm hoping Hamish will take the hint and back off.

No such luck.

'Pepper said the police came to your house with a search warrant...' It's half a question.

'Is there anything she didn't tell you?' The words shoot out of me before I can stop them.

'Sorry.' Hamish gives me a bashful look. 'I was just so worried about you both – you and Lola. Having people snooping through your stuff must have been *awful*.'

I stare at him. 'It wasn't great, no,' I say curtly. I shove the Shine brochure into my tote bag.

Time to leave.

'So… is Lola really all right?' Hamish persists. 'I just—'

'Alison, I'm so glad I caught you!' Pepper's booming voice drowns out Hamish's softer delivery as she sweeps through the door. Dressed from head to toe in scarlet, her hair freshly wound with an orange and pink scarf that streams out behind her, she strides towards her office like a fire caught up in a whirlwind. 'God, darling, what a nightmare. We *have* to talk.'

It's a command, not a request. With a sigh, I set down my bag and follow her into her office.

'What's up?' I ask, closing the door and taking the seat opposite her desk.

Pepper takes her own seat more deliberately, then leans forward, chin propped in her hands. Of the many skills she possesses, her sense of timing is one of the most impressive. She always knows when to slow things down and when to speed them up. Right now, she's controlling the moment by making me wait for her to speak.

'I just wanted to make sure you're all right,' she says at last. 'I still can't believe Brendan's dead. And poor Lola, how's she doing?'

'We're both fine,' I say, feeling mildly irritated by her questions. 'Though you should know that the police have discovered the @AvengingAngel content and are trying to find out who posted it.'

'Shit!' Pepper's eyes widen. 'Did you tell them it was me?'

'No,' I say with a sigh. 'I just hope you really did cover your tracks.'

'I did, don't worry about that.' Pepper grins, her composure regained. 'Though I didn't realise I'd have a crack team of IT experts trying to track me down. I guess my skills as a covert special agent are coming into their own at last.' She laughs.

I stare at her, my irritation rising. 'Well, I'm glad this is working out well for *you*,' I snap.

Pepper frowns. 'I didn't mean that, but don't you see? If the police know it was me behind the post, they'll want the full story. Which is going to make you a suspect, while hardly making Lola look much less like one. Far better they keep thinking there's someone else out there with a motive to kill Brendan.'

'I know,' I groan, putting my head in my hands. 'It's just… a lot.'

'Don't stress about it,' Pepper advises. 'It's only you and I who know. I posted from an internet cafe, so there's no way they can trace @AvengingAngel back to me. So long as we both keep quiet, yeah?'

'Absolutely.' I stand up, my head reeling. 'If it's okay with you, I'm going home now. I'd like to get back to Lola.'

'Of course.' Pepper makes a sympathetic face. 'Is she really doing okay?'

'Well…' I try to collect my thoughts. 'She's very upset of course. But at least the scales seem to have fallen from her eyes. In fact, I think they did a few days ago; I'm not sure she'd have gone with Brendan in the end, which is good as the police reckon he wasn't actually planning to take her.' I look up. 'Can you believe the nerve of him?'

'What an arsehole.' Pepper mutters. 'Poor Lola, it's such a lot to deal with.' She hesitates. 'I meant to tell you, the police want to interview me later. Routine they say, because I knew him and because of my connection to you and Lola.'

'Oh,' I say.

'Honestly,' Pepper says indignantly. 'You only have to take one look at Lola to know how ridiculous suspecting her of murder is. The whole idea she could hurt anyone. I mean, apart from anything else, she's half Brendan's size.'

'I know.'

'It's madness.' Pepper sighs. 'Anyway, we're agreed I won't say that I'm @AvengingAngel, yes?'

'Yes.' I stand up, ready to leave.

'Actually, Alison, there's just one more thing,' Pepper says. 'I wanted to ask about Seb. Has he stopped banging on about getting his money back?'

'For the time being.' I groan inwardly, suddenly realising that I completely forgot earlier to ask Stacy if she's found out who the executor of Brendan's will is.

'What?' Pepper asks, clearly catching some shift of expression on my face.

'Nothing,' I say. God, Seb will be annoyed; it was literally the last thing he said to me this morning.

There's a thud outside in the main office as Hamish shunts a cardboard box of flyers off the shelf by his desk. He bends down and disappears from view.

Pepper leans forward and, lowering her voice, says: 'Don't bloody shoot me, but do you think Seb might… you know… have *gone after* Brendan? Over the money, I mean?'

It's like she's punched me in the gut.

'No,' I say. 'Of course not.'

Pepper stares evenly back at me. My throat constricts.

'Have you been talking to Michael about this?' I ask.

'No, why?' Pepper's eyes widen. 'Does Michael suspect him too?'

I look away.

'He *does*, doesn't he?' Pepper leans forward, eyes gleaming. 'Think about it, Alison, Seb was out of the house when Brendan was killed, wasn't he?'

'So what?' My fists clench in my lap.

'So what was he like when he came back?'

'He was fine, in a good mood,' I say, tersely. 'It was the same as any other day. He came in for a run, then had a shower while I made din—'

'A shower?' Pepper taps her desk. 'Do you think… is there any chance he was washing off evidence?'

I stare at her. That is exactly what Michael suggested. For the first time, I wonder if there could be anything in their suspicions, then I give myself a shake.

'Stop it!' I say, forcing a laugh. 'Come on, Pepper, this is crazy. Seb had been running. Of *course* he had a shower when he got back.'

'Maybe,' Pepper concedes. 'But do you know *where* he went for a run? I mean, who says he didn't run to Brendan's house?'

'I don't want to—'

'Maybe he wanted to confront Brendan directly. Demand the money back.'

'He would have told me,' I insist, anger surging again. 'Now, please will you—?'

'I know you don't want to see it, but it kind of makes sense. Seb's stacked. He works out. As tall as Brendan, and several years younger. Maybe they got into a fight?' Her eyes widen. 'Seb could have done it.'

'Seb *wouldn't*.' I stand up.

'Are you sure? Perhaps Seb went over there riled up, determined to beat Brendan up to get the money.'

'That's—'

'And then, when Brendan refused, probably taking the piss as he did so, it pushed Seb over the edge?'

I stomp to the door. 'Pepper, you need to stop with this—'

'Oh my God!' Pepper sits bolt upright. 'I've just thought – suppose Seb arrived in time to see Lola going inside Brendan's house? He could have followed her in, done the deed and – *oh my God* – deliberately set Lola up to take the blame.'

'How dare you!' I march across the room towards her. My palm slams down on Pepper's desk.

Bam. She jerks back, into her chair. Her eyes blink with shock.

'You're not listening to me,' I shout. 'Seb wouldn't do *any* of what you're saying. He's totally honest and the least violent person I've ever met. Plus, there's no way he'd let Lola go through all the police interviews or make me deal with all the horrible upset we've just had to—' Tears prick at my eyes. I gulp back a sob. 'For God's sake, Pepper, he's my *partner*. How can you think he'd be capable of hurting me or Lola like that?'

A tense silence fills the air. Out of the corner of my eye I can see Hamish watching us through the glass. I keep my gaze on Pepper. The muscles in her right cheek twitch as they always do when she's feeling stressed or uncertain.

'You've never liked Seb.' The hurt I feel fills my voice, softer now. 'You always compared him to Michael, thought he was too narrow-minded for me.'

'That's not true, I *do* like him,' Pepper protests. She breathes out in a frustrated sigh. 'Look, I'm sorry. I shouldn't have said all that, I'm just so upset that the police could even suspect Lola for a second, my brain can't stop running over what might have happened…' She hesitates. 'And you have to admit, apart from you, no one had a bigger beef with Brendan than Seb.'

'No one we know about,' I point out. 'Remember you said yourself that there might be other rape victims out there. Not to mention all the people he owed money to.'

'True…' She trails off.

'Right.' My hands are trembling. I press them together as I take a step back. 'Look, I need to get home to Lola.'

'Alison, please.' Pepper makes a face. 'I'm really sorry.'

I give her a curt nod then hurry out of her little office and back to the open-plan area where Hamish and I work. Hamish looks up. He must be able to see how pink-cheeked and flustered I am, but to my huge relief he says nothing.

Seconds later I'm out the door and on my way home.

FIFTEEN

Despite her apology, Pepper's words echo in my head for the rest of the day.

Seb could have done it.

Lola stays in her room, not wanting to talk, so apart from taking her up some soup, I'm left to my own devices. I leave a message for Stacy to call me – hoping I'll be able to get some information for Seb before he gets home tonight. After that, I try to distract myself from Pepper's hurtful suspicions – first by pulling together the next quarter's plans for the Shine Security account, then by making a chicken stew for dinner. There are loads of ageing vegetables in the fridge and I take my time chopping and cubing them.

Seb could have done it.

I push the words away. Pepper texts me late in the afternoon, asking if I'm okay and offering another apology. I don't reply. I take Lola a cup of tea. As I knock lightly on her bedroom door I can hear her hiccup-y voice on the phone.

'It's just so hard, Daddy.' She glances up as I enter and set the tea by her bed, then turns back to her mobile. I wander back downstairs, simultaneously grateful that Michael is helping her and wishing she would talk as much – and as freely – to me.

Seb gets home just after six. 'Any news?' he asks, scowling.

'No, but I left a message for the lawyer,' I said.

Seb grunts at this, then mutters that he's going for a run. He changes into his gear then disappears out the front door.

Seb could have done it.

I go out in the overgrown back garden and forage deep behind the bushes for the thyme shrub that's planted there. I snip some, then take it back inside and painstakingly slice the leaves off the stalks.

Seb could have done it.

Damn Pepper for planting such a poisonous seed in my head. Or, more precisely, for watering the seed bloody Michael had already put there.

Except... I can't help but think that what they both said made a sort of terrible sense. Seb was – is – furious about the money and, though I don't believe for a second he would have premeditated a murder, let alone set Lola up to take the fall for one, I can totally imagine him challenging Brendan. I don't know what Seb would be capable of if provoked, but I do know that Brendan was, to his bones, one of the most provocative people I've ever met.

The kitchen clock registers 6:55 p.m. when Seb returns from his run. I hear the front door click shut, then the light tap of Seb's feet on the stairs. Josh is in the living room, watching a *Love Island* repeat with Lola, who drifted downstairs a little while ago.

I put a pan of water on the hob, then set a steamer of potatoes over the top. There's nothing more to do down here until just before we eat. I wander out into the hall. Seb has kicked off his trainers at the foot of the stairs.

As usual, a jumble of Lola's coats and jackets are in a pile beside them.

Seb could have done it.

If Brendan was stabbed, there must have been a lot of blood. I flick the nearest trainer over on its side, then the other one. The sound of TV laughter wafts from the living room. I bend down, hating myself for looking – there's nothing on the shoes apart from a few scuff marks.

I sigh as I turn them right side up again. Not only am I being ridiculous to suspect Seb, but anyone with blood stains on their shoes would get rid of them as soon as possible.

The shower is running upstairs. Unsure what exactly I'm planning to do, I let my feet carry me up to our bedroom.

Seb is already in the en suite. Water pounds loudly against the tiles.

Seb could have done it.

I stare at the bed where Seb has left his sweatpants and zipped running top – neatly folded as usual. His sports smart watch lies on the top of the pile.

I stare at it for a second. I'd forgotten about this at the time, but surely Seb should have handed this over when the police asked for all our personal devices?

I snatch the watch up and swipe at the screen. It opens. I gulp, guilt creeping up my neck and flushing my cheeks. I glance at the bathroom door. The shower is still running. I've got at least five minutes. I don't stop to think about what I'm doing – or why I'm doing it. I quickly access the location history information. Seb spent an entire evening explaining to me how this GPS function worked when he bought the watch a few months ago. 'It tracks exactly where I've been running, so I can see how fast or slow I take different bits of the route.'

Another glance at the bathroom. The shower is still hammering against the screen. I turn back to Seb's watch and open the data for Friday evening. Seb's run route plus timings are displayed. Except... I peer more closely. He didn't run very far at all. According to the location information, he ran for fifteen minutes to 6 Charbury Mews, in Gospel Oak. My heart jolts in my chest. Gospel Oak is just a few streets south of Brendan's house in Hampstead Heath. According to the data displayed on the sports watch, Seb stayed at the Charbury Mews address for an hour before running back, arriving home at five minutes to eight.

I stare at the screen. From inside the bathroom, the shower water stops.

My stomach in knots, I swipe the watch shut, put it carefully back on Seb's jacket and hurry out of the room. Questions flutter madly inside me, like panicking birds in a cage.

If Seb was near Brendan's house when Brendan was killed why didn't he tell me about it? Why, in fact, did he lie about going for a run when he was clearly going to a specific address?

What was he doing there for an hour? Or – a feeling of dread rises inside me – was it just his watch that was there for an hour, while Seb continued on, around the corner to Brendan's house...

Head spinning, I hurry away from our bedroom before Seb appears from the shower. I fetch my new phone, sit down in the kitchen and google '6 Charbury Mews'. I get nothing except the postcode and the location on a map. Who lives there? And what on earth was Seb doing there for an hour – the same hour that Brendan died? He didn't mention stopping off on his run that night.

I'm desperate to ask him, but of course I can't. Not without revealing that I was snooping on his sports watch. I take a deep breath and try to focus on the most likely explanation: he decided to visit a friend. Except, I'm fairly certain that none of Seb's friends live in the area. And anyway, if Seb *was* seeing a friend, why not tell me about it?

Could it be an affair? My stomach lurches. No. No *way*. Seb would never be unfaithful. It's one of the reasons I was drawn to him after Michael.

I hate to admit it, but its far more likely this mysterious visit somehow connects Seb to Brendan's death, just like Pepper and Michael suggested.

I'm still staring at the address on Google Maps, when Seb comes into the kitchen, hair damp from his shower.

'Is dinner ready?' he asks. 'I'm starving.'

I swallow down the desire to ask him who lives at 6 Charbury Mews and, instead, fetch the casserole out of the oven and the potatoes off the hob. Seb sits heavily down at the table and scowls at his phone. His sports watch is back on his wrist.

I call for the kids and Lola and Josh appear in the kitchen. Lola's forehead is knitted in the same anxious frown she has worn since she heard about Brendan's death and there are dark shadows under her eyes. She says she wants to take her dinner up to her room again. I let her leave without a fuss, and then of course can hardly object when Josh wants to do the same thing.

'I'm worried about Lola,' I say, quietly.

'She'll be fine.' Seb murmurs. I glance over. He gives me his 'you're fussing again' look then ladles stew onto his plate. We have dinner without speaking. Seb is hunched over his phone while I sit opposite, my appetite gone, and pick at the food. How is it possible that less than a month ago I was congratulating myself on how smoothly Seb had fitted into our lives. My thoughts drift to Lola. The police investigation must hang over her like a dark cloud, making the trauma of Brendan's death so much worse. I wish I knew what other leads the detectives are following. Surely the world must be full of people Brendan has cheated and betrayed and infuriated to the point of violence?

Dark thoughts circle my head. If only I'd had more time to examine Seb's sports watch's history, I could have seen if it was an address he visited regularly – or whether he just went there the night Brendan was killed.

I give up on my dinner, put my bowl in the sink, then turn back to Seb at the table.

'Do you have any friends in north London?' I ask. 'I mean, apart from people you've met through me, like Pepper.'

'What?' Seb frowns, his fork hovering halfway to his mouth. 'Why?'

I shrug. 'Just wondering.'

'No,' Seb says bitterly. 'I don't have a single friend in north London. There're a few people in Ealing and a couple of old uni buddies near Chiswick but most of my friends are still in Reading, which – as you know – I left earlier this year to come here and move in with you.' He turns pointedly back to his phone. I slink away.

That night it's hard to sleep. I tell myself there's no way Seb could have anything to do with the murder, but every time I try to put the subject out of my head, fresh thoughts circle my brain like vultures picking at the bones of our relationship. How well do I really know Seb? In the eighteen months since we met, I've met his parents just twice and a handful of his friends on a couple of social occasions.

Is there a darker side to him that he's kept hidden?

SIXTEEN

The next morning, I'm woken to the rattle of a cup being set down on the bedside table. 'Hi Mum.' Lola is standing over me.

'Hey.' I frown. 'What time is it?'

'Nearly nine,' Lola says. 'It's just us in the house.' She shifts awkwardly from foot to foot. As I sit up, I notice that she's already dressed – in an oversized check shirt and skinny jeans, with slanting slicks of eyeliner accentuating the cat-like shape of her hazel eyes. She's even wearing a dab of pale pink lip gloss.

I stare at her. 'You look better, love. Thanks for the tea. How are you feeling?'

'Good.' Lola gives me a quick smile. 'Er, I'm going out.'

I blink, surprised. 'Out?'

'Yeah, Maisie's off sick today,' she says with a grimace. 'I'm going over to—' she pauses, '—to help her with her A level Art project.'

I'm sure this is an excuse to see her friend, but I don't care. I'm just so delighted to see Lola engaging with life again. 'Okay,' I say. 'Call me if there's any news from Stacy, okay?'

'Sure.' Lola drifts away onto the landing. I watch as she sits on the carpet and tugs on her Docs. A moment later she's thudding down the stairs and out of the house.

I lay back on my pillow and check my phone. Seb has sent a text, presumably while on his commute to work:

> Message me the SECOND you get any info from Stacy.

My guilt surges up. I let out a sigh, then text back:

> will do x

Seb doesn't reply.

I check my work inbox then make a client call. As soon as I put the phone down, Hamish rings.

'Sorry to bother you, Alison,' he says, sounding flustered. 'It's the new Shine Security account campaign proposal.'

I'm still talking to him about a detail on one of the new Shine Security systems when the doorbell rings. I make my excuses and hurry to the front door. I'm half expecting it to be Michael, popping by to check on Lola, but it's Pepper on the doorstep. She's wearing a bright red coat with matching lipstick and an apologetic smile. Before I can speak she thrusts a huge bunch of lilies at me.

'I'm sorry, so, so, so sorry, Alison, please forgive me, I was utterly thoughtless and insensitive to go anywhere near suggesting that Seb could have *possibly* done anything remotely violent. It's only that I'm *desperate* for Lola and I got carried away and you have every right to hate me, but I'm begging you to forgive me because you're my best friend in the whole world and I don't know what I'd do or where I'd be without you.' She stops, at last, for breath. 'Did I say I'm *so, so* sorry?'

I can't help but smile at the look of abject contrition on her face. Pepper is as sensitive as she is flamboyant. My mind flits back to the tender way she cared for her dying father the year Lola was born. She might act like she's an attention-seeking extrovert, but she's also deeply caring, always willing to put her own needs aside when it matters.

I open the door wider. 'D'you want to come in?'

'Just for a second.' Pepper's heels tap across the hall as I shut the door and turn to face her. Under the coat, she's wearing black cigarette pants and a geometric pink and orange shirt. Her hair is swept off her face with an orange clip, and a single diamond sparkles at her neck. She's always been able to put an outfit together, even when we were students and had no money.

'I can't stay,' she says, a worried frown still creasing her forehead. 'Prospective client. I just couldn't get on with the day without making sure that you – we – are okay.'

I stare at her. Pepper might have been super inappropriate and pushy over Seb yesterday, but now I know that she wasn't necessarily wrong I don't have the energy to still feel angry with her.

'We're okay,' I say, smiling. 'We're always okay.'

Pepper lets out a long, theatrical sigh. '*Thank God*,' she says, then wrinkles her nose. 'Oh, well, if you're making a coffee…'

I take the hint and put the kettle on. Pepper arranges herself at the kitchen table, setting down her bag and pushing my laptop out of the way.

I fetch the cafetiere and spoon in some coffee. My mind drifts to Seb again, and to what he was doing at 6 Charbury Mews.

'What's on your mind?' Pepper asks, sharply. 'Is it Lola?'

I spin around to face her. Her pale blue eyes penetrate mine. She's always been able to read my moods. As we stare at each other, the water boils and the kettle clicks off.

'I'm fine.' I walk to the fridge and fetch a carton of milk. I can sense Pepper still watching me. 'Why?'

'Because you just put six heaped spoonfuls of coffee in that four-cup cafetiere,' Pepper says with a wry smile.

'Shit,' I say, putting down the milk and scooping some of the coffee out. 'I guess I'm distracted,' I say. I pour the hot water into the cafetiere and set it on the table.

'Is Lola here?' Pepper asks.

I shake my head. 'Gone to see a friend. She really seemed better when she got up.'

'Well, that's a good sign,' Pepper says. She frowns again. 'So, what's wrong?'

I bring two mugs and the carton of milk over to the kitchen table, then sit down by my laptop, opposite Pepper. She looks expectantly at me.

I take a deep breath. 'I snuck a look at Seb's sports watch while he was in the shower.'

Pepper's jaw drops. 'No way!' She laughs – a short, impressed-sounding chortle. I brace myself waiting for her to make the obvious comment that clearly her suspicions hadn't fallen on deaf ears yesterday, but instead, she pours herself a mug of coffee. 'What did you find out?'

I tell her.

As I explain the address Seb visited was just a few streets away from Brendan's house, Pepper's expressive eyes widen in horror.

'Oh my God,' she says, breathlessly. 'God, Alison, that is *weird*.'

'I know,' I acknowledge. 'But I keep telling myself there are lots of reasons why he might have gone there.'

'Maybe, but there aren't lots of reasons why he'd lie about it.' Pepper hesitates. 'You know, please don't start thinking I don't like him all over again, but whatever the truth behind all this is, you have to admit this is probably the most interesting thing that Seb's ever done.'

In spite of myself, I laugh.

'Thanks, Peps,' I say injecting as much sarcasm into my voice as I can. 'Did you get a refund on that sensitivity training?'

Pepper giggles, then folds her arms. 'What are you going to do?'

I take a sip of coffee, set down my mug and push myself up from the table. The idea that's been hovering at the back of my mind, finally pushes its way to the front.

'I'm going to 6 Charbury Mews right now,' I say.

'Whoa!' Pepper's eyes widen. 'Seriously?'

'Yes,' I say. 'I'm going to talk to whoever lives there. Find out if – how – they know Seb and, with a bit of luck, what he was doing there the night Brendan died.'

Pepper stands up. 'Do you want me to cancel my client meeting? I can come with—'

'No,' I say, firmly. 'Absolutely not.'

Pepper nods. 'Okay, if you're sure? Just promise you'll pop in to the office on your way home, report back. I'll be done with this client and back there in an hour or so. Deal?'

'Okay,' I agree, a little reluctantly. It's not that I mind confiding in Pepper, but I'd rather not have to provide a running commentary on my snooping. Still, she's only asking because she cares.

Pepper takes a final swig of coffee. 'Right, I'm going.' She waves her hands theatrically.

I see her out, then slip on my winter boots and apply some of the powder and lip gloss Lola left on the hall table. I examine myself in the long mirror in the hallway. I don't know what I'm going to find at 6 Charbury Mews, but I want to feel as confident as possible when I get there.

I grab my smartest coat and leave the house.

–

Charbury Mews is a short, elegant cul-de-sac, lined with ultra-modern mews houses, all glass and steel. My phone rings as I'm searching for number six. I glance down.

Michael calling.

No way do I want to speak to him right now. I switch the phone to silent and shove it deep in my bag. I raise my trembling hand to the doorbell. The chime sounds, a muffled tinkle. Footsteps patter across the floor inside and a dark shape looms on the other side of the glass door.

I breathe out, shakily, suddenly wishing I'd brought Pepper with me after all.

The door swings open. A woman stands in front of me. It's hard to tell how old she is. There are a few wrinkles on her forehead and neck, but she has a soft, youthful prettiness that I imagine could make her look about thirty in the right light. Strands of blonde hair peek out from the green scarf wound loosely around her head and her navy overalls have a paint smear across the front.

'Hello?' Her voice is smooth, with a slight hint of an Eastern European accent. It's as inviting and sensual as the gleam in her eyes. 'How may I help you?'

My heart gives a jealous squeeze, all thoughts of Brendan's murder vanishing at the sight of her face. I was wrong; it's an affair. *Has* to be. This woman is exactly the kind of approachable, ultra-feminine woman I'm certain Seb would be drawn to.

'Are you all right?' The woman smiles, softening the striking lines of her face. Her eyes are the most extraordinary shade of pale green, their light reflected in the strings of glass beads around her neck.

A lump lodges in my throat. 'I… er… I wonder if you can help me?' I stammer. 'I'm here for… It's about… I think you may know my… er… Seb…'

The woman's eyes register recognition. 'Ah, Seb,' she says softly. 'And you are?'

I take a deep breath. 'His partner.'

The woman blinks. A look of awkwardness rises in her eyes. Is that guilt?

My heart sinks.

'Seb told you?' she asks. 'About me? About this? What we're doing?'

Suddenly I want to cry. Strangely, it's not Seb I find I'm thinking of though, but Michael: the moment when I knew, without doubt, that he'd betrayed me. I press my lips together, unable to speak. The woman frowns, concern now rising up through her awkwardness. 'You'd better come in,' she says.

I take a deep breath and follow her into the dark, narrow hallway. 'What's your name?' I ask.

'Seb didn't say?' The woman looks confused. 'I'm Emmeline. Emmeline Schippel.' She pauses. 'And you must be Alison, right?'

'That's right,' I say.

A soft smile curls about Emmeline's lips. There's a reserved, almost cat-like quality to her face. Maybe she's less dreamy than I first thought. She certainly doesn't seem in the slightest bit embarrassed by my arrival. 'Let's go up.'

SEVENTEEN

I follow Emmeline to the first floor where the stairs open onto a large, light, airy living area. A pair of sea-coloured couches are set against plain white walls decorated with bright, abstract prints.

'There it is.' Emmeline waves towards the end of the room, which bends in an L-shape past the window. 'But I thought Seb was keeping it a secret?'

For a second, I'm utterly thrown. I follow Emmeline's pointing fingers, then hurry across the room. What on earth is around this corner? Does it have something to do with their affair? Or is my original theory right after all, that Seb used Emmeline's house as a base from which to run to Brendan's house and kill him?

Past the L-shaped bend in the room, the whole area is set up as an art studio, with a large easel in the corner. The easel is covered with a cloth.

Bewildered, I turn to Emmeline who has followed me around the corner.

'You're an artist?' I ask.

A smile curls around Emmeline's lips. 'A *portrait* artist, though I do some interiors too.' She sniffs, indicating the easel. 'This is what I do for Seb.'

'Oh.' My hands fly to my mouth, all my fear and bitterness falling away. Poor Seb. I shouldn't have doubted him. I stare at the cloth which, now I'm looking more closely, is clearly draped over a canvas. What has Emmeline been painting for him? A picture of me? Of the kids? Of all of us together?

'You want to see?' Emmeline asks.

I nod, eagerly, and Emmeline beckons me over to the easel. She stands to the side, then gently lifts the cloth.

Oh. The portrait is unfinished but entirely recognisable: a man's face, solid and unquestioning about the eyes, with a square jaw, the outline of what will surely be thick dark hair and a perfectly straight nose.

'It's Seb,' I say flatly.

She lets out a throaty laugh. 'Indeed! It's a present for you.'

I stare at her. Emmeline quickly explains that the portrait is for my birthday, coming up in two months, and that Seb was here last week for a sitting.

'Such a sweet man,' she says with a chortle. 'We got talking at an event a few months ago. He wanted something special for you. Do you like it? Personally, I'm pleased. I think it's good.'

I stare at the picture again. It *is* good. It's captured something essential about Seb, his sense of straightforward certainty.

'Oh my God, please tell me you like it!' Emmeline's voice rises.

'Yes, of course.' I laugh. 'It's great.'

I refuse Emmeline's offer of a glass of wine, make her promise not to let Seb know I've uncovered his secret and am soon hurrying away from Charbury Mews. As I walk back to my car, I'm consumed with guilt – how could I have thought Seb capable of both infidelity and murder? Thank goodness he never needs to know. Later I'll pick up a bottle of that Chianti he loves, try to make our evening a bit special.

I turn onto Highgate Road and hurry along to the HOPP office near Kentish Town tube. I promised Pepper I'd show up, but I won't stay long – just enough time to tell her there was nothing to worry about – then I'll head home.

Hamish looks up as I walk in. He flips the edge of his tie in the direction of Pepper's office and raises his eyebrows. 'Visitor,' he mouths.

I hurry around the corner. Pepper is leaning against the window of her office, deep in animated conversation with – I peer more closely at the figure in the chair. He has his back to me, but I'd recognise those gesticulating arms anywhere.

It's Michael.

Pepper spots me and beckons me in with a wave. Michael stands as I walk into her office. His expression is serious and even more intense than usual.

'What did you find out?' he demands. 'Is Seb the killer?'

I stare at Pepper. 'You *told* him?'

Pepper shrugs. 'I said you were following a lead regarding where Seb was when, you know, Brendan died.'

Irritation rises inside me. It's the same as with Hamish. Is she clinically incapable of keeping her mouth shut?

'Seb didn't kill Brendan,' I snap. 'There's no way. Not that I ever actually thought he—'

'Are you sure?' Michael asks.

'Yes,' I insist. 'There was a bit of a mystery about where he was when Brendan died – like Pepper just said – but I've cleared it up.'

'Don't be so cryptic, Alison,' Pepper says. 'Spill. If Seb didn't kill Brendan, is he having an affair?'

I glare at her. 'No!'

'If he is, I'll hit him for you.' Michael grins.

'Like you'd get a punch in.' Pepper snorts. 'Seb'd take you any day. He's got a bloody six pack.'

'Sod off, Peps.' Michael's grin deepens. 'I'm perfectly capable of defending Ali's honour.'

Pepper stares at him mock disapprovingly, as her phone pings. She peers at the message, then sets the mobile down, tapping her elegantly manicured nails on the desk.

'That was the Eighties on the line, Michael,' she says dryly, 'they'd like their outdated macho attitudes back.'

Michael makes a face, while I smother a giggle. Pepper turns to me, suddenly laser focused again. 'So if 6 Charbury Mews isn't an affair, what was Seb doing there?'

I hesitate. It feels disloyal to give away Seb's secret. On the other hand, I've known Pepper long enough to be sure she will carry on pestering me about it until I explain. Michael too. I don't need to give away all the details.

'He's commissioned this portrait artist called Emmeline Schippel to do a painting for me, for my birthday,' I explain.

'Emmeline Schippel.' Pepper frowns. 'That name rings a bell. Wait, does she do interiors too?'

'Yes,' I say. 'She said she met Seb at some work event.'

'Are you sure all this talk of a painting isn't cover for an affair?' Michael sounds disappointed.

'Yes,' I say, making a face at him. 'I saw it. The portrait.'

'What's it of?' asks Pepper.

'Seb,' I say, immediately wishing I hadn't given that detail away. 'It's a present for me and it's a secret so you mustn't— What?'

Pepper and Michael are both staring at me, jaws open.

'Seb's giving you a portrait… of *himself*?' Pepper asks, her eyebrows raised.

'What a colossal jerk.' Michael guffaws.

'Will you both shut up,' I say, icily. 'It's a sweet gesture.'

'It's an ego trip,' mutters Michael.

'Or an elaborate lie,' Pepper adds, adopting the same dramatic tone she did earlier. 'Are you *really* sure it's not some sort of cover story?'

'Shut up, Pepper!' My voice rises. Through the glass window, Hamish's head jerks up. He doesn't turn in our direction, but it's obvious from the alert way he's sitting that he's straining to hear every word we're saying. 'Seb was just trying to do a nice thing for me,' I insist, forcing myself to speak more quietly.

'Okay, Ali.' Michael holds his hands up in a gesture of surrender. 'If you say so.'

'I *do* say so.' I turn from him to Pepper. 'So drop it. Both of you.' I stalk out of the room. As I head back to my desk Michael's voice travels towards me, faint and low, 'She's so sexy when she's annoyed like that.'

I growl under my breath, infuriated with the pair of them. Hamish gives me a curious glance as I pass him.

'Well, that sounded a bit handbags-at-dawn,' he comments.

'Everything's fine,' I snap.

I stomp out of the office and down the stairs.

Outside in the chill December air, I realise I've been holding my breath and blow it out angrily. An 'ego trip', Michael said. Well, what does he know? He doesn't understand Seb. Or me. Or our relationship. He's *always* been jealous, making those stupid comments about Seb being muscular as if you can't work out *and* have a brain.

But Michael is the past. Gone. I need to focus on the kids, now. And Seb. Make up to him somehow for the money.

The tension in my body eases a little as I scuttle along the pavement. There's no sign of a 134 at the bus stop, so I keep walking, my hands and feet warming as I hurry home. I've been so unfair on Seb. I mean, *of course* he is angry. I took his savings without asking.

I call Stacy; she answers on the first ring. 'Hi, Alison, what is it?'

I explain that I'm following up Seb's request for the identity of the executor of Brendan's will. 'He wants to contact whoever it is as soon as possible. Find out how soon he can start trying to claw back his money.'

'Ah, yes, I'm afraid that's going to be tricky,' Stacy says. 'I've asked around and nobody knows anything about Brendan's will. Chances are we probably won't find out about the executor until probate is granted, which could be months.'

'Oh,' I say.

'Seb needs to lower his expectations, anyway.' Stacy sighs. 'I think it's highly unlikely that the executors will agree to pay him out of Brendan's estate. There's clearly no legal obligation, as the money wasn't directly stolen by Brendan. And there'll be a line of genuine creditors, people that Brendan is documented as owing money to, who'll take precedence.' She makes a face. 'Even if the executors do agree that Seb is entitled to all, or some, of his money back, they'll most likely insist it'll have to wait until after Brendan's house is sold. Which means further delay.'

'Oh.' I chew on my lip, my guilt rising again. 'Isn't there anything else Seb can do?'

'I'm afraid his only option for retrieving his money fast, is to bring charges against you.'

Great.

I ring off, then spend the next ten minutes setting up a call with my bank. I'm going to beg them to give me a loan. That way I'll be able to pay Seb back quickly and he won't have to rely on Brendan's estate. He can still request his money from the executors, and then give it to me if he gets it, but he won't have to wait.

It's the least I can do.

As I unlock the front door back at home, voices drift towards me from the kitchen. Is that Detective Inspector Barnbury? What on earth does he want now? That's three times the police have been here in four days. It's verging on harassment. As I hurry across the hall, Lola's voice rises with panic.

'No, I don't understand. No...'

I reach the kitchen. DI Barnbury and DS Strong, the female detective from the station, are by the kitchen table. Lola is across the room, leaning against the sink which is overflowing with dirty dishes. The overhead light glares down, catching the side of Barnbury's face as he leans forward against the back of a chair, lips pressed together, insistent. They all turn as I appear in the doorway.

'What's happening?' I demand.

'Mum!' Lola flies across the room towards me, an agonising mix of fear and exhaustion in her eyes. She grabs my arm. 'They've got a witness,' she cries.

'What?' I ask. 'A witness to what?'

'Someone who says they saw me leaving Brendan's house the... that night.'

I frown. 'But that's good, isn't it?' I ask. 'Proof that you left when you said you did.'

DI Barnbury clears his throat. 'Unfortunately,' he says, 'it appears to prove the opposite.'

EIGHTEEN

Lola huddles close to me, her slight frame trembling as she clings to my arm.

'What are you talking about?' I turn to DI Barnbury. 'What did this so-called witness actually see?'

'Please calm down, Alison,' DI Barnbury says. 'We just need to speak to Lola again. Under caution.'

'I don't understand, Mum,' Lola whimpers at my side. 'They're saying this "witness" says I left Brendan's house out the back just before eight. But it wasn't me.' She buries her head in my shoulder. 'I left much earlier, definitely by twenty past seven.'

I glare at DI Barnbury.

'We have to follow this up,' he says wearily. 'The witness's description matches Lola exactly.'

'Then they've got the time wrong,' I insist.

'Perhaps,' DI Barnbury acknowledges, 'but forensics are certain the murder took place between seven thirty and eight, so we have to take seriously any suggestion that Lola was in the house then.'

'But I *wasn't*,' Lola wails. 'I keep saying, I'd left by seven twenty.'

'We'll iron it all out at the station,' DI Barnbury says abruptly, his tone indicating that he's losing patience.

'But—' I start.

'No more questions,' DI Barnbury interrupts again. 'Come on Lola.'

He stalks to the door, then turns and waits. Lola disentangles herself from my grip.

'It's okay, Mum,' she says softly, a single tear trickling down her cheek.

My throat is painfully tight as I watch her, head bowed, leave the house.

'I'll ring Stacy,' I call out after her. 'Get her to meet you at the station.'

DS Strong, who I hadn't noticed in the hall before, steps out of the shadows. 'I'm afraid I need to go through Lola's belongings again. Collect the rest of her clothes,' she says.

I feel like crying myself. 'But you looked through everything a few days ago.'

'It's routine in a mur— in an investigation like this,' DS Strong says apologetically, heading for the stairs.

As she disappears out of sight, I call first Stacy, then Michael. They both say they'll go straight to the police station. I want to go there too, but Michael tells me to stay put, pointing out I shouldn't leave the police alone in the house. He sounds furious, firing questions at me that I can't answer.

Who is this witness?

Why are the police haranguing Lola on such circumstantial evidence?

Are they planning a line-up so that this supposed witness can try and identify her?

At least Stacy seems confident Lola won't be at the station for very long; like Michael, she insists there's no point me going there myself.

I hover in the hall, waiting for DS Strong to reappear. At last she comes downstairs clutching four large bags full of Lola's belongings. I watch her lug them away, then retreat to the kitchen. An hour later, Josh arrives home.

'Hi sweetheart,' I say, brightly, hurrying out to the hall again. 'Good day?'

'Fine,' he says gruffly, dumping his bag and coat by the door.

'You should know that Lola's had to go and talk to the police again…' I hesitate, uncertain how much to explain.

'Right.' Josh stomps up the stairs. What is up with him? He's not normally this grumpy. Is it the stress of the situation? Or did something happen at school?

'Josh!' I call. '*Josh!*' I'm on the verge of following him, but just then the doorbell rings.

Michael is on the doorstep, glowering with repressed fury. Stacy hovers beside him, looking anxious, while Lola is trudging up the path behind them.

I open the door wide, without a word, then lead the three of them into the kitchen. Michael folds his arms, leaning against the countertop. Stacy stares at him with concern. Meanwhile, Lola slumps into a chair, glassy-eyed.

'Are you okay?' I hurry over and sit down beside her, taking her hand.

She gazes at me, tears bubbling in her eyes. 'Why are the police doing this?' she sobs. 'Why can't they leave me alone?'

I glance at Michael, still exuding rage, then at Stacy. She looks back at me, a deep frown on her forehead.

'What happened?' I ask. 'Did you find out who this witness is?'

'No.' Stacy removes her pale blue beanie. The tip of her nose is pink from the cold outside. 'It turns out it was an anonymous call on a helpline.'

'What?' I frown. 'How can they take that seriously?'

'It's ridiculous.' Michael spits. He shucks off his jacket and sinks into the chair opposite Lola. 'Even if whoever it is did see Lola, they clearly got the time wrong.'

'Is that it?' A feeling of relief starts to spread through me. 'An anonymous caller who saw Lola but is half an hour out on the time?'

Michael and Stacy exchange a glance.

'I'm afraid that's not all the witness said,' Stacy says. 'According to the police, the anonymous witness described Lola as wearing only a thin top and jeans, which they noted at the time as being odd, because it was so cold that evening.'

'But—' I start.

'They also claim Lola was carrying a plastic bin bag in her hand.' Michael interrupts.

Stacy nods. 'DI Barnbury is convinced that this bag contained Lola's coat.'

'But Lola already *gave* them her coat,' I protest. 'I remember – it was your black pea coat. The police took it away that first night, when they interviewed you.'

'The police think I lied,' Lola says in a small, fragile voice. 'They think I went to Brendan's house in a different coat, then lied about it.'

I grip the table in front of me. 'But surely it's obvious what Lola was wearing on Brendan's entry cam video?'

'Unfortunately not,' Stacy explains. 'If you remember, Lola's height… the camera only shows her face.'

'Why does it matter?' My head spins.

'Because the police think the *actual* coat Lola wore that night may contain relevant evidence.' Michael rolls his eyes.

'In other words, Brendan's blood.' Lola shudders. 'The police think I got his blood on my coat, then dumped it in a bin on my way home.'

'So where is it then?' I ask.

'The police were vague on that point, which makes me think they haven't been able to find it,' Stacy says.

'They're still convinced that I lied, though,' Lola mutters. 'They found stuff I wrote on my phone. Just private things that didn't mean anything, but they're twisting them to make me look like some crazy, deranged—' She presses her lips together, clearly close to tears, then pushes her chair back and hurries out of the room.

I stare after her.

'Let her be for a moment,' Michael advises.

I turn to Stacy. 'What kind of things did Lola write?' I ask.

Stacy looks uncomfortable. She glances at Michael. I experience a sharp, fleeting stab of jealousy. 'I'm Lola's mother.' I sound harsher than I mean to. 'I need to know.'

Stacy nods. 'I can't show you the exact words Lola wrote without her permission, but it's basically a series of... of... I guess I'd call them obsessive reflections.'

'What does that mean?' I demand.

Michael lays a hand on my arm. 'Easy,' he says.

'I'm sorry.' I meet Stacy's gaze. 'Just give us the gist.'

'Lola wrote a series of poems about her feelings for Brendan,' Stacy says quietly. 'Some of her thoughts are quite extreme. She focuses on how he makes her feel a passion she's never known before, how she would die for him…' Stacy hesitates. 'Even kill for him.'

'Oh, God,' I say.

'It's just teenage nonsense,' Michael says. 'Bad first love poetry.'

A wave of nausea rises inside me. 'Should we be worried?' I ask Stacy.

'Not about the writings,' Stacy says. 'There's nothing specific that relates to the crime in any way. If anything, Lola's thoughts on Brendan suggest how deeply she cared for him.'

'Good, okay.' I breathe out. 'What about the witness you mentioned?'

'I don't *think* that should be a problem either,' Stacy says. 'Firstly, the witness statement was anonymous – just a random person leaving a description which happens to fit Lola, but which could clearly describe a whole bunch of other young women too. Secondly, the witness specified a time they saw Lola leaving Brendan's, but Lola says she left earlier, so that's just their word against hers. And, thirdly, even if the witness did see Lola and even if she was carrying a plastic bag, it's only conjecture that this bag contained a coat, bloodstained or otherwise.'

'It's complete supposition,' Michael says angrily. 'They were totally out of order to question Lola about it.'

'I wouldn't go that far,' Stacy says tentatively. 'But the bottom line is that there's no proof of *anything* the witness said.' She pauses. 'I asked and there's no CCTV on the route between Brendan's house and yours. So no way of confirming what Lola was wearing or carrying. It's all back streets or through the park.'

I let out a sigh of relief. 'So the police don't have anything?'

'Just a load of circumstantial nonsense about a knife and a coat,' Michael says grimly.

'A knife?' My stomach lurches. '*What* knife?'

'The police have confirmed that the murder weapon was a missing knife from the set on the counter in Brendan's kitchen,' Stacy says quickly.

An image of the gleaming, stainless-steel knives in their block flashes in front of my mind's eye, the thin 'Z' shape design creeping along the handle.

'How can they be sure, if it's missing?' I ask.

'The blade would have caused exactly the wound that killed Brendan,' Stacy explains. 'One stab wound, in the thigh, about two centimetres deep that severed his femoral artery. Then made worse because the assailant took the knife out. Brendan would have died within fifteen minutes or so.'

'So fast? From just one wound?' I spin around to see Lola is at the kitchen door. I have no idea how long she's been standing there listening, but her already pale face is now entirely drained of colour. 'Surely that means whoever killed him knew what they were doing.' She slides over and sits beside me at the kitchen table.

'Exactly,' Michael says.

'So… so…' My head spins. 'All that obviously means it wasn't Lola, doesn't it? Lola wouldn't know any of that stuff about femoral arteries. She's doing A levels in English, History and Drama for goodness' sake.'

Lola rolls her eyes. 'Just cos you're studying arty subjects doesn't stop you from looking stuff up about anatomy, Mum,' she says, sounding just like Michael.

I put my hand on her shoulder. She stays stiff and hunched over. 'That horrible detective asked me about that stupid knife the first time he interviewed me,' Lola goes on, her voice now low and bitter. 'I told him then, I don't remember seeing it at all.' She shudders. 'I keep thinking about Brendan left like that, bleeding to death in his kitchen…' Her voice cracks and she swallows hard, clearly trying not to cry.

I reach for her Lola's hand. She grips my fingers tightly.

'Again, it's pure supposition on his part, but DI Barnbury thinks the knife that killed Brendan may have been in the bag Lola was supposedly holding,' Stacy goes on.

'Along with her bloodstained coat,' Michael adds bitterly.

Lola shakes her head, slumping deeper into her chair.

There's a long pause, then Michael stands up. 'I'm sorry but I have to go. I'm meeting the main source for my hacking story again and he won't wait if I don't show up.' He looks at Lola. 'You okay, Babycakes?'

She nods.

I follow Michael to the front door. He turns to me as he's leaving and says in a low voice, 'Just so you're aware, the police have now officially released the cause of death and called for more witnesses, so there's no way the story won't come up in the press again.'

'Shit.' I make a face. 'I'll find a way to prepare Lola.'

'I already did,' Michael says. 'At least no one seems to have got hold of her name yet, but it's only a matter of time. The reporters are already pushing for details about the prime suspect.'

'And that's Lola?' My whole body feels numb.

Michael meets my gaze for a second, then reaches down and plants a swift kiss on my cheek. 'Look, I'm sorry I upset you earlier. Tell Seb to look after you when he gets in.'

Seb. All my earlier plans to make up to him by cooking a nice meal and buying the Chianti he likes flood back.

I close the front door on Michael and check the time. Seb will be home in about twenty minutes or so. That's not enough time to get dinner ready *and* pop out for the wine.

I walk back in the kitchen, where Stacy is patting Lola's arm. 'I don't know,' she's saying. 'But you have to stay positive.'

'Oh, Lola,' I say, sitting down next to her.

'That detective went on and on at me, Mum,' she says. '*Much* meaner than last time.'

I glance anxiously at Stacy. 'What's going to happen next?'

She clears her throat. 'My best guess is nothing. I think Barnbury was fishing today, hoping Lola would crack. But he's got nothing. There are several bits of evidence that don't fit his theory too.'

'Like what?'

'Brendan's entry cam, for instance. You remember that it recorded Lola on her way into the house?' I nod. 'Well, the camera was destroyed shortly afterwards. Smashed off the wall and onto the ground, apparently.'

'Who did that?' I ask.

'They don't know,' Stacy says. 'Whoever it was kept themselves out of sight while they did the damage. But it wouldn't make sense for Lola to do that *after* she'd already been recorded coming inside, so it strongly suggests someone else arrived at the front door.'

I sit up. 'And the police are definitely looking into that?'

'I'm sure they are.' Stacy smiles reassuringly.

I sit back. 'So what do we do?'

'We wait,' Stacy says. 'We let the police search whatever they want. Assuming they don't – as I'm sure they won't – find any forensic evidence linking Lola to the murder, there'll be nothing to back up a word the anonymous witness said.'

'Why aren't there any other suspects?' Lola groans. 'Why's it all about me?'

'I'm sure the detectives are following other leads,' Stacy says. 'There's the @AvengingAngel rape claim for instance; they'll still be tracking down the person who posted that. We just need to let the investigation into you play out, it won't last forever.'

Lola nods, blankly. I squeeze her hand again.

A few minutes later Stacy leaves, after urging us both not to worry. I see her out, then come back into the kitchen to find Lola pouring herself a large glass of wine. She glugs it back.

'I'm so sorry you're going through all this,' I say.

She takes another long swig, draining half the glass, then tops up the drink, turning her back as she sets the glass on the countertop. I resist the urge to tell her to go easy. In fact, I'm heading to the cupboard to fetch a glass for myself, when I suddenly realise Lola's shoulders are shaking.

'Sweetheart?'

She turns, her face red and crumpled with a furious misery. 'They're going to find a way to charge me, Mum, I just *know* it. And then I'll be in prison for thirty years and by the time I come out I'll have grey hair and you and Dad will be dead, and I'll be completely alone with no life and that's if I even survive one night in prison because… because I just *can't*—' She stops, her chest heaving with angry, tearless gasps. 'How has all this *happened*?'

A furious helplessness rises inside me. How dare Brendan be dead? And how dare anyone think my fragile daughter could have anything to do with it?

'Listen, Lo,' I say trying to keep my voice steady. 'I know everything feels awful at the moment, that you're coping with losing Brendan and all these police questions, but you've got to see the bigger picture here.'

She looks up. 'What do you mean?'

'The police are just following the leads they have. You were with Brendan the night he died. That *inevitably* makes you a person of interest.' I pause for emphasis. 'It does *not* make you guilty, even if it's easy to imagine that's what DI Barnbury thinks.'

'But—'

'Even if, er, the @AvengingAngel post turns out to be a dead end, I'm sure the detective won't have any trouble finding a long line of dodgy guys Brendan had connections to. Not to mention owed money to. People who are much more likely to have committed a murder than an eighteen-year-old schoolgirl half his size and with no criminal record.' I inject some steel into my voice. 'I promise you, DI Barnbury will soon move on.'

'Do you really think so?' There's grit in Lola's voice, but I still see the tiny wobble of her lips.

A memory flashes back; a moment from Lola's childhood, not long after Josh's birth, when we went to the park and a drizzle started and Lola looked up at me with that same, trusting look in her eye that she has now and asked me to make it stop raining.

'I *know* so,' I say. And as I speak, I see very clearly what I need to do now. I'm not having Lola's future ruined by having the death of a horrible man, who frankly deserved what he got, pinned on her. Lola had nothing to do with Brendan's death, but I can't prove that to the police.

What I can and *will* do, is find out who *did* kill him.

NINETEEN

As Lola curls up in her chair, peering at her phone, my mind races ahead. How on earth am I going to track down Brendan's killer? Until last week I hadn't seen him for almost thirty years. And I don't know anyone, other than Lola herself, with whom he'd been involved recently.

I have no idea where to begin.

'Mum, what's for dinner?' Josh is standing in the kitchen doorway.

I frown. 'Er, I don't know yet.'

'Can I go to Anil's?' he asks.

I try to focus. 'Um. I guess, yes, but make sure you're back by nine thirty.'

'Nine thirty? *Seriously?*' Josh scowls at me. 'So stupid Lola gets to run off on an international drug – sorry, music – tour, but I'm treated like an eight-year-old? It's not fair.'

Lola, who would normally jump right on her brother for trash talking her like that, slumps deeper into her chair, the picture of despondency.

'Stop it, Josh,' I snap. 'Can't you see your sister is going through a very difficult time?'

'Yeah? What about what *I'm* going through?' Josh demands, then turns on his heel and marches away.

I stare after him, shocked to my core. Josh is my even-tempered child, all sunny disposition and positive outlook.

He's me without the worry and Michael without the self-centred intensity.

'He's just angry because the police took his stuff,' Lola says, a sob rising in her voice. 'It's my fault.'

'I'm going to talk to him.' I hurry away, up the stairs to Josh's room. I knock, but he doesn't answer, so I inch open the door and peer around. Josh has his headphones jammed over his ears, as he shoves a gaming controller into a backpack. His room, normally neat and tidy, is almost as messy as Lola's: crumpled clothes and dirty plates surround the bed; the only clear patch of carpet is just in front of the wardrobe, whose doors and drawers are all flung open. I feel a pang of guilt that I hadn't noticed what a state the place is in.

Josh looks up as I walk inside. He tugs off his headphones. 'What is it?' he asks sullenly.

'What's the matter?'

'Nothing,' he mutters.

'Tell me,' I insist. 'Has something happened? At school? With a friend?'

'Kind of,' Josh answers unhelpfully.

I nod as if he's revealed something huge. 'Wow, well it must be hard to deal with.' I pause. 'Do you think it might help to talk?'

Josh shakes his head.

'Okay,' I sigh. 'Well, I'm here if – when – you're ready.' I stand up and turn towards the door.

'Pepper says I shouldn't,' Josh blurts out.

I turn back to him. 'Pepper says you shouldn't what?'

'Bother you right now.' Josh grits his teeth.

I sit down on the end of his bed, patting the duvet to indicate he should seat himself too. 'Go on,' I say. 'Pepper is wrong. I mean, I get why she's trying to make my life easier but I promise I'd far rather you told me if something's upsetting you.'

Josh chews on his lip, then flumps down onto his mattress. I notice with another guilty pang that his right sock has a massive hole in it that his big toe is poking through. 'It's just… she says she wants me to message her, then we make a plan and she says she'll be there, but then she isn't.'

I stare at him, bewildered. '*Pepper* is doing that?'

'*No*, obviously not.' Josh glares at me. 'Pepper's second cousin, Nadia.'

A faint memory glimmers at the edge of my brain of a lunch party Pepper threw a few weeks back. Her cousin's daughter, Nadia was there, the same age as Josh. I'd noticed them chatting, but not thought any more of it.

'You've been seeing Nadia since that party?'

Josh nods, his cheeks pinking.

I blow out my breath. More details of my children's lives I know nothing about.

'We went out a couple of times, but now… I dunno…' He looks at me with despair in his eyes. 'About ten days ago she suggested we met at the park, but then bailed at the last minute. And last Friday she sent me a text saying she'd be at Pepper's after my football practice, but when I went round there nobody was in. Since then, she's totally ghosted me.'

'Oh, Josh.' *How do I not know this?* 'I'm so sorry, why didn't you say something before?'

He shoots a withering glance at me. 'Do you remember what happened last Friday?'

'Oh,' I say. 'Brendan.'

173

Josh nods. 'That's why Pepper said not to bother you. Cos you were upset about that, and Lola and the police and everything…'

'How come Pepper knows about all this? Has Nadia talked to her?'

'No!' Josh glares at me again. 'God, Mum. No way would Nadia talk to her. I told you. I went round to Pepper's house that evening because Nadia said she would be there, but no one was in.'

'Are you sure?'

'Yes, I rang the door and I knocked. I even texted Pepper when Nadia didn't reply saying I was outside, but she didn't answer.'

'And since then, you haven't heard from her?'

Josh shakes his head, a pink flush reddening his cheeks. 'I just don't get it, Mum. Why would Nadia say she would meet me then just not turn up?'

I smile, ruefully. 'I don't know, my love, though…' I take a deep breath. 'I'm wondering if maybe Nadia just doesn't know how to tell you she'd rather be friends?'

Josh's cheeks turn from pink to magenta, his dark eyes filling with unhappiness. He stands up, avoiding my gaze. 'I gotta go to Anil's, Mum.'

'Sure.' I decide to hold off on any orders to tidy his room until tomorrow.

I follow him downstairs and chivvy him into his coat.

Lola drifts past us, a plate of toast in her hand. 'I don't want any dinner, Mum,' she says before I can speak.

Dinner. Seb will be home soon and I have nothing ready, when I wanted to prepare a special meal for him. As Lola vanishes upstairs, and the front door shuts behind Josh, I hurry back to the kitchen. I turn on the oven, then dart from store cupboard to fridge, fetching tomatoes and feta and red onion. It'll have to be a ready meal from the freezer, but I'll do a nice Greek salad to go with it.

I'm chopping the onion into fine slivers when Seb appears.

'Is it just us for dinner?' he asks.

'Yes. Listen, Seb, I want to say again that I'm so sorry about—'

'Did you talk to Stacy? Because I asked you to call as soon as you had news.'

'Yes, sorry.' I'm about to tell Seb that not only did I speak to Lola's lawyer, but that she was round here again because of the new witness and the police coming for more of Lola's things. Then it strikes me that Seb isn't really interested in any of those details, so I take a deep breath and simply outline what Stacy told me about getting his money back.

'Basically, it'll be a long shot – and even if it works it'll take time,' I say ruefully. Seb's face falls. 'But I know you can't wait. And you shouldn't have to. So I've been onto my bank and I promise—'

Seb's phone rings. He holds up his hand to indicate he needs to take the call, then walks into the hall. 'Hello?' I hear him say.

I finish slicing the onion, my heart filling with hope. Surely now I've decided to pay Seb back, we'll be able to start clearing the air? I just need to convince him I'm serious and we can move forwards. I wander to the fridge to get the cheese. As I close the door, chunk of feta in hand, Seb stalks back into the kitchen. His shoulders are stiff, his jaw clenched.

'I don't believe this!' he spits.

'What's the matter?' I ask, frowning. 'Who was that on the—?'

'Emmeline Schippel,' he snaps.

Oh, no.

'She was fixing my next appointment and let it slip that you went to see her today.' He glares at me.

I gulp. Damn Emmeline. She promised she'd keep her mouth shut. 'I can ex—'

'She says you turned up at her house this morning and forced her to show you the painting. She says you bullied her into it.'

'I didn't *bully* her into anything,' I exclaim, putting down the cheese that is still in my hand.

'She said she felt bad, that she'd been put in a really difficult position.' Seb pauses. 'What the hell, Alison? How did you even *know* about her?'

'I'm sorry,' I splutter. 'It's just… things have been so difficult… you know, Lola and Brendan and… and the money.'

'Too bloody right.' Seb folds his arms. 'But what's my money got to do with Emmeline Schippel? And you haven't answered my question. How did you know I knew her? Did someone say something about her?'

'No.'

'It was your ex-husband, wasn't it? Did he have me followed? Is that it?'

'Of course not.' I bite my lip.

'Alison, I'm not letting this drop. Answer me now,' Seb insists. 'Who told you I'd visited Emmeline?'

'No one,' I say. There's a long pause, then I take a deep breath. 'I looked at the GPS history on your sports watch while you were in the shower.'

Seb gasps. 'You did *what*?'

I hurry on. 'I'm really sorry, Seb, I—'

'Why?' Seb's voice cuts through the air like a whip. 'Did you think I was having an affair?'

'No, well, I... I just wanted to see where you were that night. Like I said, it was stupid and—'

'*That* night?' Seb frowns. '*What* night? Oh...' His eyes widen. 'Did... did you think *I* had something to do with Brendan's death? God, is that why you were checking up on where I was?'

'No, no of course not,' I say quickly.

'*Right.*' Seb stares at me. Contempt fills his face.

My heart slides into my stomach. A few, long seconds pass, then Seb draws in a sharp breath.

'Well,' he sneers, 'after all that effort to trace my movements, it must have been a bit of a shock to discover that all I was doing was trying to give you an original, expensive and thoughtful present.'

I hang my head. 'Seb, please listen. I can explain—'

'I don't want to hear it.' Seb shoves the nearest chair. It scrapes horribly across the tiles. 'This is... it's...' He marches to the kitchen doorway, then turns back to look at me, his eyes gleaming with angry hurt. 'If you think that I'm capable... If we can't even... I mean, what's left? What do we even have?' He hesitates, then strides away, his footsteps echoing up the stairs.

I stand, frozen, by the fridge. In the eighteen months we've been together, Seb and I have hardly ever argued. It's one of the things that drew me to him after years of endless spats with Michael.

I try to focus. I should give him a few minutes to calm down, then go up to see him, try and explain how confused and upset I've been, appeal to his understanding, his compassion. Heart thudding, I try to finish making the salad, but I can't focus. My thoughts tumble over each other. Jesus, why can't one thing go right? A wave of exhaustion washes over me, but I push it away. I don't have time to feel tired.

Seb reappears in the doorway. 'Alison?' His expression is stony. To my horror, a small, weekend bag hangs from his hand.

'What are you doing?' I ask.

'I need some time apart to think,' Seb says quietly. The cold, righteous calm of his voice sends a shiver down my spine. 'Because this... this snooping on my watch, tracking my movements, it's part of a pattern going back *forever* and I need to work through what it means and whether I can cope with it.'

'*What?*' Panic rises inside me. 'What are you talking about?'

'I'm talking about the fact that you don't trust me,' Seb says slowly. 'That you never turn to me when there's a problem. You'll go to your best friend and your ex-husband but not me.'

I stare at him. I want to protest but, unfurling from somewhere deep inside me, is the recognition that what he says is true.

'You don't tell me about needing my money – you just take it and give it to Brendan,' Seb goes on. 'You don't tell me you think I might be capable of murder. Jealousy I could maybe get my head round, but *that*?' He gives a weary shake of the head. 'It's a pattern of mistrust for which I have given you literally no reason.'

'No,' I protest. 'No, I get that I've messed up, Seb, and you're *totally* right about the money. Taking that was unforgiveable, but I'm going to get a loan from my bank and pay you back as soon as—'

'Stop it, Alison,' Seb interrupts. 'This isn't how I'd planned to say it, but there's something else, something I need to tell you.'

I brace myself. 'Okay.'

'Once I got Mum's money, I… I've been planning to ask you to marry me.'

'Right.' I nod slowly. I'm aware this is not the joyous response anyone offering up a proposal is probably looking for, but then it's not really an actual proposal, is it?

'I'd thought we could spend some of my money on a wedding. You know, involve the kids, invite all our friends.' He pauses, a wounded look on his face. 'Then I thought we might take a month off and do some travelling, before putting a deposit down on somewhere – outside London, obviously. And only once Josh left school. Maybe back in Reading?'

'Right,' I say again. I stare impassively back at him. I don't know how to respond to what he's saying out loud, but my whole body is screaming the truth of how I feel: *No to Seb. No to travelling with him. And definitely no to marrying and settling down with him in Reading.*

Seb gives an injured sigh. 'Your actions have *seriously* caused me to reconsider all of the above. Bottom line is, Alison, you clearly need help to deal with your issues and I'm not sure if I can be around for that any longer.'

I glance at the bag in his hand. 'What are you saying?'

'Like I said, I need a bit of time to think.' Seb gives me a final, reproachful look and walks away.

My heart thuds against my ribs. I hurry after him. 'Where are you going?'

Seb ignores me. A moment later he reaches the front door and lets himself out of the house.

I'm left in the silence of the empty hall.

Alone.

TWENTY

I wake the next morning to a text from Seb. Apparently, he's staying with a friend from work.

Just for a few days he writes, *please take the time to have a serious think about us.*

I don't know whether to laugh or cry. It's like I'm living in two separate worlds: Seb's world, which revolves around the two of us and my 'trust issues'. And the real world, containing almost everyone else I know, where the very air exudes worry about Lola being the prime suspect in a murder investigation.

Of course, Seb is justified in getting angry about my keeping things from him – just as he was about the money – but why can't he see how hard everything is right now? He hasn't even asked how Lola is.

I close the text without replying, then try to put Seb out of my mind. What matters right now is Lola. The police clearly believe she is guilty of killing Brendan. Which means it's down to me to prove that she isn't. And the only way to do that is to identify the actual murderer. DI Barnbury said, when he interviewed me, that Brendan had borrowed money from a number of his friends. Maybe Michael was right when he suggested the killer was someone coming round to collect an overdue debt and discovering Brendan about to flee the country.

Josh leaves for school and Lola is still asleep upstairs. I settle myself down at the kitchen table. I'll reply to a few emails, just enough to keep on top of my Hot Pepper PR work, then I'll start my investigation. First step: trawl Brendan's social media and make a list of any friends, in particular looking out for references to money lent and money owed. I'm ten minutes in to the work emails, when Lola shuffles into the kitchen, still in her PJs. I glance at the time. It's only just after nine a.m.

'You're up early,' I say.

Lola peers sleepily at me, stifling a yawn. 'I'm going over to Maisie's again.'

'Okay.' Should I point out that if she's feeling up to helping Maisie with her sixth form art project, she should probably be putting some energy into keeping up with her own studies?

No. She's only had a few days off school so far. Baby steps. I'm glad she's seeing her friends, trying to keep a hold of some part of normal life through all the turbulence.

Lola makes us both tea, then shuffles away again. Half an hour later she's left the house and I'm almost done with my work. I receive a fine for going down that school street last week. It feels like that happened in another lifetime. I pay up immediately. At least I won't have to tell Seb about it. As I close my laptop, my mobile rings.

It's Pepper.

'Turn on your TV. Hurry!' She directs me to one of the news channels as I scurry into the living room, my phone still clamped to my ear. My jaw drops as I access the item Pepper has urged me to watch.

'...this development in the investigation into the murder of Brendan Zeno has set the online world alight.

The case took a turn when details emerged of a social media post, published across a range of platforms the day before Zeno's death, which claimed the former musician had abused and raped her. The anonymous post, written under the username @AvengingAngel has given rise to speculation that Zeno may have been deliberately targeted. Today, we learn that at least four further women have come forward, sharing claims online that Zeno abused them.'

I suck in my breath. 'It worked, just like you said. There are other women just like me.' The thought that I wasn't the only person Brendan manipulated and attacked is strangely comforting.

'Of course,' Pepper says softly.

On the TV, the newsreader is still talking: 'A police spokeswoman says the Met are taking all claims seriously and urging @AvengingAngel – and other women affected by their post – to call a helpline. Details are on the bottom of the screen...' As the newsreader continues, tying Brendan's story to other abuse scandal cases, Pepper lets out a low whistle.

'Do you realise this makes me a police suspect?' she asks.

'Do you think we should come forward now?'

'No.' I'm surprised how vehement Pepper sounds. 'Once we explain what we did, the police will be less inclined to look somewhere other than Lola for Brendan's murderer. We want them pursuing all potential avenues for as long as possible. Anyway, for all we know, Brendan's murderer *is* one of the women he abused. She would certainly have a motive.'

The news moves onto a new topic and I switch it off. As I set the remote down, Pepper apologises for winding me up over Seb's portrait yesterday.

'It's fine,' I grunt, 'I overreacted.'

And, by the way, he's left me.

I don't say this, but Pepper – true to form – senses something is wrong.

'So how are you, though?' she asks. 'You sound weird.'

'I'm just tired,' I say, quickly launching into an explanation of yesterday's second round of police questioning and the news that an eyewitness to Lola's departure from Brendan's house has come forward. 'They got lots of details wrong, though, so the lawyers aren't as worried as they might be.'

'Still, that's a lot,' says Pepper with feeling. 'And for Lola, too. Is she with you now?'

'She's at Maisie's,' I say.

'Then come into work,' Pepper insists. 'Take your mind off things.'

I frown, glancing at my computer screen. Just one more thing to check and then I can begin my investigation into Brendan's contacts. 'Actually, Peps, I'm all set up for working at home.'

'I know,' Pepper says, 'but...' she sighs. 'Okay, full disclosure, I know we'd agreed you'd WFH, but I'm seeing a prospective client tomorrow and I'd really like to show you some of their stuff, get your advice. Please, it'll only take an hour or so.'

I hesitate. It's the last thing I want to do, but the insistence in Pepper's voice tells me it's important. 'Fine,' I say. 'Just for an hour.'

Pepper is on the phone when I get to the HOPP office. As I slide into my seat, Hamish – who says he doesn't know anything about the prospective client – tells me he's drafted a press release for the new Shine Security sensor camera.

'I'll make coffee while you check it over, yeah?'

'Sure, thanks.' I open the attachment he's just sent me. Shine Security is one of our most demanding clients. A lucrative contract – though not a glamorous one – that we were once in danger of losing thanks to Pepper's total lack of interest in electronic gadgets. Luckily, managing director Ben Royston has been impressed by Hamish ever since he joined us, recognising that HOPP's assistant account manager has a genuine fascination with how stuff works. I scan the press release.

'You've done a good job, the attack lines are great,' I say, when Hamish returns with a mug of coffee in each hand.

He sets my mug down beside me. 'Thanks. The pic could be sexier.'

'Security cams aren't supposed to be sexy, they're supposed to be reliable.' I consider the photo Hamish has inserted into the press release. This camera might be an upgrade, but from the outside it looks like all its predecessors, as well as most of the other security devices on the market: white, with a narrow aperture for the lens, designed to fit tidily and unobtrusively high up on an outside wall. It's just like the one outside Brendan's house that I waved at the day Pepper and I went to visit him. The one Stacy said was destroyed the night Brendan died.

'It doesn't matter how high-tech these things get,' I muse. 'They're still not going to work if someone knocks them off the wall, are—?' I stop, struck by the wide-eyed look of surprise on Hamish's face. 'What is it?'

He frowns, then waves his hand airily. 'Nothing, just weirded out by how interested everyone's suddenly got in security cameras.' His gaze drifts towards Pepper's office, where Pepper is still talking animatedly on the phone, her free hand gesticulating wildly.

'What d'you mean?'

'Nothing.' Hamish raises his eyebrows, lowering his voice conspiratorially. 'It's just Pepper said almost exactly the same thing to me only a few days ago.'

'Really?' I frown. 'Pepper never asks about Shine.'

Hamish shrugs, sipping at his coffee. 'Well, she did last Friday. We were talking about doorbells. She said hers was broken, and she wondered if Shine made them.' He lifts his chin and assumes a haughty voice that's a remarkable imitation of Pepper's own. '"*Never hurts to buy from the client, Hamish.*"'

I make a face, to acknowledge his mimicking skills. Hamish grins. 'Then she asked how much it would cost to get a security camera as well. And I gave her a rough estimate and she said, well, just what *you* said, really: what's the point of paying all that when all a burglar has to do is knock it off the wall.' Hamish chuckles. 'Great minds, eh?'

A chill creeps over me. Last Friday was the day Brendan died. And didn't Stacy mention yesterday how the camera above his front door was smashed off the wall soon after Lola was filmed entering the house that evening? Yes – her point was that this strongly suggested a second person arrived *after* Lola – possibly the murderer themselves.

'Alison?' Hamish is staring at me curiously.

'I'm fine, er, just give me a minute.' I turn and scuttle away, out of the HOPP office and onto the first-floor landing. The ladies is the second door on the right. I hurry inside and stand, facing the mirror. I put my hands on the cold sink and let out a long, slow breath.

How come Pepper – who never shows any interest in gadgetry – was talking to Hamish about knocking cameras off walls just a few hours before Brendan's own security cam was destroyed? I guess, if her doorbell really *was* broken, it makes sense she might be thinking about both an upgrade and a purchase from Shine Security. So it's probably just a mad coincidence.

Except… I grip the sides of the sink. What did Josh say about going over to her house that night?

No-one was in… I rang the door and I knocked. I even texted…

I hadn't thought much about it at the time, but now… What if Pepper wasn't there because she was at Brendan's house?

The bathroom door swishes and sucks. Pepper strides in, towering over me in heels and a pink trouser suit. An expression of concern creases her forehead.

'Are you feeling okay, Ali?' she asks. 'Hamish said you looked a bit sick, then ran off.'

I meet her gaze, unable to speak.

Pepper raises her eyebrows. 'What is it? Don't tell me old Seb's got you pregnant?' She grins, to indicate this is a joke.

'Er…' I hesitate. A big part of me wants to ignore what I've just learned and tell my best friend everything else that's on my mind: that my relationship is hanging by a thread and that I'm desperately worried about Lola being the prime suspect for Brendan's murder.

But look where I ended up when I hid stuff from Seb.

'So, what is it?' Pepper asks, just a hint of impatience in her voice.

'Josh was upset last night, about your cousin's daughter, Nadia…'

'Oh, God.' Pepper rolls her eyes. 'I thought they might have been seeing each other.'

'You did?'

She nods. 'Something Nadia said. Well, that her mum told me she'd said.' She sniffs.

I let go of the sink and turn to face her. 'Josh happened to mention that you weren't at home when he called round last Friday. He thought Nadia would be there, but *no one* was in.'

'Bollocks.' Pepper frowns. 'That's rubbish. *I* was in, but the doorbell is broken and I was playing music through my headphones so I didn't hear him call or knock.'

Is she telling the truth? It's hard to be sure with Pepper, she's such a good actress. 'I'm just trying to get a handle on last Friday night,' I say carefully. 'Make sense of what's happened.'

'Right.' There's a real edge to her voice now, as if she can hear my suspicions. 'Well, to recap for you: I *was* at home. All evening. I just didn't notice Josh's message until later.'

'You're sure?'

Pepper's expressive eyes widen. 'Of *course*,' she splutters. 'What are you getting at?'

'Nothing.' I lean back against the bathroom sink as Pepper noisily washes and dries her hands. She sounds convincing, yet I've heard her sound just like that with clients, making claims that aren't exactly lies, but that aren't the whole truth either.

Plus, it hits me, the other day she was pushing me to think Seb might be guilty of Brendan's murder. In fact, she was even more insistent about it than Michael. Then there's her @AvengingAngel post, which she clearly went to great lengths to avoid being associated with and which she keeps saying we shouldn't tell the police about. I thought she did that for me, to help Lola, but could it have been a clever and premeditated device for ensuring the police had a fresh lead to follow? Has, in fact, everything she's done since I told her about Brendan dating Lola been designed to point the finger away from herself as his murderer?

She strides to the door, then turns to fix me with a steely glare.

'Has it occurred to you that maybe Josh is stirring the pot?' Pepper asks, her voice thin with suppressed anger. 'I'm not saying he realises the impact, but perhaps he's telling you stuff to make you suspicious. After all, he's not getting a lot of attention right now, so—'

'Don't lay this on Josh,' I snap, rearing up off the sink. 'He only mentioned that you weren't at home in passing, when he was telling me about Nadia. Which reminds me, by the way, I'd rather you didn't tell my kids to avoid talking to me. I'm their *mother*.'

The atmosphere tightens. Pepper holds her hands up.

'Bloody hell, Alison, I'm just trying to help.'

'Like you were trying to help when you kept insisting Seb could have killed Brendan?'

The words shoot out of me like bullets. Pepper stares at me, her expressive face wreathed in shock and hurt. My heart thumps. Pepper and I have only fallen out seriously one time during the nearly thirty years we have known each other. It was a year or so after Lola was born, when

Pepper expected me to resume the regular weekly drinks we'd enjoyed before I fell pregnant, and I had to explain that I was no longer available in the way that I used to be. That Lola – not socialising – was my priority now.

'That isn't fair,' Pepper says, echoing the words she used all those years ago. 'You're implying I deliberately tried to make Seb look guilty of Brendan's murder, but why would I do that? Unless—' Her eyes widen. 'Unless you think *I* killed him?' She gasps. 'Why on *earth* would I do that? I mean I adore Lola, but you can't think for a second I'd go that far to protect her?'

'I don't know what to think.' The words come out sounding heavy and bitter.

'Right,' says Pepper. 'You know, Alison, sometimes you can be *such* a passive-aggressive bitch.'

I gasp as the bathroom door swings open. A woman from the office on the floor above appears. She glances curiously in our direction, as if sensing the tension between us, then heads into a cubicle.

'I'm going to go home now.' I glare at Pepper. 'You can deal with your prospective client by yourself.'

'Fine by me.' Pepper snaps and she stalks into one of the remaining cubicles.

I hurry back to the HOPP office, bustling around my desk to grab my tote bag from the floor by my chair. I'm determined to be out of here before Pepper reappears from the bathroom.

'Is everything okay, Alison?' Hamish has sidled up beside me. 'You looked kind of weird earlier.' His eyes burn with curiosity. 'Did you see Pepper? She came to look for you? I–I, er, heard shouting…?'

Could he be any nosier?

'I'm fine, everything's fine,' I snap, picking up my bag. 'I'll be working from home for the rest of this week.'

Hamish opens his mouth, presumably to ask another bloody question under cover of his deep concern. But before he can speak I'm through the door, down the stairs and out onto the damp, chilly pavement, heading for home.

TWENTY-ONE

The rest of the day passes slowly. I put the horrific idea that Pepper might be capable of murder out of my head and concentrate on investigating the women who have come forward on social media saying Brendan abused them. As far as I can work out, they all encountered him in the music industry during the height of his fame – or shortly afterwards. But it's hard to get details, or to winnow out specific victims from the many angry voices shouting online that Brendan should have been murdered years ago. It's even harder to read the words of the many people who are furious on Brendan's behalf; I feel sick to my stomach as I scroll through post after post insisting that the women accusing him are liars and should themselves be killed.

After three hours trawling through various platforms, I have got precisely nothing except a stress-induced headache. I don't even have the actual name of anyone claiming Brendan attacked them, though I can see from other comments that the police have been in touch with those people, urging them to make contact via their helpline. Have any of them done so yet? Will an investigation follow?

I close down all the threads I've been poring over. Maybe Michael can do some digging, using his contacts as a journalist; I'll ask him the next time I see him.

Leaving the posts about Brendan as an abuser aside, I begin trawling through his old social media feeds. I'm looking for any hints about money either loaned or owed. There's nothing here either. I retrace my steps and make a list of people with whom he was obviously in regular contact, as opposed to the gushing fans who appear in most of the interactions. After a couple of hours, I have twenty names – and no idea what to do next. How do I work out which of these people he owed money to? If, in fact, it *was* any of these people. My mind careers about like a Catherine wheel, sparking in one direction after another. DI Barnbury said Brendan was in debt to several friends, but that doesn't mean he didn't borrow from loan sharks as well. Or other contacts he knew *outside* of his social media.

This thought brings me back to Pepper. Could she have loaned Brendan money? No, surely not, she knew him too well to take such a risk. Anyway, she made it clear the other day she doesn't have any spare cash.

I spiral about, from frustration and distrust to self-doubt and back, until Josh and Lola get home. Rousing myself to make some dinner, I tell them Seb is away at a conference. Neither of them suspect this isn't true. Neither of them ask when he'll be back. The truth is, I have hardly thought about Seb all day. It's actually a relief that I don't have to deal with him right now. More than that, I realise, I don't miss him. Not really.

Which doesn't say much for our relationship.

Lola, Josh and I eat together, then the kids drift away, leaving me alone again, with my careening thoughts. Lola pads downstairs just before eight p.m. to tell me that Stacy wants her, Michael and myself to come to the solicitor's office tomorrow morning.

'I've called Dad already,' she says. 'He'll pick us up at ten.'

'Why?' I frown. 'What's the meeting for?'

'Stacy wants us to meet her boss, Meena somebody.'

'Okay, but why?' My heart thuds. 'Why do they feel we need to meet someone more senior?' What's going on now? It doesn't sound good. Surely the only reason for us to see a more experienced solicitor is if the firm thinks the police are actually close to charging Lola with murder?

'Stacy said it wasn't anything to worry about,' Lola says, uncertainly. 'They just want to go over some details. I asked what they were, but she said they'd rather talk it all over face-to-face.' She gazes at me anxiously. 'It's not a big deal, is it, Mum?'

Of course it bloody is.

'No, sweetheart.' I try to sound as reassuring as possible, but inside I'm wishing that all lawyerly communications didn't have to come through Lola. If *I* had been talking to Stacy, I'd have insisted on her telling me what was going on then and there. 'I'm sure it's just them being thorough.'

–

The leaden sky matches my mood the next morning, all dark, grey clouds and spits of rain. I make an effort to look smart – earrings and a jacket plus a touch of mascara and lipstick. I notice Michael's eyes linger on my face when he turns up to collect us. He's smiling, far cheerier than I'm expecting.

'It's good news we're seeing Meena Gupta,' he enthuses as he drives us away. 'She's got a top reputation. Really knows what she's doing. You're in good hands with her, Babycakes.' He glances over his shoulder to where Lola is curled up on the back seat.

My heart gives an unexpected tug at his attempt to reassure her. Lola nods, smiling – though I'm not sure whether the smile is genuine, or simply for her dad's benefit – then draws her headphones over her ears. The hiss of a superfast drumbeat drifts towards us.

Twenty minutes later we're walking into the foyer of Wilson, Gupta and Partners, where Stacy is waiting. She greets us with warm smiles and, I note idly, no hint of her former interest in Michael. She leads us into a conference room where Meena Gupta rises from the polished wooden table and extends a perfectly manicured hand. She's seriously groomed, in a grey silk suit, with a Strathberry handbag at her feet.

Introductions over, we all sit down and everyone looks expectantly at the senior lawyer.

'Stacy's brought me up to date and I've read over all the files,' Meena says. Her bird-like head flicks from Lola to me and Michael and back again. 'Do you have any questions on the situation so far?'

I clear my throat. 'No, er, just, it's great that you're getting involved, but we… I was wondering if something has happened that we should be worried about?' I ask, meeting Meena's sharp dark-eyed gaze. 'It's six days since Brendan was murdered and the police have already interviewed Lola twice. Do you think they're about to charge her or something? Is that why you called us in?'

Beside me, Lola shuffles awkwardly in her seat.

'We called you in to bring you up to date on our strategy for Lola's case. Belt and braces, so we're all up to speed.' Meena purses her lips, skilfully avoiding the first part of my question. 'Shall I outline where we're at?'

I nod and glance at Lola. She tugs her jumper lower, over her wrists, her mouth set in a grim line. She looks several years younger than she actually is, a little girl in a room full of adults.

Meena clears her throat. 'Lola's interview under caution two days ago was a blatant attempt to prompt a confession. It failed, of course, but the police are still very focused on accumulating enough evidence to convince the Crown Prosecution Service to take the case forward.'

'Jesus,' Michael says.

Meena holds up her hand. 'Don't worry, there's good news.'

I nod encouragingly at Lola, a tiny flicker of hope sparking.

She looks up, the sullen look still on her face. 'What?' she asks. 'What's the good news?'

'The police's case rests on four key pieces of evidence,' Meena says briskly. 'I'll go through them one by one. Firstly, Brendan Zeno's security camera. According to the video footage that the security company have now provided, no one entered Brendan Zeno's home between the time that you went in, Lola, at 7:03 p.m. and the point that the camera was destroyed, precisely thirty-three minutes later, at 7:36 p.m.' Meena pauses. 'This makes Lola the last person *known* to have seen the deceased alive.'

'I don't see how that's good news,' Lola mutters.

I pat her hand across the table, then turn to Meena. 'The footage by itself doesn't prove anything, does it? But the breaking of the camera works in our favour. I mean, why would Lola destroy it *after* it had filmed her. It would make far more sense to do it beforehand.'

'Quite.' Michael nods.

'Which is exactly what we suspect the real killer did,' Meena says. 'You're right, Alison, that broken camera is probably the best piece of evidence we have.'

'What about the others?' I sit back, feeling more confident.

Meena taps on the pile of papers on the table in front of her. 'The police's second key piece of evidence is the anonymous witness who claims to have seen Lola leaving Brendan's house just before eight p.m. We think that person is probably the murderer and that he or she is deliberately setting Lola up. Our working theory is that the witness who claims to have seen Lola leaving the house *later* than was actually the case – and wearing different clothes – is almost certainly the same person who destroyed the video camera, entering the property at the front just a few minutes after Lola exited from the back.'

My throat tightens. 'How... how can you be so sure?' I ask.

Meena adjusts her folder with an elegant fingertip and smiles. 'Well, the front door wasn't broken down, which means somebody on the inside must have let the perpetrator in. Our narrative suggests that Brendan himself was that person. Which means he was alive *after* Lola left the house.'

'We think the perpetrator was watching the house, that he waited for Lola to leave, then came in, killed Brendan and fled,' Stacy adds.

'That does, actually, make sense,' Michael says.

I gaze at Lola. She nods, slowly.

'You said there were four pieces of evidence,' I say. 'You've tied together the anonymous witness and the damaged video cam. What are the other two?'

'The knife used to commit the murder – which is missing – and the neighbour who supposedly heard a woman threatening to kill Brendan at some point after seven o'clock.'

'That's not a very specific timeframe,' Michael chips in.

'And he's not a very reliable witness,' Meena adds. 'He's over eighty and wears a hearing aid. So I don't think we need to worry about him.'

'Will the CPS buy all this?' I ask.

'So long as the knife doesn't show up, I think they will,' Meena says. 'When it comes down to it, our version of events is far more plausible than the police's theory that an eighteen-year-old with no record of violence killed her boyfriend, then for some inexplicable reason destroyed the camera that had already recorded her entering the property.'

'I have a question,' Michael says.

Everyone looks at him.

'This person who set Lola up,' he says. 'How did they know Lola would be going to Brendan's house? I mean, you're saying the murder was planned in advance, but how could they have known Lola would be there, at exactly that time?'

'We have two working theories. One, that they had been watching Brendan's house for a while, waiting for someone to go inside,' Meena says. 'This would mean Lola was just unlucky.'

'And what's the second theory?' I ask.

Meena hesitates. Before she can speak, Lola leans back in her chair and says grimly. 'That someone knew about me and Brendan and was following me until I went to his house.'

'That's right,' Meena acknowledges.

A shiver snakes down my spine. The atmosphere in the room stills.

'Do you think that's likely?' Michael asks, sounding horrified. 'That Lola was deliberately framed?'

'No,' Meena says emphatically. 'We have to cover all bases, but for me there are too many moving parts with that theory, things that don't add up. Remember Brendan was going away the next day, so the murderer didn't have a big window in which to operate. It wouldn't have been very efficient to follow Lola around all the time on the off chance she would pitch up at Brendan's house at just the right moment.'

'What about the women who've come forward on social media claiming Brendan abused them?' Michael asks. 'Surely the police are investigating them too? I'm not saying it was necessarily one of the women, but maybe an angry partner...?'

I stare down at the conference table. The wood is so highly polished I can see my own reflection in it.

'I've actually spoken to the detectives about that line of enquiry,' Meena says. 'A few women have come forward, enough for the police to see a pattern and look into Brendan's past behaviour.'

I glance up at her, hope surging through me. 'But that's good, isn't it? I know they've been thinking that @AvengingAngel was Lola, but surely other women coming forward gives them a whole load of new suspects.'

Meena wrinkles her nose. 'Apparently all the women the police have spoken to not only claim they didn't see the @AvengingAngel post until *after* Brendan's death, but have alibis for the evening of his murder. As far as that strand of their investigation goes, the police are focusing their attention on establishing the identity of @AvengingAngel herself. They think – and I agree – that it's highly suspicious a direct threat against Brendan was made publicly the day before he died. At the moment, of course, they still suspect @AvengingAngel is Lola, but I understand they're very close to identifying the IP address for the post. At the very least, that should provide some fresh evidence. And, if they latch onto a new prime suspect, it might even mean they eliminate Lola from their enquiries.'

'Yes,' breathes Lola.

'That's great news,' says Michael. He smiles at me. 'Isn't it, Ali?'

I nod, not trusting myself to speak.

–

As we leave the solicitor's office, Lola tugs at my sleeve. The dark clouds from earlier have cleared and the sun is now shining brightly. I shield my eyes from the glare as I turn to face her.

'I said I'd go to Maisie's again, Mum, I'll see you later.' She takes a step back.

'Don't you want to talk about what the lawyers just said?' I ask.

'We could debrief in the car, I'll give you a lift?' Michael offers.

A weary look crosses Lola's face. 'I can get the train.' She points to the overground station across the road. 'Honestly, I just want to go to Maisie's. She's totally obsessed with her art project. It's brilliant. We don't talk about my stuff at all.'

Poor girl. 'Okay, sweetheart,' I say, though I'm also thinking that this evening we're going to *have* to talk about her getting back to school.

'Have a good time,' Michael says gruffly, bending down to kiss her cheek.

Lola gives us a wave and hurries over the road and into the station. I follow Michael along the pavement to his car.

'Do you think she's okay?' I ask.

'As okay as can be expected.' He stands beside the driver's door, smiling at me in the sharp sunshine. 'Look, I'm sorry I said I thought Seb might be, you know… It was stupid of me.'

I gaze into his apologetic eyes. 'D'you want to get some lunch?'

Michael's eyes register surprise. He moves closer, his hand now just centimetres from mine on the bonnet. His fingers touch the tips of mine. 'Sure,' he says, 'I'd love to.'

I frown, removing my hand from the car. 'I thought you could help me with something,' I say, pointedly. 'I've gone through Brendan's socials and made a list of any potential suspects. I know the police claim they're investigating everyone he came into contact with, but I thought you might—'

'I've already checked through every single contact of Brendan's I could find,' Michael says flatly. 'No leads.'

'Oh.' I look up, into Michael's dark eyes, as intense as the day I met him.

'Was that the only reason you wanted to have lunch?' he asks softly.

I shake my head, thinking of my suspicions about Pepper from yesterday. 'Not exactly.'

'Come on, then.' He points to the cafe over the road. 'Let's go there. You can tell me what else is on your mind.'

TWENTY-TWO

The cafe is smart and vegan, with plump wedges of banana bread and gleaming chocolate cake ranged along the counter. We order bowls of soup, then head for a free table. There's only one couple nearby, settling their bill. I press my finger to my lips, indicating we should wait until they've gone before talking. Michael nods and peers at his phone. My whole body tenses. The couple leave and the waitress brings our soup over. Michael grins, appreciatively, at her as she sets them down. He has the sexiest smile – it's one of the first things I noticed about him all those years ago. It's a smile that draws you in. Not lightly mocking, like Brendan's, or dazzling and exuberant, like Pepper's; more a slight, suggestive upturn of the lips, an invitation to get to know him rather than an announcement of his personality.

Put another way, he's a flirt. Always has been.

Our waitress smiles back, then sashays away. Michael turns to face me. 'So go on,' he urges. 'You suspect someone, don't you, Ali?'

I nod, slowly.

'Who?' he frowns.

I lean forward. 'Michael, I know it sounds crazy but I think she… she might have—' I stop.

'For goodness' sake, Alison, *who?*'

I take a deep breath. 'Pepper,' I say at last, my voice cracking.

'*What?*' Michael's eyes widen with shock.

'Just listen.' Words spill out of me like water as I explain all the small clues that add up to my suspicion that Pepper might have murdered Brendan. 'So you see,' I say, drawing to a close. 'She had motive – she loathed Brendan being with Lola – as well as means – she talked about destroying security cameras on the day of the murder – and opportunity, at least according to Josh, who is certain she wasn't at home at the time it took place.' I gaze into Michael's eyes. 'It all fits, apart of course, from the fact that I can't believe she'd be capable of either stabbing someone – or framing Lola.'

'Wow.' Michael stares at me.

A faint smell of baked pastry wafts towards us. I realise that I've barely eaten for the past few days and, in spite of the knot of anxiety in my stomach, my mouth is watering as I take a bite of the roll by the side of my soup bowl.

'What do you think?' I ask.

Michael says nothing, just takes a sip of his soup.

'*Well?*' I urge.

Michael wrinkles his nose. 'I don't know.'

'But you think it's possible?'

'I guess.' Michael frowns. 'But do you really think Brendan being with Lola would have been a strong enough motive for Pepper to kill him?'

'Maybe she had other reasons, too.'

'Like what?' he asks.

The answer is on my lips, but I can't say it. It's not just the fact that I've kept the rape a secret for such a long time. I realise with a jolt, that the real reason I don't want to explain everything to him is that it will mean acknowledging what an idiot I was back then – how eagerly I soaked up Brendan's attention, how I betrayed Michael every time Brendan looked at me – until the very last minute, when it was too late.

To cover my confusion, I take a spoonful of soup. It's leek and potato, hot and flavourful. 'I know we've been friends with Pepper a long time but… maybe there's stuff we *don't* know…'

'Maybe.' Michael shrugs, looking doubtful.

We sit in silence, the cafe filling up around us. An idea seeds in my head. A mad, ridiculous idea that I can't shake off. Michael slugs down his coffee.

'So what do you want to do?' he asks. 'With your suspicions of Pepper, I mean. Do you think we should talk to her? She'll be mightily pissed off with us but—'

'I want to take a look in Pepper's house,' I interrupt. 'While she isn't there.'

Michael splutters coffee over the table. 'Break in? You're kidding.'

'It won't be breaking in,' I say. 'I have a spare key. Anyway, Pepper and I had a bit of a bust up yesterday. She knows I've got… doubts. She's not going to say yes if I ask permission to snoop around her home.'

'But… but—' Michael stutters.

'The police have searched my house and your flat,' I say firmly. 'But they've shown no interest in Pepper's place. *Nobody's* looked there.'

'Come off it, Ali.' Michael laughs. 'What would we be looking *for*? Bloodstained clothes under the sink? The knife used for Brendan's murder in her sock drawer?'

'No,' I say. 'Obviously not. If Pepper killed him with that knife, she'd have got rid of it by now,' I say.

'O-kay.' Michael spreads his hands out on the table. His gold wedding band glints under the electric lights. When did he start wearing *that* again? 'So what *would* we be looking for?'

'Something specific,' I say. 'Something recent. Something that explains why Pepper might want Brendan dead *now*.'

Michael stares at me. 'You really want to look through her stuff behind her back?'

'It's our only option,' I say, staring at the steam wreathing off my soup bowl. I suddenly have no appetite. 'I *know* it's an abuse of friendship and trust, but Lola's *future* is on the line.'

Michael looks down at his soup. 'That's true,' he says, his voice low and suddenly very serious.

'All we'd be doing is taking a quick look through Pepper's things,' I go on. 'And if, by chance, Pepper somehow finds out, we can pretend that we called round when she wasn't there and just waited inside for a bit.' I reach for my phone.

Michael watches as I scroll the screen. 'What are you doing?'

'I'm checking the HOPP work calendar,' I say, scanning the screen. 'Looks like Pepper is in the office right now then has a client meeting at four thirty. She won't be home until six at the earliest.' I look up. 'We've got four hours. If we're going to go snooping, there's no better time than now.'

Michael gazes at me. It's a strange look: part wary, part admiring.

'Okay.' He rises to his feet so fast he knocks the table and soup slurps over the side of my bowl. 'I'm in.' He grins. 'Let's go.'

Pepper's ultra-modern town house is eerily silent. The last time I let myself in here alone was back in the summer, while she was sunning herself in Tuscany and I came to feed her cat, Druska, once a day.

'This is weird,' Michael says with feeling. 'I'm getting flashbacks to the autumn of ninety-eight.'

'What?'

'My celebrity-bin-searching period.' He sighs. 'Okay, where do you want to start?'

I lead Michael into the kitchen. It's in its usual state of colourful and artfully ordered clutter. Even with the four hours we have, it's going to be an uphill struggle to find anything incriminating.

'Where do we begin?' Michael asks, doubtfully.

'I guess— Oh!' Druska leaps out of nowhere onto the counter, making me jump. She purrs as she slinks over, rubbing her back against my arm. 'Hey, pretty girl,' I say absently. Her name means 'salt' in Lithuanian, a joke which I've heard Pepper explain a million times.

'So I had a builder from Lithuania once who thought my name was *hilarious*,' she always says. 'He kept saying "Pipirai, Druska" and laughing, so when I got the cat it was the obvious choice.'

'Ali?' Michael frowns. 'Are we going with "buried deep in a drawer" or "hidden in plain sight"?'

'Both,' I snap.

Michael rolls his eyes. 'So we're looking everywhere, then.'

I glance sideways at him. 'Are you going to moan or help?'

He grins. 'Okay, I still think this is ridiculous, but how about I look through the ground floor, you check out upstairs?'

Druska follows me up the stairs, her lithe body curling around my legs, almost tripping me up. She must think I'm here to feed her.

'Sorry Druska,' I murmur. I go into the explosion of reds and oranges that is Pepper's bedroom. Despite the colourful sense of chaos, it's actually as neat as a pin. How like Pepper is that? All flamboyant excess on the surface, underneath, everything controlled and pared back to the bone. There really aren't many places she could be hiding something. I rustle through the wardrobe, pulling out the shoe rack, then delve into each neatly arranged drawer in turn.

Pepper's bedside cupboards reveal nothing more than some books and a small pink vibrator. I flush with guilt at this reminder of how badly we're invading her privacy. I check the time. Over half an hour has already passed.

Michael appears in the doorway. 'Found anything?'

'Only my conscience,' I mutter.

He grins and pads away. As his footsteps echo down the stairs, I check the time again. We still have two more hours before Pepper should be home.

I move to the larger of Pepper's spare rooms. Druska makes another brief reappearance, then – clearly accepting at last that I'm not about to give her any food – disappears again. I check under the bed, flicking open and rummaging through two suitcases full of souvenirs and summer clothes, before replacing them carefully. I scan the bookshelves to make sure there's nothing hidden between the books and the wall, then turn my attention to the bathroom.

Nothing significant here either. Guilt rises, fast and hard, like a riptide.

I push it away. Just Pepper's home office to go. As I cross the landing, the soft thud of sofa cushions landing on the carpeted living room floor drifts up towards me. I check the time. Another thirty minutes, then we leave.

Pepper's home office was originally a third bedroom, but Pepper has always used it as a study. One whole wall is lined, top to bottom, with deep shelves. Rows and rows of box files cover the shelves, each one labelled in hot pink marker. Pepper's whole life is here. *Sale of Dryden Road*. That's the house she grew up in, where her dad died soon after Lola was born. *Barsington Grammar... Uni Admin... Theatre Studies Year One notes...* and on and on, with separate files for everything, from early, pre-online bank statements and tax returns to her parents' wills and old family photos. There are even files called *Audition Notes* and *Agent Admin*, from the days when she was still trying to be an actress.

It's all yet more evidence of Pepper's organised – some might say controlling – nature.

I move to the end of the shelving unit. I'll start at the top and work methodically along, then down. I reach up to the top shelf. The first file is marked *Queer Stuff*. Intrigued, I pull it out and flip the lid. It's full of photos and programmes from about fifteen or sixteen years ago, that period when Lola was very little and Pepper and I stopped seeing so much of each other for a while. I flick through the flyers for TransPortal, remembering the time Pepper persuaded me to visit the club with her and how I'd wandered open-mouthed in wonder at the glittering dancers as they glided, flipped and tumbled across the long, glassy stage.

I shut the box with a snap. This is no time to get nostalgic. I reach up to fetch the next box along, when the edge of a smaller, yellowed box file catches my eye. It's shoved behind the others, out of sight unless you remove the files in front. Curious, I stretch to pull it out. This is different from the brightly coloured boxes along the rest of the shelves. Not only is it battered and, clearly, very old but it's labelled with just a single letter: 'B'.

I open it carefully.

A folded sheet of paper and a bulging envelope meet my gaze.

I lift out the paper and unfurl it. It's a list of five dates, roughly two or three months apart, starting about a year and a half after Lola was born. Beside each date is the number 20,000.

Weird.

I take out the envelope. There's something soft inside it. I lift the flap, a sense of dread washing over me, and draw out an object heavily wrapped in bubble wrap. I slowly unwind the wrap, then stare down at the object inside.

It's a small Ken doll with a photo of Brendan's face from when we were at uni stuck over the plastic head. The doll is wearing clothes like Brendan's from that time, too, including what looks like a clumsily stitched attempt at a grubby white T-shirt with a green peace sign scrawled on the front. Brendan definitely had one like that. He wore it all the time.

A memory slams into me, hard, of Pepper and I as students, making stupid voodoo dolls of two annoying guys in our student flat for a laugh. Did we make one of Brendan back then? My mind scratches about for the memory... No. I'm sure we didn't. I peer closer. The doll is covered in tiny silver – Jesus – pins. It's only bloody stuck full of pins.

Stab wounds.

Frozen to the spot, I lift the doll out, pinch one of the pins and slowly draw it out a centimetre. It glints in the light. Did we actually put pins in our dolls thirty years ago? Surely we'd lost interest in the game by then. Moved on to beer and pizza and gossip instead.

My hands shake.

'It's not what you think,' Michael's voice rises, urgent, from downstairs. 'Just listen.'

Shit.

The front door closes.

Shit. Shit. Shit.

'How did you bloody get in here?' Pepper sounds furious. 'Did Alison let you in? Where the hell is she?'

'Upst—'

The rest of Michael's reply is drowned out as Pepper roars my name, pounding angrily up the stairs.

I freeze, unable to move, the voodoo doll of Brendan still in my hand.

TWENTY-THREE

'Alison!' Pepper yells again. 'Is this about yesterday?' Her footsteps draw closer. I can't move. A moment later she's there, in the doorway. We stare at each other. The utter fury on her face gives way to horror, as she sees what I'm holding.

Michael appears behind her.

'Listen, Peps—' He's trying to sound conciliatory. Pepper throws him a furious glance. Then Michael spots the little voodoo doll too. 'What the hell is that?'

I hold up the miniature Brendan for him, turning the doll so the pins extending from its body catch in the light.

'Jesus Christ,' Michael says.

A long pause follows. Michael and I stare at Pepper who blinks, the colour draining from her face.

'Get out of my house,' she says at last, her voice shaking with fury.

'Tell us why you have a voodoo doll of Brendan,' I demand.

'Are you serious?' Pepper spits. 'For God's sake, you were with me when we did that. It was a *million years ago* when we were in our second year. We were mucking about. We made stupid effigies of those arsehole guys in our flat. Don't you remember?'

'We didn't do one of Brendan,' I insist.

Pepper presses her lips together, an uncharacteristic uncertainty hovering about her eyes suddenly.

'When did you make this?' I glare at her, holding out the doll again.

Pepper stays silent. Her expression is mutinous. And fearful.

'You have to admit, that pin is kind of specific,' Michael says, clearly trying to sound more conciliatory again. '*Weirdly* specific, bearing in mind Brendan was stab—'

'I don't owe you any explanations.' She glares from me to Michael. 'Neither of you.'

'Then we'll give this—' I shake the doll '—to the police.' My heart thuds. 'Please, Pepper.'

'Owning a Ken doll and drunkenly voodoo-ing it up isn't a crime,' Pepper scoffs. 'Unlike breaking and entering.'

'For goodness' sake, Pepper, I had a key, which,' I let out a sigh, 'I have because we're friends, and there's something here you're not telling us which I don't want to believe is that my very best friend in the whole world might have killed someone and set up my daughter to take the blame, so *please* tell us what Brendan did that made you want to make a doll of him and stick pins in it?'

I stare at her. Is it possible that Brendan came on to Pepper too? That he led her on? Raped her? Pepper was always so sure of herself, even when we were students. I can't believe that she would have fallen for Brendan's charismatic 'you're-so-special-until-you're-not' routine like I did. If she'd wanted to shag him, she would have done.

Unless he attacked her, not like me after a slow-burn seduction, but more suddenly and out of the blue. And then – I gasp, the thought horrifying me – what if Pepper kept the truth of that from me out of shame, just as I kept my truth from Michael? And what if that shame built and burned inside her until eventually, tipped over the edge by his manipulations of me and Lola, she decided to kill him? Knowing Pepper, she'd have planned it carefully. And maybe part of that plan was her creating the @AvengingAngel post, not to protect me from exposure or to help Lola, as she claimed at the time, but to deflect attention away from herself.

'I *can't* tell you what Brendan did.' The words burst out of Pepper. 'Show the police the bloody doll if you want. It's from a quarter of a century ago, plus, *ha*, your fingerprints are all over it now, Alison.' Her voice rises. 'Not that *sticking a pin in something is a sodding crime anyway.*'

'Not good enough.' Michael takes a step closer to Pepper, his voice now low and intense. 'We're not asking because we're interested in whatever beef you had with Brendan. All we care about is Lola. So you've got five minutes to convince us you had nothing to do with Brendan's murder.' He pauses. 'And if you don't, never mind the police. I'm going to make sure the tabloids not only get a good look at this doll but every scrap of information Ali and I can dredge up about your relationship with Brendan.' He pauses. 'I can't imagine the publicity will help your PR company very much. Who wants to have their promotional work organised by the crazy voodoo lady?'

Pepper's jaw drops. She turns to me. 'You're going to let him blackmail me like this?'

I stare, stonily back at her. 'We need to know the truth.'

Another long pause, then Pepper holds up her hands to admit defeat.

'Fine,' she says. And the three of us sit down in the living room.

Pepper clears her throat.

'As you know, Brendan and I were never really friends back at uni, and once he got popular and dropped everyone from his past,' she glances at Michael who makes a face in acknowledgement, 'I thought I'd never see him again.'

'So?' I lean forward. 'What happened?'

'We bumped into each other at some event, just after my dad's terminal cancer was diagnosed,' Pepper says. 'You were busy with Lola, totally caught up in all the challenges of having a baby, a *new* person in your life, while I was facing letting go of the most important person I'd ever known.'

I nod, remembering. 'That was a difficult time,' I say softly.

'I broke down in front of him – Brendan,' Pepper explains. 'I don't know why. I think it was knowing him from the past, yet not really knowing him at all.' She sighs. 'Anyway, he was lovely, you know how he could be? Mr Charm. Saying all the right things, making me feel special and… and that he cared.'

I look away.

'Go on,' Michael urges.

'So Dad was very sick and you weren't around much, Alison – not that I'm blaming you.' Pepper shoots me a quick look. 'Dad knew he only had a few months left and one day he said that he wanted me to help him… end things.'

I gasp.

'I said no, at first, but then…' She shakes her head. 'I don't expect you to understand, but he was in terrible pain and frightened of it getting worse and he started begging me to get him something that would put him to sleep forever.'

'Oh Pepper.' I cover my mouth with my hand, flooding with guilt. 'I had no idea.'

'You had enough problems.'

'But you went through all that alone?'

'Brendan,' Michael says darkly.

'That's right,' Pepper makes a face. 'He came round to see us. Sat with Dad so I could get out of the house a bit. I ended up hinting at what Dad wanted and Brendan just listened, he didn't push me, didn't judge me.' She hesitates. 'In fact, he gave me the details of someone who could supply the drugs we needed so I could set up a meeting.' She sighs. 'I thought he was being such a great friend. I was so grateful. He made it easy for me to get the pills and then, a few days later, I helped Dad take them.' She looks down at her lap. 'He slipped away quietly in the end, just a few weeks before he would have done naturally anyway.'

'So Brendan knew exactly what you were planning?' I frown. 'I don't understand. What does all that back then have to do with that voodoo doll?'

Pepper heaves a sigh. 'Dad died and Brendan came to the wake at his house.' She looks at me. 'Do you remember, you two couldn't make it because Lola was sick?'

I nod, feeling ashamed.

'The whole thing felt a bit surreal, but at last everyone left – or I thought they had. I went into Dad's room. The one we made up for him on the ground floor. And I was sitting on the bed, when who should come in but Brendan.'

'What did he want?' Michael asks.

'He started asking me about the house. He knew Dad was leaving it to me and he wanted to know how soon it would be until probate was granted and what I thought the property was worth.'

'Sensitive,' I say wryly.

'Sounds like Brendan,' Michael adds.

'I told him I wasn't thinking about the house and its value today and he gave me this horrible mean smile and said: "I'm afraid you're going to have to think about it".'

I stare at her. 'What did that mean?'

'It turned out,' Pepper goes on, 'that Dad had told Brendan all about the terms of his will, and what I would inherit, and how he and I had talked about me selling the house and setting up a business. Brendan insisted that once I'd got hold of the money from the house, he wanted one hundred grand paid into his bank account.'

'No way.' I look at Michael.

'What on earth made him think you'd give him anything?' he asks Pepper.

Pepper sighs. 'That's exactly what I said. So Brendan played me a recording of my conversation with the drug dealer who got me the stuff I needed for Dad. He'd totally set me up, to the point of making sure the dealer used a fake name and couldn't be traced.'

'What a bastard,' I mutter.

'And just as I'm reeling from that, Brendan walks over to the bookcase opposite Dad's bed and pulls out the video camera he'd stashed there. He then proceeds to show me the recording he'd carefully timed – having got the whole plan out of Dad, so he knew exactly what I was going to do and when I was going to do it.' Pepper's voice cracks. 'Brendan said that if I didn't give him the money he wanted he'd present everything he had to the police, along with a bunch of lies about my dad telling him he was scared I might kill him off.'

Michael lets out a low whistle. 'That is some long con.'

My jaw drops. 'Brendan did all that?'

Pepper nods. 'The secret video recording he made in Dad's bedroom actually showed me handing Dad the pills that killed him, watching him swallow them and sitting beside him while he died.' She pauses. 'It wouldn't have counted in a court of law, but Brendan had all the other stuff to add to the mix, too. I figured that even if I didn't end up in jail I'd be totally cancelled. That I'd never get my business off the ground.' Tears prick in her eyes.

I swallow hard, trying to dislodge the lump in my throat. Poor Pepper. She must have been devastated, especially when she was feeling so raw about losing her dad. Especially when she didn't have a best friend to turn to.

My body fills with shame. I wasn't there for her. I was so caught up with Lola, I didn't see *any* of this.

'So you paid Brendan what he asked?' Michael asks.

'I did.' Pepper's face convulses with shame. 'I made the voodoo doll of Brendan not long afterwards. I came across the dolls when I was sorting out the house. I switched one of them to Brendan's face and drew that stupid peace sign on his T-shirt, just like the one he used to wear. I don't know why, I just felt so out of control... so angry.' She looks up. 'But I didn't kill him. If I'd been going to do that, it would have been back then.'

I glance across the room at Michael. He is sitting like I am, rigid with shock.

'Well?' Pepper sits back. 'What do you think of me now?' Her tone is lightly ironic, deliberately casual. But there's vulnerability underneath the archness, a deep layer of pain in her voice.

I gaze at the Brendan doll, hanging limply from my hand. I lay it down on the glass coffee table. 'I'm so sorry all that happened, Pepper.' The words sound empty. 'I wish… I'm sorry you felt you had to keep it all to yourself.' I look up and Pepper's eyes meet mine.

'I couldn't involve anyone else, especially then,' she says. 'I was guilty of a crime. Telling you would have made you guilty too.'

I nod, slowly. 'I just can't believe you've had to live with it all this time.'

'*I* can't believe you didn't kill the bastard years ago,' Michael mutters.

'I could never have done that,' she says, her voice growing throaty. 'Knowing how it feels to end a life, the last thing I could ever do is end another.' She presses her lips together, tears trickling down her cheeks. I gulp, my own throat swelling. In all the years I've known her, I have *never* seen Pepper properly cry. Not even at her dad's funeral.

'Oh, Pepper.' I'm out of my seat and over to where she's sitting. I put my arm around her. 'I'm so sorry.' My own voice cracks as she sniffs back her tears, leaning against my shoulder. And then I look over at Michael and he meets my gaze, and I can see the same thought firing in his head, that is rising now in mine:

If Pepper didn't kill Brendan, who did?

TWENTY-FOUR

By the time Michael and I leave Pepper's house it's dark outside and the air has grown cold and damp, threatening rain. I shove my hands in my pockets as we hurry to Michael's Audi. What do I do now? Lola is still the police's prime suspect for Brendan's murder. All I've achieved today is to delay my search for the actual murderer.

Well, I'm not going to waste any more time.

'Looks like we're back to square one,' Michael says, as he opens the driver's side door. His eyes are deep with concern.

'I know.' I sigh, getting into the passenger seat. 'Listen, I know you said you'd checked out Brendan's contacts, but maybe there's something you missed? Remember the police say he had huge debts. That's a big motive for someone to kill him, isn't it?'

'I guess I could take another look, but I've already checked under every stone I could find.' Michael frowns as he sits behind the wheel, his face filling with the same fierce intensity that made me fall for him all those years ago. 'It's a dead end, Ali. The police know it too – that's why they keep coming back to Lola.'

'Oh,' I say.

We set off. A drizzle patters around us as we make our way through the gloomy streets. Neither of us speaks until Michael pulls up outside my house.

I rest my hand on the door handle, about to press it down, then turn to say goodbye.

'Listen,' Michael says. 'I'm certain of two things: whoever killed Brendan framed Lola. That's the first thing. The other is that it must be someone that nobody has so far suspected. Not us. Definitely not the police.'

'Right.' I nod. 'So, what do we do?'

Michael shifts towards me, closing the space between us. For a second his face is dangerously close to mine. I feel the pull of his eyes, his mouth…

'I don't know,' he whispers. 'I don't know what to do.'

For a second, I imagine kissing him.

No. The small voice sounds in my head. I turn away, fumbling for the car door handle again. 'We… we'll work it out,' I stammer, then I say more firmly, as I open the door and look over my shoulder at him, 'Let's talk again, soon.'

'Okay.' Michael clears his throat. I can't read his expression. 'I've got another interview with the guy for my hacking story tomorrow morning, but I'll call you in the afternoon. We can get together then.' He hesitates. 'Maybe I can stay for dinner? You, me and the kids?'

'Sure.' I get out of the car. 'See you tomorrow.'

I don't watch as he drives away. Feeling confused, I make my way up the path to my front door, only turning to look along the street when my key is in the lock.

Michael's car has already disappeared from view.

Was he coming on to me? Or did I misread him? Maybe he's just wound up tight because of Lola. That's what we both need to focus on anyway. Protecting her. Finding Brendan's actual killer.

The following morning Lola announces she's going out – this time to see her friend Anya.

I make a face at her. 'Are you telling me Anya needs help with her A levels too, just like Maisie did last week? You know you're going to have to get back to school sometime, don't you?'

'Of course I do.' Lola sounds injured. 'That's why I'm going to Anya's, to go through some things for History that I need to catch up on. I'm going to go back to school on Monday.'

I smile, trust Lola to wrong foot me yet again.

'That's great, sweetheart.' I hesitate. 'I realise you might not want to discuss it with me, but might you talk to Anya or Maisie about what happened with Brendan? Maybe it would help.'

'I can't, Mum.' Lola shakes her head, her lips wobbling slightly. 'None of my friends know about Brendan. I didn't tell any of them when we got together, and… and they don't know anything now.'

'Oh.' I'm genuinely surprised. 'I'd have thought you—'

'It's too painful to talk about,' Lola says, an edge now to her sadness.

I stare at her, feeling bewildered. 'Okay,' I say.

Lola sighs. 'I'll see you later Mum.' And before I can say anything else, she leaves.

In the kitchen I pour a second cup of coffee, feeling troubled. I badly want Lola to be over her grief. After all, she was only with Brendan for a few weeks. Why does she feel so strongly about losing him? I guess, despite all the manipulations and betrayals, he found his way under her skin, like he did with me.

I sip my coffee. I should check my emails, but work is the last thing I want to do. Our end of month salaries have just been paid, so I go to my latest bank statement, work out the largest amount I can afford – it isn't much – and transfer it to Seb's account. It might take me the next twenty years, but I'm going to fulfil my pledge to pay him back. Having made the payment, I text him to let him know.

Seb doesn't reply.

Michael messages me at lunchtime to say he's still deep in his hacking interview and will be over at about three p.m.

> We can talk about how to help Lola then.
> Keep the faith xx

I smile to myself. At least I'm not alone. Michael cares about protecting Lola as much as I do, even if neither of us have much clue as to what we can do. I turn to work at last, going through all my emails, then checking a couple of promotional schedules for dates and action points. The press release Hamish wrote for Shine Security that I approved earlier in the week pops up on my screen. The Shine logo reminds me of the security cam outside Brendan's place, which sends worry for Lola spiralling inside me again.

I wander into the living room, trying to get out of my own head and switch on the TV. *Singing in the Rain* is on TCM. Exactly what I need.

The doorbell rings just as Gene Kelly has splashed his way through the iconic title song. It's just gone two p.m., far too early for the kids to be back. Or Michael. I pause the TV. Who on earth is it? Someone selling cleaning products on the street? Oh, God, surely not a reporter? No. Michael would have told me if the papers had found out about the police interest in Lola.

I go out to the hall and peer through the peephole. It's Seb, standing on the doorstep and smoothing back his hair as he checks his reflection in the chrome knocker. My heart sinks. Apart from when I transferred the money and texted him this morning, I haven't given him – or our relationship – a single thought for the past forty-eight hours.

What does he want? Another angsty conversation about my failings as a partner?

For a moment I think about pretending to be out. Then my phone rings, loudly, in my hand. *Seb calling.* Which, clearly, Seb himself will be able to hear, since he's barely two feet away.

Reluctantly, I open the front door.

'Hi.' Seb makes brief eye contact as he steps inside. He doesn't kiss me. Instead, his eyes dart around the hallway. 'I didn't want to use my keys, trying to be respectful.' A quick, eager glance. 'They said at HOPP you were here. I was going to call, but I wanted to talk properly, in person. Are you alone?'

I nod.

'Er, thanks for the money this morning. I appreciate it,' he says gruffly. He shoves his hands deep in his pocket.

'It's just a start,' I say. 'And I want to say I'm sorry again. It doesn't matter how desperate I felt, it was totally wrong to do what I did. Everything you said about that was right.'

'Right,' he says. 'Thank you.'

We stand in awkward silence.

'It wasn't really the money,' Seb stammers. 'At least, not entirely.'

I raise my eyebrows. 'Oh?' As I speak, I realise that I don't really care what Seb says next; it's irrelevant. The next thought hits me like a sledgehammer: Seb, himself, is irrelevant.

He shuffles his feet from side to side, a deeply troubled expression on his face.

I wait, uncertain what to say. I should never have got together with him a year and a half ago. It was stupid of me. Well, not so much stupid as self-deluding. I thought maybe we had a future, but, standing here now, I realise the truth with a jolt: being with Seb was only ever a reaction to the hurt of my break-up with Michael. I was only interested in Seb in so far as he *wasn't* Michael.

I don't miss you, Seb. The unspoken words run through my head. *I don't love you. I'm sorry, but I don't.*

'Where are you staying?' I ask to break the silence. 'Have you found a new place?'

'My problem was you keeping things from me, not trusting me.' Seb gazes sorrowfully at me, ignoring my question. 'But… but I don't like us being apart,' he goes on, his voice husky. 'If you promise me you'll never lie again, or keep a big secret from me, then… then I'd be prepared to give you a second chance, to try again.' He offers me a nervous smile. 'What do you think?'

No.

I stand, gazing at his handsome face for a few seconds. I should feel guilty, that in rejecting him, I'll be hurting him a second time in as many weeks. But I don't. Not really. Right now, Seb isn't even my third or fourth priority. Even so, I take a deep breath. I owe it to him to find the right words. To be kind.

'I appreciate the offer, Seb, it's generous of you. And you should know that I – I don't regret us being together…'

He makes a face. 'I feel there's a "but" coming.'

I take a deep breath. 'I don't think trying again is going to work.'

'But I've only moved in with friends. I can easily come back. Maybe we can still have, you know… that future together we talked about?'

I frown. Did he not hear me?

'It's over,' I say flatly.

Seb blinks. 'You're breaking up with me?'

'Yes.'

A look of shocked humiliation fills his eyes. 'Right,' he says, sounding dazed. 'I see.'

He digs his hand in his pocket and pulls out his front door key. 'Here.' He hands it over. 'I guess we can talk about my share of bills and stuff like that another time?'

'No need,' I say quickly. 'I'll do the sums and reimburse you if necessary.' I pocket the key. 'Do you have your car with you? For your things?'

'I do, but… but I can come back another time for my stuff?' he suggests hopefully.

I meet his gaze. I need to be firm. It's better for both of us.

'I think you should take everything now,' I say.

Seb gives a swift, embarrassed nod, then disappears up the stairs. Twenty minutes later, accompanied by two bulging suitcases, three bin bags and his vintage Darth Vader model, Seb leaves the house for the last time.

TWENTY-FIVE

Michael slumps into a chair at the kitchen table.

'It doesn't help that I'm knackered,' he complains. 'That hacking guy talked really fast and I didn't understand half of what he said.'

'Right.' I sigh, putting my head in my hands. It's almost four p.m. and the light is fading from the day outside. Lola and Josh aren't home yet and Michael and I have spent the past hour going over and over what we might do to help our daughter.

We've come up with precisely nothing.

I haven't told Michael that Seb and I have just broken up for good. Michael might take it as a sign that I'm open to getting back together with him. And that isn't an option.

At least, I don't think it is, though it's hard to be sure when Michael is sitting right next to me like this, his presence filling the room. He opens his eyes and finds me looking at him. That sexy smile of his curls across his lips.

'Hey, Ali…' he starts. 'I'd like – that is, I wonder if—'

Before he can finish his sentence, the door slams. A moment later, Josh hurtles into the kitchen.

'Hey, Dad!' he calls, apparently unsurprised to find Michael here. He makes straight for the fridge, as usual, quickly pouring himself his usual post-school bowl of cereal. He and Michael are soon sitting together at the table as Josh proudly shows off the TikTok videos he's made of him and his friends with celebrity faces imposed over their own.

'This is impressive, Josh,' Michael says. 'You know, I was interviewing one of the UK's leading hackers earlier? He's extraordinary.'

'Cool,' Josh says.

I roll my eyes but say nothing. It's nice to feel a slight sense of normality returning. This was always the dynamic: Michael egging on Josh's naughtiness and me playing sensible mum.

Lola returns from Anya's soon after and is equally pleased to see her dad, though more quietly. She greets him with a kiss, then sidles up to me and lays her head on my shoulder. I feel so close to her. Close to all of them.

The four of us eat dinner without mentioning Brendan or the police investigation. Michael leaves soon after and I tell the kids that Seb and I have split up. I feel awkward doing it, unsure how they'll react, but they both take the news in their stride. Josh looks mildly embarrassed that I'm talking about relationships, then shrugs, uninterested, when I asks if he'd like to see Seb at all – this isn't, I realise, something Seb has mentioned himself. Perhaps it's not surprising. Seb's relationship with Josh was only ever superficial.

Lola simply asks, very sweetly, if I'm okay, then drifts off again.

It's funny. And strangely easy. Seb is gone. And we've all just adapted, the waters closing around his absence as if he'd never been there.

–

It's a quiet weekend. Despite all our worst fears, the police stay away. Lola might still be their prime suspect, but they clearly aren't any further forward in gathering evidence against her. Lola herself spends her time catching up on the History and English assignments she has missed, ready to return to school at the start of the week.

Monday morning comes around quickly. Once Josh and Lola have left, I spend an hour cleaning and vacuuming, then decide to go in to work. This is partly to check in with Hamish and partly so that I can sit down with Pepper and let her know, face-to-face, that I'd like to spend the rest of the week based at home again. It's not for Lola this time. It's for me – a way of decompressing while we're not in crisis. That's if I *can* decompress. I'm only too aware that, if the police find another piece of evidence they can use against Lola, we'll be plunged back into hell all over again.

I'm so preoccupied with these thoughts as I leave the house, that I completely forget to bring my normal reusable mug of coffee with me. Shaking my head at my brain fog, I stop for a flat white at the van parked opposite Kentish Town underground station. There's a short queue, delaying me further, and it's almost eleven a.m. when I finally arrive at the office. I plonk my faux leather tote on my desk and hang up my coat. Hamish is busy on a call. He looks up and waves at me. I raise my hand in response, but my eyes are drawn to Pepper's glass-walled, breakout office space. She's in there, at her desk. Has already seen me, in fact. She's gesticulating enthusiastically for me to come through.

'Hi.' I walk in, feeling suddenly self-conscious. Pepper and I parted on good terms after she revealed how Brendan blackmailed her, but I know her too well to think that there won't be any fallout. My guess is that she'll feel awkward about having exposed such deep, dark secrets.

'How is everything?' Pepper asks. Then, without waiting for a reply. 'Thank God you're here. I'm having a total 'mare with bloody Busby,' she says with a sigh. 'Do you think you could talk to him, you handle him better than me.'

'Sure,' I say, feeling relieved, if a little unsettled. Perhaps I'm wrong. Pepper is behaving as if yesterday's revelations never happened. 'What's the problem?'

'Hamish will fill you in.' Pepper waves her hand vaguely in the direction of the outer office. 'Basically Busby just needs some ego-stroking, I think.' She sighs. 'I've tried, but it's not working. And I have to see a prospect. I'll be back in half an hour.' She starts putting on her coat.

I sigh inwardly. John Busby is the rather neurotic owner of a small chain of bakeries HOPP took on recently as a new client. It's not exactly a surprise that Pepper is finding him tricky to deal with; whenever I've seen them together he's always seemed a bit overawed by her brisk, confident manner. A minute later and Pepper sweeps out of the office, while Hamish runs me through the Busby Bakes problem. I'm only half focused on what he tells me.

I sit down at my desk, shove my bag to one side and make a few notes for the call I'm about to have with John Busby. At least a successful conversation with him will make it easier to announce that I'm intending to spend next week working from home. As I prepare, Hamish fusses over me, offering me a chocolate truffle from a pack that's been sent to the office. Much to my relief, he doesn't mention Lola or the investigation into Brendan's death. After a few minutes, he settles down to work on a draft presentation for renewal of one of our biggest accounts – a branding agency – and I make the call.

It takes almost thirty minutes, but at last Busby calms down. As I set down the phone, Pepper whirls back into the office after her meeting with the potential client.

'I did it!' she cries, waving her arms excitedly. 'They're taking us on!'

I smile at her. Pepper triumphant, a new contract under her belt, is Pepper at her flamboyant best.

'That's great,' I say. Across the room Hamish nods. 'And John Busby's all sorted, too,' I add.

'Brilliant! You're a star, Alison. You *both* are.' She glances at Hamish, then sits on my desk and entertains us with the whole story of her victory, complete with theatrical gestures. She's brought a load of flyers from the new client with her. 'Research to show us what *not* to do!' she says with a throaty chuckle, tipping them onto my desk.

I point out that we should set up an admin file before these get lost in the general clutter.

'You're so *organised*, Alison,' Pepper trills. 'Where would HOPP be without you?'

'Behind on its filing,' I say with a grin, getting up from my desk.

As I cross the room to fetch a fresh box file from the stack next to the photocopier, Pepper announces cheerfully that she's going to order in pizza for lunch, her regular way of celebrating when she lands a new client. 'We deserve the treat,' she enthuses with an expansive flourish, banging her hand down on my desk and scattering the flyers. 'You call Romana's, Hamish.' She makes a face. 'Shoot! They're cash only and I don't have any.'

'I'll pay,' I say. 'I'll sort it through petty cash later.'

'Thanks, Ali.' Pepper leans towards my tote bag, still resting on my desk. She's about to rummage for my purse. It's a typically impulsive move. And not a little presumptuous.

'Wait!' I take a step forward, feeling irritated. It's not a massive deal, but I don't really want Pepper getting a glimpse of the mess of dirty tissues, tampons and scribbled shopping lists inside. 'I'll do it.'

Pepper freezes, an exaggerated, theatrical stillness. 'Come on, Ali! Dontcha trust me?' She turns back to my bag, parts the sides and peers inside.

The smile falls from her face. 'Shit.'

'What?' I ask.

Pepper's mouth opens and shuts, but she doesn't speak. Instead, she points at my bag.

'Are you okay, Pepper?' Hamish looks up.

'What is it?' I hurry to my desk and snatch the tote out of her hands. Heart thudding, I peer inside. There, nestled between my red purse and a tube of hand sanitiser, is a kitchen knife, its sharp blade glinting under the overhead lights.

With a gasp, I reach inside and grasp the knife's handle. The stainless steel is cold in my hands. I draw out the knife and turn it over. A thin 'Z' shape design zigzags along the handle. It's not from our kitchen at home.

And yet I've seen it before.

I feel numb, like I'm watching something happening to someone else.

Hamish gasps. 'Why are you carrying *that* around?' he asks, faintly.

'Good question.' Pepper looks at me, eyebrows raised. 'Alison?'

'I don't know how this got in here. It's not my knife. It's…' I trail off, my voice sounds hollow and flat in my ears.

The others don't answer. They just stare at me. The blood is pounding in my ears. I've never held this knife before, but I know exactly where I saw it last: in the knife block on the countertop in Brendan's kitchen.

This is the knife that killed him. It has to be.

I uncurl my fingers. The blade gleams in my hot palm. Sharp. Lethal.

'Alison?' Pepper stares at me, wide-eyed with shock. 'What the hell?'

Feeling numb with shock, I stare down at the slim blade in my open palm. It glints under the electric lights.

Pepper draws her blouse over her hand, then picks up the knife between her fingers. I notice, dully, that she is deliberately avoiding leaving her fingerprints on it.

She follows my gaze to the thin 'Z' design, carved into the handle. 'You know what this is, don't you?' she asks in a low voice.

'What are you talking about?' Hamish asks.

'It's Brendan Zeno's murder weapon,' I say, my throat is dry and scratched.

Hamish blinks rapidly, then backs away.

I look up at him, then at Pepper. 'I had no idea this was here.'

'Of course you didn't.' Pepper sets the knife down on the desk behind her. She meets my gaze. 'Do you have any idea how it got into your bag?'

I shake my head. *Try to focus, Alison.* 'It wasn't there when I left the house,' I say.

Pepper nods. Her surface movements are calm and deliberate, but I can see the shock in her eyes.

232

'What should we do?' I'm not really speaking to the others. It's more a question to myself.

Across the room, Hamish clears his throat. He's gazing fearfully at me, as if I'm some sort of wild animal that might pounce at any moment.

'Obviously,' he says, 'we need to call the police.'

'No,' I say.

Hamish stares at me, eyes widening.

'*What?*' Hamish splutters. 'Why on earth not?'

I take a deep breath. 'I just need a moment.'

'But—' Hamish starts.

'Quiet.' Pepper holds up her hand to stop him talking. 'Go on, Alison.'

I force my thoughts to knit together. 'Someone must have put the knife in my bag.' I pick the tote up carefully and peer inside. Nothing else has been added. Nothing is missing. 'I carry it on my shoulder, it would be easy enough to slip a knife in from behind.'

'You think someone did that on the way to work this morning?' Pepper asks.

I nod. It's the only explanation. But who would do that? And why?

Pepper sighs. 'I'm afraid Hamish is right. We really don't have any choice but to call the police.'

'Okay.' I nod again. 'It's just…' I chew on my lip.

'You're worried it will make you look guilty?' Pepper's voice is surprisingly gentle.

'I'm worried it will put the police focus right back on Lola,' I say.

Pepper frowns. 'How about I drive you to the station?' she asks. 'It will look less like you're covering anything up if you voluntarily take the knife to them.'

It's the last thing I want to do, but she's right.

'Whatever you do, please can you get that knife out of here.' Hamish shudders.

'Come on.' Pepper nudges the blade into a jiffy bag, again avoiding planting her own fingerprints on the handle.

Five minutes later the two of us are in the car. I call Michael on the way to the station. He offers to meet me there, but there's no point. I ask him to call Meena instead. It's a lawyer I'm going to need.

'What you could do is let the kids know where I am. And help them sort dinner later if I'm still at the station,' I say.

'My God, Ali,' Michael says with feeling. 'Who do you think planted the knife on you?'

'Isn't it obvious?' My voice drops to a whisper. 'It's Brendan's killer. Who else would have his murder weapon?'

TWENTY-SIX

'Let's go over your movements one more time, Mrs White,' DI Barnbury says.

I glance at Meena Gupta. The lawyer nods. I shuffle, feeling awkward, in my chair. We're in the same room as on my previous visit, a large table complete with glasses of water and recording device, bare walls all around. It's almost five p.m. I've been here for hours, mostly waiting to be interviewed while the police, presumably, do a rush job on a forensic examination of the knife. Meena said they'd be examining the blade for minute traces of blood, as well as checking the knife against the pattern of Brendan's fatal wound.

Just over an hour ago, DI Barnbury appeared and said, very solemnly, that though they don't yet have forensic confirmation, they are convinced the knife is the murder weapon.

He's been asking me the same question in various forms ever since: *How did it get into your tote bag?*

I've lost track of the times I've answered that I don't know.

The detective keeps coming at the question from different angles, as fox-like as the last time we spoke. He's accompanied, again, by DS Strong, who sits silently, watching me the entire time. She never speaks, just stares at me. It's deeply unnerving.

'Talk me through everything you did, from the last time you looked into your bag before the discovery of the knife,' DI Barnbury says briskly.

'As I told you before,' I say wearily, 'my bag was in the kitchen at home overnight. The last time I remember looking into it was when I put my keys back after locking the front door and leaving the house for work. I had some heavy files in there, but I had to move those to put the keys in the inside pocket. I'd have definitely noticed if an eight-inch knife was inside.'

'Right.' DI Barnbury gazes sceptically at me. 'And you say you walked all the way to work?'

I nod.

'Was it normal for you not to check your bag on the way?' he asks. 'You didn't use your purse to buy anything on the way?'

'As I've already explained, I'd forgotten my normal travel mug of coffee so I stopped to buy a drink from the Coffee Carnival van near the office. I had to rummage for my purse, take out my card to pay and there was definitely no knife then eith—' I suck in my breath, a fresh realisation chilling me to the bone. 'It must have been *then*,' I gasp. 'I put my bag down between my feet when I tapped the card against the reader. Then I dropped my purse back in without looking inside the bag. *That* must have been when someone came up behind me and slipped in the knife.' I stare at him, willing him to believe me. 'I bet if you take a look at the CCTV on the High Street you'll be able to see someone coming up behind me.'

DI Barnbury still looks unconvinced. 'What happened after that?'

'I carried on walking to the office.'

'What about when you arrived. There's a main front door and the office door? Didn't you need to get keys out of your bag for those?'

I sigh. 'Someone was coming out the main door as I went in, so I walked straight through,' I explain. 'And the HOPP office door was unlocked, because Hamish and Pepper were already inside.'

'That's your boss, Pepper Curran and your assistant Hamish Gartshore.' DI Barnbury looks up. His expression changes and I sense he's about to ask something new. I tense up. 'Were Ms Curran or Mr Gartshore alone with your bag at any point?'

My head jerks up. 'You think one of *them* put the knife there?'

Jesus. Hamish doesn't have a motive. But could Pepper be guilty of Brendan's murder after all?

'I'm not thinking anything,' the detective replies smoothly. 'Just trying to get a clear picture of events.'

I frown, remembering the appalled look on Pepper's face when she saw the sharp, steel blade in my bag. Then the terror of Hamish's expression.

There's no way either of them could have faked such horrified reactions.

'Please, Mrs White?' DI Barnbury asks, a hint of impatience creeping into his voice. 'Could Pepper Curran or Hamish Gartshore have put the knife in your bag?'

'I don't see how,' I say. 'The bag wasn't out of my sight for more than a few moments the whole time I was in the office.'

'Mm.' DI Barnbury taps his fingers against each other, leaning back in his chair. 'You didn't leave your bag at all, perhaps to go to the toilet?'

'No, but even if I did, why would either of them put the knife in my bag? Why would either of them even *have* the knife? It doesn't make sense.'

'No, it doesn't.' DI Barnbury meets my gaze. 'But it also doesn't make sense that someone would have put the knife in your bag on the street. They would have had to follow you, waiting for the right opportunity. And once the knife was in your bag, they couldn't control when you found it or what you might do with it. For all they knew, you'd discover it straight away and slip it into the nearest bin.'

'What are you suggesting?' There's a tremor in my voice.

'That it would make far more sense if *you* put the knife in your bag, that you knew it was there all along.'

I wriggle uncomfortably in my chair. 'Why on earth would I do that?'

DS Strong and DI Barnbury exchange meaningful looks.

'Let's go over what happened when the knife was discovered one more time,' DI Barnbury says flatly.

I draw a deep breath and go through the details once again.

'Very well.' The detective's voice is heavy with meaning as I finish. 'The picture is starting to clarify, I think.'

'Is it?' My stomach knots with anger. 'Because the picture I'm looking at shows the police wasting their time asking me the same questions over and over again, while whoever put the knife in my bag is still out there*, getting away with Brendan's murder.*'

Silence descends on the room.

Meena puts a hand on my arm, a clear plea for me to stay calm, then turns to the detective. 'I think Alison has answered all your questions, DI Barnbury. She'd like to go now, get home to her family.'

DI Barnbury stares at her, his expression unreadable. I pick at the skin around my thumb. My mind drifts to the kids. What will Michael have said to them about where I am? The truth? Or some fudge of a white lie? Whatever, Josh will still need his dinner. My mind darts to the leftover lasagne in the fridge. Hopefully somebody will have spotted that.

'Just another few minutes,' DI Barnbury says lightly, 'then Mrs White can go.'

Meena shakes her head but sits back in her chair.

'Getting back to the discovery of the knife,' DI Barnbury intones. 'If someone else really slipped it into your bag, how do you explain that yours are the only fingerprints on the handle?'

'Obviously the person who planted it used gloves,' I say. 'My fingerprints are only on that knife because I took it out of the bag. Pepper and Hamish both saw me do that.'

'Indeed, they have both confirmed that,' the detective acquiesces. 'We've taken statements.' He pauses. 'However, Mr Gartshore also says that you were quite insistent beforehand that no one should look in your bag.'

'Only because that's… it's *private*. Anyone would say the same thing.' My voice rises.

'You also told him that you didn't want him to call the police,' he continues coldly.

'I just… I just needed a moment to think.'

'Think about what?' DI Barnbury leans forward. 'How to explain away a murder weapon?'

I glare at him. 'If you're so bloody convinced I killed Brendan then why don't you arrest me?' I demand, the words exploding out of me. 'At least come straight out and accuse me.'

'Alison.' Meena's voice is low, another plea for me to calm down.

I ignore her, turning to the detective as hot, angry tears prick at my eyes. 'I didn't kill Brendan. And I didn't put the knife in my bag.' My voice rises again. 'I don't know how it got there but it wasn't *me*.'

DI Barnbury's gaze is cool, unflappable, infuriating.

'It doesn't even make sense that I would kill Brendan,' I protest.

'Doesn't it?' DI Barnbury leans forward, intent on my face. 'As far as you were aware, he'd taken the money you'd given him and was backtracking on the deal to leave Lola. Perhaps you thought killing him was the only way to get Lola away from him?'

'No.'

'Or perhaps it wasn't planned, perhaps you were just furious that you'd been double-crossed, so you went over to demand your money back? Then you got there and saw Lola going inside, and something snapped inside you? You could have destroyed the video camera, then gone inside and—'

'And killed him? And let my daughter take the blame?' I snap. 'No way. No *way* would I do that.'

There's a long pause, then DI Barnbury lets out a soft sigh. 'No,' he says. 'I don't think you did that.'

I sit back, feeling confused.

'So why are we here then?' Meena asks testily.

Another long pause. DS Strong whispers something in DI Barnbury's ear. He nods, then turns back to me. I'm surprised to see that there in his eyes, mingling with the suspicion and the frustration, is a soft gleam of pity.

My guts twist into a knot.

'For the record,' Meena says, 'my client has come here in good faith and I'm not happy with the manipulative way you're conducting this inter—'

'Let's move on,' DI Barnbury cuts in. 'And let's all agree that Alison is at heart a good person and a loving parent.'

I stare blankly at him.

'And having agreed all that…' the detective fixes his gentle gaze on my face, 'let's also agree that you were in possession of this knife in order to dispose of it.'

'What?' I stare at him. '*No.*'

I glance at Meena. She frowns. We both look back at the detective.

He clears his throat. 'I think that Lola gave the knife to you, Alison,' he goes on. 'I think that at some point over the past week, she confessed to you that she murdered Brendan Zeno. And I think that you offered to get rid of the knife for her. *That's* why it was in your bag.'

I stare at him. 'That's ridiculous,' I say.

'Yes,' Meena adds. 'If Alison had taken the knife to get rid of it, why not do just that? Why carry it into her office?'

A slow smile creeps around DI Barnbury's face. 'In order to frame someone else. Part of your plan to protect Lola.'

My heart thuds against my ribs.

'Pure supposition,' Meena snarls.

'It fits,' the detective insists. 'Lola couldn't bear the burden of what she'd done. She admitted she was the killer and that she still had the knife.'

'No.' I shake my head.

'I'm also certain that she told you she was behind the @AvengingAngel post, claiming Brendan raped her and making threats that he should "pay".'

'That *wasn't* Lola!' The words burst out of me.

'Quite,' adds Meena, sharply.

'I'm afraid it seems more and more likely that it *was*,' the detective counters. 'We've now managed to locate the internet cafe where the post was made, but whoever used it paid cash, then logged on with a random email address. There's no CCTV either inside or outside the cafe.' He pauses, leaning forwards and fixing me with an intense stare. 'It's clear to us that @AvengingAngel covered her tracks with an extraordinary amount of care. Why would anyone go to all that bother just to malign someone? It seems clear that whatever else @AvengingAngel's motive was, hiding her identity so that she couldn't be linked to the murder was key.'

'But I *know* @AvengingAngel wasn't Lola,' I splutter. 'For one thing, she thought Brendan was taking her away with him when that post was made.'

'That's what she says now,' DI Barnbury says, 'but our forensic psychologist thinks the post was a sort of confession in advance, a coded cry for help. Take the username, for instance. It's linked to the nickname Brendan had for her: Angelface. Did you know that?'

My stomach falls away. Did Brendan really use that term for Lola?

'The social media post also fits with the private writing about Brendan that we found on her phone. Did you see any of that?'

'No, but I heard there were some poems, right?' I ask, remembering Stacy telling me about them. 'Extreme' was the word she had used; Michael had dismissed them as 'teenage nonsense'.

'I'm not sure I'd use the word "poetry",' DI Barnbury says with a grimace. 'These were violent fantasies about what Lola would do if her relationship with Brendan was threatened.' He pauses. 'It all adds up: our investigations suggest that Lola premeditated the murder then carried it out and has been lying about it ever since. But – and this fits with the psychologist's profile too – the weight of her crime grew too great this week and Lola unburdened herself to you a few days ago. Together, you worked out a plan to divert suspicion on someone else. You decide to plant the knife she used to kill Brendan on Ms Curran, but she found it before—'

'No.' I sit up, my heart thudding. This has gone too far. 'Your so-called psychologist has got it all wrong. For one thing, Lola is categorically *not* @AvengingAngel.'

'No?' The detective frowns. 'How can you be so sure?'

I take a deep breath. It's time to come clean.

'Because Pepper Curran wrote that post. She didn't realise I'd made a deal with Brendan to pay him off and thought that broadcasting Brendan was an abusive rapist might bring other women forward, which in turn would convince Lola to leave him.'

DI Barnbury purses his lips. With a jolt I realise he doesn't believe me.

Beside me, Meena bristles. Without turning to look at her face I can tell she is furious to have lost control of the interview like this. It strikes me – far too late – that I should have told Lola's lawyers about the posts from the start.

DI Barnbury shakes his head. 'Give it up, Alison. Stop trying to incriminate Ms Curran.'

'I'm not,' I plead, close to tears now. 'Pepper was trying to help me; to help Lola.' My voice cracks.

DI Barnbury studies my face carefully. 'I don't understand. Are you saying Ms Curran made up the claim that Brendan Zeno was a rapist? Or that he raped her?'

'Neither.' My cheeks are burning and I can't bring myself to meet his eyes. I take a deep breath. 'I'm saying that he raped me a long time ago and Pepper was the only person who knew.'

The atmosphere in the room changes. I can feel everyone's eyes boring through me. I keep my own gaze fixed on the chipped edge of the table immediately beneath me. 'Pepper suggested we put the truth out there anonymously, so I didn't have to go through the exposure of saying publicly what happened to me,' I explain. 'She thought other women might see the post and come forward with their own experiences – which they have – and that Lola would see those responses and realise, once and for all, what a cruel, lying, abusive bastard her boyfriend was.'

I look up at last.

DI Barnbury is staring at me. The sceptical look in his eye has vanished. 'I'm sorry you went through all that, Alison. But I have to ask. Did you explain what you were doing to Lola?'

'No.'

'Had you… did you tell her Brendan raped you years ago?'

'Yes, but she didn't believe me.' A sob wells inside me. I swallow hard.

Meena shuffles in her chair. 'I think that's enough for now.' She sounds flustered. 'I'd like to talk to my client in private.'

'Very well.' DI Barnbury tilts his head to one side. 'I can see this is a very emotional subject for you, Alison, but you need to understand that it doesn't really change things for Lola. We have plenty of evidence against her without needing her to be @AvengingAngel.' He pauses. 'In fact, if what you've just told me is true and,' he adds hurriedly, 'and I do believe you, it gives Lola even more reason to hate Brendan and you even more of a motive for helping your daughter get away with his murder. That's if, you didn't help her commit—'

'I'm calling a halt on proceedings.' Meena jumps to her feet, tapping me sharply on the arm.

I stand up, feeling dazed. 'I wouldn't murder anyone,' I say. 'Neither would Lola. And I wouldn't frame my best friend either.'

'Wouldn't you?' DI Barnbury gives me a rueful smile. 'Because from everything I know about you, Alison, I'd say you'd do pretty much anything it took to protect your daughter.'

TWENTY-SEVEN

The next fifteen minutes or so are a blur as Meena signs me out of the police station and bustles me into her car. As we drive home through dark, wet London streets she hisses a series of angry questions at me.

Why didn't I come clean about @AvengingAngel before? Why didn't I tell her about Brendan raping me? Who else knows? What exactly did I tell Lola – and when?

She makes some effort to frame her questions with sympathetic words and phrases, but the sympathy doesn't extend to her tone of voice. I answer as best I can, feeling numb.

At last Meena stops.

'Okay,' she says with a sigh. 'The police are clearly still fishing for evidence against Lola. With or without your testimony over @AvengingAngel, and whatever the detective inspector says, they don't have anything concrete against Lola. They don't even know for sure if the knife in your bag is definitely the knife used to kill Brendan yet.'

'What d'you think they'll do next?'

'They'll check out the CCTV near that coffee van you mentioned. Maybe that will show someone placing the knife in your bag, like you thought. And they'll wait for the forensic report on the knife – that might throw up some fresh clues for them to follow.' She hesitates. 'If they still think it's Lola after all that, they'll probably call you in again, try a second time to get you to admit Lola's confessed to you.'

'But she hasn't,' I protest, 'for the simple reason that she doesn't have anything to confess!'

'I know.' Meena sighs. 'Look, I understand talking about… your experience, what happened in the past with Brendan is painful, but please don't keep anything else from me. All right?'

I nod, then turn my head to stare through the window as the rain pours down, gleaming on the dark, dirty pavements that we pass.

–

Meena drops me at home just after six p.m., with the none too reassuring advice that I should call her immediately if the police make contact again. I barely notice the raindrops as I walk up the front path to the door. Not only is Lola still under suspicion, but the reality of what happened today is sinking in – and creeping me out. If the police are so convinced Lola committed Brendan's murder, they can't be putting much effort any more into finding the actual killer. Three thoughts circle my head, each more terrifying than the last. One: somebody followed me to work earlier without me noticing, with the express intention of sliding a murder weapon into my tote bag. Two: that person almost certainly murdered Brendan. And three: if they did all that, what else are they capable of?

I let myself into the house. Lola and Michael are waiting in the kitchen. Lola hurries over and gives me a hug.

'Are you okay, Mum?' she asks, her sweet face wreathed in concern.

'I'm fine,' I say, forcing a smile onto my face.

Michael fetches me a glass of water and mutters something about the leftover lasagne being in the oven. There's no sign of Josh, but Michael tells me he's been up in his room since getting back from school.

'He's in a great mood. He's been out with that Nadia girl,' Michael explains. 'It's all back on, apparently. Which is good, isn't it?'

'I suppose so.' How come Michael is now clearly Josh's preferred confidant, as well as Lola's? Resentment wriggles inside me.

'Anyway, he doesn't know where you've been all afternoon,' Michael says, quietly. 'I figured you'd put him in the picture if you wanted.'

I nod. 'Thanks,' I say. 'Better he doesn't know unless he has to.'

It's not just that I'd rather protect Josh from having to worry about me, but also that standing here in the soft light of the kitchen, feeling properly warm for the first time in hours, I am suddenly and overwhelmingly exhausted. I can see Michael and Lola are hoping for a full breakdown of my police interview. But all I want is food and sleep.

Lola's phone rings and with a quick 'Sorry, Mum, won't be long,' she drifts away to take the call. I sink into a chair at the table, peeling off my coat, while Michael offers to make me a cup of tea. It strikes me as weird that he is making himself so at home in my kitchen. But only slightly. After all, we did use to live together. And, anyway, I'm too tired to care.

'Are you okay, Ali?' Michael asks, filling the kettle.

'I'm fine.' I try to put a bit of reassuring steel in my voice, but I just sound shattered.

'I think everything that's happened today is actually good news.' He sets the kettle on its stand and flicks it on. A low rumble rises and falls away.

I stare at him. He looks freshly shaved and is dressed in a suit and open-neck shirt, everything sharply cut and well-pressed. There's an irksome cheeriness to his manner.

'How is a murder weapon in my handbag good news?' The question spills like acid out of my mouth. Michael blinks, clearly taken aback. I glare at him. 'Sorry, but you're not the one who just spent the afternoon in a police interview room.'

'I know, Ali,' Michael says. 'Sorry. All I meant was it was a good sign that they've let you go. It means the police must realise that the knife was planted on you.'

'No,' I say. 'They think Lola gave it to me to plant on someone else.'

'What?' Lola is in the doorway, off her phone. Her eyes are wide with shock.

'Oh, sweetheart, I didn't know you were there.' I glance, frowning, at Michael.

'At least the police have kept both your names out of anything they say to the media,' he says quickly. 'Which means they really can't be that certain.'

This isn't true and Michael knows it. The police have all sorts of reasons for not making our names public at this point. Still, at least Michael's trying to reassure Lola. My irritation at him lifts a fraction.

Lola nods, gazing up at him. 'Do you really think so?'

'Of course,' Michael insists. 'And as a bonus it means the press still don't know that you're a suspect.'

For now, I think. I close my eyes, trying to ease the pressure that is building around my right temple. Michael finishes making the tea, sets a mug in front of me, then slips away.

Lola and I are left alone. We sit in silence for a while, then Lola nestles closer to me, resting her head on my shoulder.

'I'm so sorry about all this, Mum,' she says softly. 'I wish I'd never met Brendan.'

I take a sip of my tea, then put the mug down and draw her to me. 'It will pass,' I say. 'I'm fairly certain the knife was put into my bag on the street and once the police have examined the relevant CCTV they should be able to work out who put it there.'

'Identify them, you mean?' Lola shivers.

I nod. 'Even if they can't see exactly who it is, it will give them something to go on.' I squeeze her tight, smoothing a stray strand of hair off her face. 'Most importantly it will prove that it wasn't *you*.'

'It *wasn't* Mum,' Lola says, her voice suddenly erupting with emotion. 'I'd never do anything like that to you.'

'Of course you wouldn't, sweetheart.' I kiss her cheek. 'None of this is your fault. You do know that?'

Lola meets my gaze. Her eyes are troubled. 'But if I hadn't met Bren—'

'No.' I press my finger against her lips. 'Remember, it was me and your dad who met him first. If *we* didn't have that connection, you might have been more wary of him when he came up to you in Camden Market.'

Lola says nothing. There's still a terrible unhappiness in her eyes.

'There's something else,' I say, biting my lip. 'The police seemed convinced you wrote the @AvengingAngel posts, so I thought it was best to come clean about that.'

Lola frowns. 'What do you mean?'

I explain what Pepper did – and the when and the why of it. As I speak, I'm bracing myself for Lola to shout at me for interfering or making things worse. Instead she just stares, sadly, at me.

'Did Brendan really… you know, rape you, Mum?'

I nod, a lump forming in my throat. 'He did. It happened when I was the age you are now. I only ever told Pepper about it.'

'Not Dad?'

I shake my head. 'I know you've grown up in a world where you see women standing up for themselves and being brave and making accusations, but it wasn't like that when… I'm not saying I couldn't have said something all those years ago, or that I shouldn't have, just that it was… that it felt impossible…' I trail off.

Lola's face crumples. 'I just can't believe I fell for him. I feel so stupid.'

'No,' I say. 'No, don't think that.' We sit in silence for a while holding each other. Lola feels fragile in my arms. Ground down and exhausted and frightened and unhappy.

I hate Brendan for doing that to her. And I hate whoever killed him and set her up to take the fall, for making it worse.

–

Two days have passed since the discovery of the knife in my bag. Much to my surprise, Lola has rallied after the initial shock. She has – as she said she would – carried on going into school. I'm the one who isn't coping; I can't settle at anything or concentrate for more than a few minutes at a stretch. Pepper has called a couple of times, but I've ignored the messages she's left.

Random thoughts constantly scratch at my brain. Has the forensic report on the knife come through? What will it show? If there's no trace of Brendan's blood on it, surely that means there's no way of proving it was used for his murder? Which makes it turning up in my bag more a cruel joke than a serious attempt to incriminate me and Lola, doesn't it? And what about the CCTV on my journey to work? Have the police managed to find the right bit of film that will show who planted the knife?

If only I had answers, all this fear and stress would start to ease. I take a shower, lifting my face to the hot water and closing my eyes, willing the cascade to wash all the confusion and worry in my head away.

As I'm getting dressed after the shower, my phone rings. It's a withheld number.

'Hello?' I say, warily.

'It's me, Mum,' Lola says, sounding distraught. 'I'm at the police station.'

'What's happened?' Panic fills me.

'The police came to school, dragged me away in front of everyone.'

I gasp.

'Everyone saw.' Her voice trembles. 'I called Meena and she got the officer at the station to let me call you but there's nothing you can do. Nothing anyone can do.'

'What do you mean?' My throat is tight. 'What did the police say? Why did they take you in again?'

There's a long pause. 'To do what they've been wanting to do for the past two weeks,' she says bitterly. 'Oh, Mum, they've charged me with murder.'

TWENTY-EIGHT

I sink onto the bed as Lola sobs on the other end of the phone.

My head spins. 'Ch—charged you with murder?' I gasp. 'No, they can't.'

'That horrible detective says I'm going to jail. I–I...' she trails off, her voice fading to a muffled mumble.

'Lola?' I grip the phone more tightly.

'Alison?' Meena, comes on the line. Her voice is crisp. Businesslike. 'I'm with Lola at the station. There wasn't time to call you before. Obviously, it's not good news.'

'I don't understand,' I gasp. 'Didn't the police find the CCTV of the coffee van?'

'They did. And footage of you walking along the street.' Meena pauses. 'The film clearly shows there was no one behind you at any time. Nobody close enough to plant the knife in your bag.'

'What?' My hand flies to my mouth. 'That can't be right.'

Meena sighs. 'The forensics on the knife came back, too. There are microscopic traces of Brendan's blood in the groove between the blade and the handle. No trace of Lola's DNA, thank goodness, but it's definitely the murder weapon.'

'Oh my God.' How can this be happening? 'So... so...?' I can't think clearly enough to formulate a question.

'DI Barnbury is sticking to his belief that *you* put that knife in your bag in order to plant it on Pepper Curran, to make her look guilty of Lola's crime. They've taken that narrative to the CPS who've agreed to take things forward.'

'Oh my God.' I sink onto the bed.

'As Lola just told you, she's been arrested and charged with murder,' Meena goes on. 'I'm working on her bail right now.'

'This can't be happening.' I say the words more to myself than to her. 'I'll come to the station. I'll call her dad.'

'No need,' Meena says briskly. 'Lola's already spoken to her father. And I'm hoping that bail will be set in another couple of hours. Then I'll bring her home.' She pauses. 'You should know that, if the case progresses, there's a good chance they'll go on to charge you as well.'

Oh, God. 'Really?'

'I hope it won't come to that,' Meena says. 'Now, I have to go. Speak later.' She rings off, leaving me numb with shock, my insides shrivelling in fear.

–

The story hits the news the following morning. Lola, who arrived home on bail late last night – at least she didn't have to sleep in the police cell – stays in bed. All the confidence she's displayed over the past few days has vanished.

'They all saw me being arrested at school,' she keeps moaning. 'They all know I've been charged.'

Michael, who spent most of yesterday trying to stop the story coming out in the press, arrives after lunch. He speaks to Lola upstairs, then reappears in the kitchen, where I'm staring numbly at my third cold cup of tea of the day.

'I'm taking Lola out for the afternoon, then I'll collect Josh from his school. They can sleep over at mine.' He hesitates, resting his hand on my shoulder. 'It'll give you a bit of space.'

I nod. 'If the kids are happy with that.'

'No worries.' Michael strokes my hair. It's too intimate a gesture and I know I should pull away, but instead I close my eyes, letting his touch soothe me. For a moment I think of Seb. It's strange that Michael hasn't mentioned him. Or perhaps Pepper has told him we've split up. Whatever, I'm grateful not to have to talk about it.

'Thanks, Michael,' I say. 'I don't know how I'd get through this without you.'

The words hang in the air between us. Then Michael takes a step away, his hand falling to his side. He says gruffly. 'It's the least I can do, Ali. They're my kids, too. And you're still...' He trails off.

I'm what? Still your wife, even though we're divorced?

A beat passes where I both want and don't want him to say it.

'Anyway,' Michael goes on, 'I'll get Lola and go. Check in with you later.'

A few moments later the house is empty. I sit down on the sofa. I close my eyes again, just for a second.

The trill of a text wakes me. Bleary-eyed, I sit straight up, my heart thudding. But it's just a message from Pepper:

How are you coping? What a shitshow.
Hope you're ok. As you're on your own, I'm
taking you for a drink tonight. Dinner too. I
bet you haven't eaten all day. See you at
Monarca. 8 p.m.

I stare, groggily at the text. It's Pepper at her imperious best, issuing an invitation to the private club that she's a member of. How on earth does she know I'm on my own tonight? Michael must have told her. They seem to have been telling each other everything recently.

It feels wrong to go out when Lola has been charged with this terrible crime. But, oh, God, Pepper's face when she peered into my handbag and saw that knife. Did that really only happen three days ago? It feels like three years and I haven't spoken to Pepper since. I owe it to her to let her know what's going on.

I text back my thanks and tell her I'll see her there, then head upstairs to splash some water on my face. I have an hour to get ready and I use the time to tidy up, which makes me feel a little better. I brush my hair and make the bed and fold up the clothes scattered on the chair in the corner. I scan my wardrobe and pick out a clean top. An hour or two with Pepper is exactly what I need. She'll insist that everything will be okay. And that, more than anything, is what I want to hear right now.

–

I arrive early at the club to find that it's fairly empty. To my surprise, Pepper is already here – she normally runs at least ten minutes late for all social engagements. She's sitting in an armchair by the fire, sipping at a whisky. That's strange too, her usual order is fizz or a cocktail. She's staring at the flames as I approach, swirling the amber liquid in her glass, deep in thought.

'Hey,' I say.

She looks up and her expressive face gives away the anxiety in her eyes immediately. It's a jolt. I'd anticipated she'd be smiling, eager to take away my concerns, not full of her own. But of course, she'll be almost as worried for Lola as I am.

'Are you all right?' I ask, taking off my coat and sitting down in the armchair next to hers.

'Fine,' she says, too brightly. 'I've just been so worried about you. Michael texted me. Told me they've charged Lola with murder.'

'Right.' Is it weird that Michael and Pepper are in constant contact at the moment? No, they're probably just trying to save me from having to explain everything twice. Having said that, from the way Pepper's bright eyes are peering at me, I'm guessing she's going to want to know all about the police interview.

She gives me a sympathetic smile. 'What a nightmare. You must need a drink.' Without waiting for my reply, she glances across the room to the bar area. A waitress materialises immediately. Unlike me, Pepper has an unfailing ability to be seen in public places – she never has any problems getting served, commanding any space she enters with a combination of physical presence and the confident assumption that people will pay her attention.

'I'd like a Sauvignon Blanc, please.' I smile at the waitress, as her gaze flickers over to me. 'A large one.'

The waitress nods and trips away.

'So how are you doing?' Pepper asks. 'Michael told me the police think Lola gave you the knife to incriminate me.'

'That's right,' I say, flatly.

Pepper shakes her head wearily. 'It's just *ridiculous*.'

'The whole thing is ridiculous,' I groan. 'Lola's a *baby*.' I glance up, expecting Pepper's expressive face to be emanating concern.

But Pepper isn't looking at me. She's gazing into the fire, chewing on her lower lip. 'It's not good that they've charged her,' she says, absent-mindedly.

I frown. What is she talking about? 'No, *obviously* it's terrible. Lola could end up in prison.' If Pepper can hear the exasperation in my voice, she doesn't react. She just carries on staring into the fire, looking preoccupied.

'It's not good,' she repeats. 'Not good for anyone.'

Anyone? I stare at her. What is she talking about? And then it dawns on me: when she says 'anyone', she really means herself. Is she seriously making what's happening to Lola about *her*?

'You sound upset,' I say, crisply. Then I inject as much sarcasm into my voice as I can. 'Is there some sort of problem at work?'

Pepper looks up at last. Her eyes are ice cold. 'A co-worker brought a murder weapon to my office three days ago and hasn't been seen there since,' she snaps. 'So, on balance I'd say yes, there is some sort of problem at work.'

I swallow hard. *Shit.* I wasn't thinking – with only three of us full-time in the office, any single person's absence inevitably has a big knock-on effect. The waitress returns and Pepper and I sit in tense silence as she places a glass of pale yellow wine in front of me. I watch her leave, then say quietly: 'I'm sorry I've not been in, everything's just

258

been so frantic. Er,' I cast my mind back to the call I made on Monday. 'Is everything okay with John Busby?'

'Fine, fine.' Pepper waves her hand dismissively. 'But I do think we should talk.'

I frown. 'Talk about what? The Busby account?'

'No!' Pepper stares at me. 'Talk about *you*, Alison. You're my best friend and my colleague at work and you're so strung out right now you're basically hanging on by a thread.' She pauses. 'I'm really worried about you.'

'I'm okay,' I say, feeling awkward.

'No, you're not. Neither's Hamish,' Pepper says. 'He totally freaked after you'd gone to talk to the police. We both had to give statements. Which was a nightmare. It felt like everything I said was making you out to be some kind of psycho-bitch from hell. Just *awful*.' She pauses. 'I know it was worse for you, of course, it's just—'

'I know,' I say, now feeling guilty. 'I hadn't really thought about Hamish,' I admit. 'He did look absolutely terrified when I found the knife. Is he okay?'

'Not really.' Pepper sets her glass down on the table between us. It glows in the firelight, a deep honey gold. 'He been in, but he's off his game. Says he's having nightmares, that he's considering taking some time off…' She pauses, shaking her head. 'I can't have *both* of you out of action.'

A sliver of dread trickles down my spine. 'What are you saying?'

Pepper meets my gaze. There's something deeply unnerving about the slow, deliberate way in which she is acting. 'I know this is all very difficult for you,' she mutters, 'but I think we need to make a decision about work.'

'Work?' My throat is dry. I reach for my wine. It's cold to the touch. The Sauvignon inside has a crisp, vaguely lemony, scent. I take a long swig.

'I think that you should take a leave of absence for as long as you need, but definitely until everything with Brendan's murder is properly resolved.'

A creeping feeling of dread pools like cold sick in my belly. 'You're firing me?' I fix my gaze on her eyes. There's a wariness. And pity for me.

'No. Of course I'm not firing you.' Pepper frowns. 'I just, well, you know yourself you haven't really been able to focus on work recently, and—'

'I thought that was okay.' My insides tighten. I take another large gulp of wine. It leaves a sour taste in my mouth. 'I thought *you said* it was okay for me to take time off?'

'I did and it was,' she says quickly. 'It *is*. That's what I'm trying to say – take the time off. Properly. Do what you need to do at home. Come back when it's all over.'

'And what if I don't want to?'

Pepper shakes her head wearily. 'Why wouldn't you want to? I'll put you on sick pay, you won't miss out. Look, please don't make this a big deal. I'm saying take some time. That's all. Look after yourself.'

I clench my fists. Everything she says sounds kind and reasonable, but is that really what's driving her here?

'Do you think I was doing what the police think?' I demand. 'Deliberately trying to cover up for Lola by framing you?'

Pepper blinks, clearly horrified. 'No,' she says. 'Of course not.'

'Do you think Lola killed Brendan?'

Pepper hesitates, then looks away.

'*Oh my God!*' My voice rises, catching in my throat. '*Is* that what you think?'

'For goodness' sake, Alison,' Pepper hisses. 'Please stop shouting.'

I am suddenly aware that the drinkers on the far side of the club room are watching us. I force my voice lower, fury coursing through me.

'How could you think Lola would—?'

'It's not that. Can't you see, Alison? This is *exactly* what I'm talking about.' Pepper's voice takes on a haughty edge. It's the first moment since we met up tonight that she's looked and sounded like herself. 'Listen! Whether or not *I* think Lola could have killed Brendan is irrelevant. The police clearly believe she did. That's what matters.' She pauses, her tone softening. 'I'm being completely honest with you, here. What's happening now is bad for my business. Lola's name is in the press, and it won't be too long before some client or other makes the connection. It's easier if you're just… taking a sabbatical or something. And, like I said, it'll give you some breathing room, too.'

Is she serious? 'What about you and me outside of work?' I demand. 'Do you want to give me some breathing room from that?'

I'm half-ready for Pepper to snap angrily at me. But she just gives me a sad smile.

'Of course not,' she says. 'I'll always be your friend.'

Our eyes meet. I know I'm overreacting, it's not like Pepper is pulling away entirely. I just can't bear the thought of not having work at the moment – it's the one constant, steady element in my life right now. Not to mention a major distraction from everything else.

'Sure,' I say. 'Whatever you need to tell yourself.' I drain my glass and leave.

TWENTY-NINE

The next morning marks a fortnight since Brendan's murder.

It's weird being home alone; weirder still not to have any work to do. I potter around the house, gathering clothes from overflowing laundry baskets, then put on a wash. While the machine is spinning I clear and clean the fridge. I peer into the vegetable crisper. Those limp carrots and the soggy bag of outdated salad will have to go. I carry them all to the food waste caddy. As I tip the food inside, last night's conversation rolls around inside my head.

In the cold silence of the house, I try to see Pepper's decision to keep me temporarily at arm's length from the business from her perspective. Of course, Pepper is worried about HOPP. She's right to be. Concern for her company's standing and concern for me aren't mutually exclusive. And while asking me to take a leave of absence is a lot for me to deal with, I can see why she might think I'd be grateful for one less thing to worry about. Not to mention the logic of her making every effort to keep Hamish on board when I'm below par myself.

At least Pepper doesn't believe I was prepared to frame her with that bloody knife.

I chuck on clothes and boots, then walk to Waterlow Park. The air is cold against my cheeks, burning my ears. Hardly anyone else is out, just a few joggers and grim-faced mums with mud-splattered pushchairs. The sky glowers grey, close overhead. As I turn for home, still preoccupied, the first drops of rain start to fall. By the time I let myself through the front door it's lashing down.

Michael texts to say he's cooking Lola bacon and pancakes for brunch. I have a sudden yearning to be with them both.

I shower, then call Michael. He answers on the first ring.

'Hi, I was about to call you,' he says.

'Can I come over?' I ask. 'I'd really like to see Lola. Is she okay?'

'Listen, Ali.'

'What?'

'Are you at work? In the office, I mean?'

'No.' I open my mouth to explain that Pepper effect-ively – if temporarily – fired me last night, then shut it again. I don't want to have to deal right now with Michael's reaction when he hears. He's bound to be angry that Pepper has upset me. 'I'm not going to work today. Why are you asking? And you haven't said if Lola's all right?'

'She's fine. Well, she refused to go to school earlier, which after her very public arrest there the other day I didn't want to argue about, but she's gone to meet Anya and Maisie during one of their free periods. She'll be back in a couple of hours.'

'Oh.' I sit down.

'Now, listen,' Michael goes on. 'You and I are certain, aren't we, that Lola was deliberately set up for Brendan's murder, that it wasn't just a chance burglary gone wrong?'

I sigh. 'Michael, yes, of course, but I don't feel like going over it all again. Lola's been charged now. This is really serious and—'

'Please,' he interrupts. 'How do we know the murder wasn't part of a burglary gone wrong?'

I blow out my breath, feeling irritated. 'We know because there was no sign of a break-in at Brendan's house, and nothing was taken.'

'Exactly,' Michael interrupts, 'and, later, an anonymous witness called the police helpline and claimed to have seen someone answering Lola's description leaving the house *later* than she actually left.'

'Which adds to the proof that Lola is deliberately being set up,' I say. 'We know all this. So what?'

'So, I've been thinking about that knife in your bag,' Michael goes on. 'The DI thinks you got it from Lola, that she's admitted to you she killed Brendan with it and that you were carrying it in your bag in order to frame somebody else for the murder.'

'That's right,' I say.

'But *we* know it's *Lola* the murderer is trying to frame.' Michael pauses. 'So why not plant the knife on *her*? Why put it in *your* bag?' Michael asks.

'Because... well, maybe I was easier. Maybe whoever it is doesn't – didn't – have access to her,' I suggest.

'It's got to be more than that.' Michael clears his throat. 'Think about it: the whole set-up only makes sense if whoever put the knife in your bag *knew* when it would be discovered. There had to be witnesses. That was the whole point. Which means they had to be able to control precisely when the discovery happened. Whoever it was must have chosen to put the knife in *your* bag because they were confident they could engineer its discovery in a way they couldn't if they'd tried to frame Lola directly.'

'Hang on,' I say. 'How could *anyone* have that level of control over my handbag and when someone would look inside it? Even if they put the knife in there, how would they know when it would be discovered? Or who'd discover it?'

'They wouldn't.' Michael hesitates. 'Not unless they were in the room. Manipulating everything.'

I hesitate, the enormity of this claim sinking in. 'But… but that means the knife was put in my bag in the HOPP office.' I suck in my breath. 'Jesus, it was *Pepper* who discovered it.'

'I know,' Michael says, flatly.

My head spins. Surely it's impossible that Pepper killed Brendan after all, that she planted the knife in my bag, that she only cares about herself, not what happens to Lola or me.

'*Shit.*' I want to protest, but the truth is that what Michael is saying makes sense of everything; not just the discovery of the knife, but Pepper's early attempts to throw suspicion onto Seb, her carefully anonymous setting up of @AvengingAngel as a suspect, the fact that she wasn't at home when Brendan was killed, having previously asked Hamish questions about video entry cams and, of course, her fury at Brendan for blackmailing her years ago. Except…

'No, Michael, *no*,' I protest. 'Pepper already told us last week that the whole issue between her and Brendan was over when Lola was still a baby,' I point out. 'Why would she suddenly want to kill him now?'

'I've been thinking about that too,' Michael says. 'What if something happened that gave her a fresh motive?'

'You mean, like Brendan starting up the blackmail again?' I wrinkle my nose. 'What makes you think he'd have done that?'

Michael pauses. 'Because that's more or less what he did with you.'

'Okay, but… even so, Pepper would just pay and—'

'She'd pay *at first* maybe,' Michael says. 'But you know what Brendan's like. Perhaps he went back for more. Maybe several times. Eventually Pepper cracked.'

'And lied about it? To us? To everyone?'

'I know.' Michael sighs. 'But you have to admit, if anyone could carry off a lie like that, it would be Pepper. She's great at sales – at selling a story. It's what she *does*. What she's always done.'

'No.' I shake my head. 'Pepper would never set up Lola to take the fall for her.'

There's a pause. I can hear Michael's breathing, quick and shallow.

'If she has,' he says, 'I'll never forgive her.'

I stand, the phone frozen in my hand. 'No,' I say, 'neither will I.'

'So, what do we do with our suspicions?' Michael asks.

'Tell the police that we think Brendan might have been blackmailing her?' I suggest. 'We'll have to explain why, which…' I trail off, not wanting to put my thought into words: *If we tell the police that Pepper helped her father end his life, she'll hate us. Hate me.*

'There'd be no way back from that, Ali,' Michael says, flatly. 'Anyway, we have no proof.'

'I know.' I chew on my lip.

'I've got an alternative suggestion,' Michael says. 'If Pepper had bank-transferred a large lump sum to Brendan, the police would have already found it in his bank statements and asked her a load of questions, but she has only been interviewed twice – once, very briefly, after Brendan died. And then again, this week, over the knife in your bag. So it seems likely to me that if Brendan *had* been blackmailing her again, she gave him cash.'

'Okay, but how does that—?'

'Where would Pepper have got that cash from?'

I frown. 'Well, I know from things she's said recently that she doesn't have any savings and her only source of income is the business, so I guess she would have to siphon off funds from one of the HOPP clients. Maybe several of them, altering the invoices to cover her tracks.'

'Exactly,' Michael exclaims. 'Which is why, before we go to the police, I think we should check HOPP's bank statements,' Michael says. 'See if Pepper made any big, odd-looking withdrawals over the past few months. Money that she could have used to pay off Brendan.'

'You mean go snooping again?' I groan. 'It's a big risk for such a long shot.'

'I know, but it's the only thing that will give us anything close to proof Pepper was being blackmailed.' Michael hesitates. 'I don't know about you, but I'd like to feel more sure she actually had a motive for murder before we land her in it with the police.'

It's a fair point. 'Okay,' I say.

'So where are all the HOPP accounts kept?' he asks.

'It's all on Pepper's desktop computer at work,' I explain. 'Hamish downloads certain files to his laptop every month so he can work on the financial admin, and the bookkeeper who comes in every month has access to them too. I don't go anywhere near that side of things.'

'Then let's look on Pepper's computer,' Michael says.

'You mean go to the office?' A chill snakes down my spine. 'Come on, Michael, we already broke into her house and—'

'It's not breaking in. You *work* there. I thought you could sneak a quick look while she's out of the office.'

'Yeah, well, she's basically told me to take a sabbatical, so…'

'…so she's found a way of keeping you out of the office.' Michael clears his throat. 'Interesting.'

'I guess…' An idea takes root in my head. 'I guess we could sneak in while nobody's there.' Silence on the other end of the line. Outside, rain lashes against the window, loud and persistent. 'Michael?'

'Right,' he says. 'And if we find something, we screen grab it and take it to the police. Show that idiot Detective Barnaby what a proper investigation looks like.'

'It's Barnbury.' I frown. 'Screen grabs of bank accounts aren't admissible as evidence.'

'But they'll show reasonable grounds for suspicion,' Michael insists. 'Then the detectives can get a search warrant and swoop in without warning. That way they can pick up Pepper's desktop before she has a chance to delete anything.' He falls silent.

I nod, slowly. A week ago I couldn't have imagined myself sneaking around the office, but now, with Lola charged, maybe the stakes are too high to not take the risk.

'Think about it, Ali,' Michael says, his voice low and serious. 'This could be our only chance to clear Lola's name.'

'I know,' I say.

'So are you in?'

I take a deep breath. 'For Lola, yes,' I say. 'I'll do it for Lola.'

THIRTY

Michael and I watch the Hot Pepper PR offices from Bella Bacio across the street. Just one hour has passed since we made our plan, but it feels like an eternity. I'm on pins, wired with anxiety as I keep my eyes peeled on the building front door. I still have access to the HOPP online diary, so I already know that Hamish is out at a business lunch, while Pepper is working in the office.

It's Friday, which means Pepper will be going to Beauty Diva along the road for her weekly manicure at one p.m. Our plan is to slip inside the office as soon as she leaves. The desktop computer locks after five minutes, but I should have time to access the accounts before that happens. Then we'll have roughly twenty minutes before Pepper returns.

'I feel like a spy in a movie,' Michael mutters. He takes a swig of his coffee. 'Except all this waiting is more boring. Suppose Pepper changed her appointment?'

'It's *always* at one on a Friday,' I say, fiddling nervously with a napkin. 'They know her. It means she doesn't have to keep making fresh appointments.'

Michael nods and takes another swig. He hasn't shaved this morning and dark stubble, flecked with grey, is visible on his chin. I have a flashback to our student days, when we would spend hours in bed; I can almost feel the press of that rough skin against my cheek, my thighs.

I shuffle in my seat, hoping he can't see any evidence of the heat rising up my neck. Despite the concern for Lola that I can see deep in his eyes, that 'spy' remark suggests a part of him is enjoying our staking out the HOPP office. He has that look I remember from when we were first married, and he was a virgin news reporter on the trail of a big story: serious but excited. 'It's such a buzz,' he explained to me once, 'the hook of that moment you get a big lead.'

It's strangely easy to be here with him, even under such bizarre circumstances. I check my phone for what feels like the millionth time since we arrived. 12:54 p.m. I peer through the window. No sign of Pepper.

The cafe behind us is silent except for a young waitress taking an order across the room, her low murmur rising just above the sound of the traffic sweeping past outside.

12:55 p.m. Still no Pepper.

12:56 p.m. Michael sets down his empty cup. After the earlier rain, the sun is now out and the light through the window glints off the metal band on his finger. I suddenly realise that he's wearing his wedding ring again and look away quickly.

'Maybe she cancelled her appointment this week?' Michael suggests, uncertainly.

I snort. 'Yeah, right, have you ever seen Pepper without perfect nails. She never—Look!'

He follows my gaze to where Pepper is emerging onto the pavement. Her orange coat flares out behind her as she strides purposefully along the street.

'Come on.' Michael stands up.

Together, we hurry outside and across the road. Work keys clutched in my clammy palm, I let us in to the building's main front door then lead the way up to the

HOPP office on the first floor. I stop for a second inside, staring at my desk by the window. It's piled high with folders, a dumping ground. I hurry into Pepper's sectioned-off office. Sunlight streams in through the window. Her computer is on the desk and it's still open. I click on the keyboard to get rid of the fractal screensaver. The faint scent of Pepper's perfume lingers in the air – Tom Ford's Black Orchid.

'You in?' Michael appears in the doorway.

'Yup.'

'I'm going to keep an eye on the street out here, watch out for Pepper coming back,' he says. 'I'll let you know how we're doing for time, okay?'

'Fine.' I don't look up as Michael slips away. I access the HOPP bank accounts and open the outgoings spreadsheet that covers the past quarter. I scroll through the accounts, wishing I was as fast as Hamish or as familiar with the set-up as Pepper. As far as I can see, there's no record of any big withdrawals. I start over, double-checking every transaction. A sudden thought strikes me. What if Pepper did an off-the-books cash deal with one of our clients? The money from that wouldn't show up here, but a gap in payments would still be a discrepancy I should be able to spot. I peer at the screen more closely. I know the names of every client and supplier. And virtually every piece of work. It's all itemised here. Is anything missing?

Outside, in the main part of the office, Michael is standing close to my desk and peering intently through the window at the street below. Ten of our twenty minutes have already passed.

Anxiety tightens in my chest as I run down the list of names and accounts for a third time. More minutes tick by. I can't see anything out of the ordinary.

'We need to go.' Michael is in the doorway.

'But I need more time.'

'We don't have any,' he says, turning away.

I quickly close the open files, then follow Michael across the room.

As Michael reaches Hamish's desk he points at the laptop, peeking out from under a pile of client company reports. 'Didn't you say Hamish downloads accounts to work from home sometimes?' he asks, his voice urgent.

'Yes, but—'

Before I can finish my protest, Michael has snatched Hamish's MacBook off his desk.

'What are you doing?' I stare at him, aghast.

'Giving you more time with the accounts,' he says.

'*What?*' I glance across to the window and the street beyond. 'But Pepper will be back in—'

'We're taking it with us.' Michael shoves the laptop into his backpack.

'*Stealing* it?' I stare at him. 'That's Hamish's property.'

'We're *borrowing* it.' Michael shoots me a look. 'We'll take a peek, then put it back here before Hamish gets back from his meeting. Pepper won't notice it's missing.'

'How are we going to—?' I start, but Michael is already hurrying out of the office.

My heart hammers as I race down the stairs after him. What on earth is he thinking? Outside the cold air slaps at my cheeks. I hunch down in my coat, following Michael across the road and back into Bella Bacio. It's busy now, the waitress taking an order from a large, noisy group of suited office workers near the counter. Michael makes his way back to our window table and sits down. The cups of coffee we abandoned earlier are still standing there. I peer through the window. Pepper is striding along the road opposite, heading back to the office. I turn away, leaning against my chair to make sure that if she were to glance across, she wouldn't spot me. Michael, concealed from the window by a plant pot, has already opened the laptop. He grimaces at the screen.

'What the hell did we just do?' I demand.

'Cool your jets,' he says, not looking up. 'I'll pop back to HOPP in a couple of hours. Pretext of saying "Hi" to Pepper. It'll be no problem to get this back on Hamish's desk without her seeing.'

'Oh, great.' I shake my head. 'Pepper won't smell a rat there at all.'

'Actually, she won't. I've been dropping by a lot, recently,' Michael says.

'Really?' A hot, unwanted jealousy rises inside me. 'I noticed she seemed to know everything I've been telling you about Brendan's murder investigation.'

Across the room, the young waitress finishes taking the large group order. She hurries into the kitchen without looking over at us.

'You sound like you mind, Ali,' Michael says lightly, the hint of a smile curving his lips. 'You'll be relieved to hear that mostly I just talk to Pepper about you, asking if she thinks you're okay.' Michael prods at the laptop.

'I don't care what you talk to her about,' I snap.

Michael looks up, an infuriating grin on his face. 'Yes, you do, Ali.'

I look away, heat burning my neck, rising into my cheeks. If Michael notices, he doesn't comment. Instead, he closes the laptop and slides it back into his rucksack.

'What are you doing now?' I demand. 'I thought we were going to look at the accounts here?'

'The laptop's locked,' Michael says.

'Great,' I mutter. 'So our latest bit of criminal activity was a complete waste of time.'

Michael's eyes twinkle. 'Not at all. Thanks to the story I've been working on for the past few weeks, I happen to know one of the best hackers in the business.'

My jaw drops. 'You want to *hack* into Hamish's computer?' I stare at him. 'Are you serious?'

'Are you saying you *don't* want to?' Michael frowns.

'I guess... now we've come this far,' I splutter. 'But how exactly will—?'

'My main contact for the hacking story, his name is Pol,' Michael explains. 'He's one of the top hackers in the country, I don't think Hamish's MacBook is going to stump him.' He gazes at me, his triumphant expression reflecting classic Michael: infuriating and charming in equal measure, and always with an answer for everything.

I nod, fresh hope fizzing through my body. 'Where is this guy – Pol – based?' I ask.

'Dalston Junction.'

I do a quick mental calculation. 'Okay, so it's probably going to take thirty minutes by car there *and* back, and it's one twenty now. That gives us an hour max for Pol to hack in and for us to examine the invoices. It's not much time.'

'It's better than nothing.' Michael grins. 'Are you in?'

I nod.

'Nice one, Louise.' He cocks his head to one side. 'Or are you Thelma?'

I grin back. 'Oh, you are *so* Thelma!'

We scurry outside, pulling our hoods up – just in case Pepper is looking from her office window – and hurry around the corner to Michael's car.

He clicks the doors open and I reach for the handle.

'Come on then, Thelma,' I say. 'Take me to the scene of our next crime.'

THIRTY-ONE

I assume Pol is going to be young and geeky looking, with the pasty appearance of someone who has spent too much time indoors. Instead, he turns out to be a hand-some thirty-something, with a tan and shiny dark hair that reaches well past his shoulders. Despite the cold outside, he's dressed in a faded T-shirt and long shorts, a pair of battered Converse on his feet. He meets us at the door of his east London lock-up, then peers up and down the road full of boarded-up houses, before dragging us inside.

There's no natural light in here and it's hard to see at first just how big the garage is. Pol doesn't speak as he leads us across the room to a bank of computer terminals set against the far wall. They cast a blue glow over the rough concrete floor and the shabby sofa that stands to the side. Empty pizza boxes and takeaway cartons are piled on the floor and the low, chipped table beside the sofa.

'Everything okay, Pol?' Michael asks cheerfully. 'This is my wife, Ali.'

'Hi, Pol.' I glance sideways at Michael. Technically, of course, 'my wife' isn't correct since we are divorced, but the words sound strangely natural.

'Where's this laptop you want looking at?' Pol screws up his angular face. Michael had already told me that Pol is the product of a wealthy background; highly educated at the world's best schools, but long ignored by his jet-setting parents. I'm still not prepared for how posh he sounds.

Michael chuckles, drawing Hamish's MacBook out of his backpack. 'No time for small talk, I see.'

Pol takes the laptop, then looks up at Michael. I idly wonder if he's gay, his gaze is almost ferocious in its intensity. Then he looks at me in the same fierce way and I realise his interest in us isn't sexual; he's just curious, as if we were exotic animals in a zoo. I'm beginning to see why he's only dressed in a T-shirt. There are at least six computer terminals in here and they generate an oven's worth of heat.

'Are you trying to insult me with this crappy Apple?' His voice cuts through the air. 'I could have hacked it remotely.'

'Fair enough,' Michael says evenly. 'We just want to be able to look at the contents, so all you have to do is—'

'Find a way inside, I get it,' Pol interrupts. 'Just so we're clear, I'm doing this as a favour, but it's my last one. After this we're done, okay?'

'Sure,' Michael says.

Pol sniffs contemptuously, as he opens the laptop on the empty table in front of him. Without looking up, he motions us towards the large, stained sofa across the room. 'You two can sit over there.'

Michael and I perch on the squashy couch, which is sandwiched between two towering stacks of boxes. A half-eaten pizza lies, cold and congealed, on the topmost box. A massive screen is set too close in front of us, several sets of games consoles scattered among the food debris. I tuck my legs up underneath me and lean into Michael.

'This is weird,' I whisper.

He turns his head and I'm suddenly aware of how close we are. He shifts, just a tiny bit closer, so his lips almost brush my cheek. 'I only bring you to the interesting places.'

For a second there's a charge between us, so strong I can almost touch it. Then I pull away, heart racing. I glance at Pol, hunched over Hamish's laptop, hoping Michael can't see my burning cheeks in this dim light.

'Do you think Lola's all right?' I ask, more to cover my confusion than anything else.

'I think she's doing okay.' Michael touches my arm with the tip of his finger, lowering his voice to a low growl. 'I've never stopped wanting you.'

I gulp, skin tingling where he's touching me. Then I pull away again. 'How long do you think Pol will be?' I ask. I can hear how strangled my voice sounds.

'Let's ask him.' Michael gets up fast, like I just burned him. 'Pol, how're you doing?'

'Uh-huh,' Pol grunts. 'Don't pester me.'

Michael takes out his phone and strolls across the lock-up, peering at the screen. I sit back and close my eyes. My heart is still banging against my ribs. I let out a long, slow breath. I don't want to think about wanting Michael.

'It's open,' Pol calls out. 'What are we looking for?'

Michael and I hurry over to Pol's cramped work area. I lean over the desk, peering at the screen past Pol's shoulder.

'This year's quarter four accounts,' I say.

Pol's fingers move across the keyboard at lightning speed. He finds the relevant folder in seconds, then gives me his seat so I can scan what's inside.

I work my way through every file in turn. A metallic taste builds in my mouth. There's nothing here that differs from the accounts on Pepper's computer. Nothing out of the ordinary, no odd amounts or names I don't recognise. I reach the end of the last file and push the laptop away in frustration.

'It's a dead end.'

'It can't be.' Michael bends down, peering closely at the other files and folders on Hamish's desktop. He draws up another chair and sits down beside me. Pol wanders across the room to the sofa. The sound in the lock-up is strangely deadened. Muffled. As if the whole place is sound proofed which, on reflection, it probably is. Pol settles himself down, puts on a pair of headphones and picks up one of the games consoles. Seconds later the flashing lights of a video game illuminate the room. Michael taps away at the folders on Hamish's desktop.

I let out a long, slow sigh. This has been a total waste of time.

'Ali, look!'

'What?' I follow his gaze to a folder in the corner of the screen. It has a one-word title: *Lola*.

My stomach falls away. I glance at Michael. 'What's *that*?'

Michael leans over the keyboard. For all the strength in his voice, I can't help but notice his fingers tremble, very slightly, as he opens the file.

A file full of JPEGs fills the screen. Michael pulls up the first photo. My hand flies to my mouth. Lola is looking coyly up at the lens, her hand self-consciously on her shirt. Michael swears under his breath and swipes through the next few pictures: Lola sitting at my desk, tousling her hair and grinning; Lola looking over her shoulder at the HOPP photocopier and winking suggestively.

'Oh my God!' I breathe.

'What the *hell*?' Michael's voice drops so low he sounds almost hoarse.

I glance over at Pol. He's engrossed in his video game and paying us no attention.

'She can't have realised how sexualised these are,' I say faintly. 'To her this is just… smiling for the camera.'

'But she's at work, in your office.' Michael frowns. 'Why is she smiling and having her picture taken there?'

'I imagine because Hamish asked her to.' My voice rises. 'He's totally abused his posi—'

'Look!'

I follow Michael's pointing finger and peer at the next photo. Lola is outside the office, staring across the street. She's dressed in a blue dress and white cardigan, her hair neatly brushed. The memory stirs inside me, fluttering just out of reach… then: 'That's from her last day at work back in August.' I say, turning to Michael. 'I remember she was really self-conscious about that dress.'

'I don't think she knew that picture was being taken,' Michael growls. He swipes to the next picture, clearly taken through a window, of Lola chatting to her friends in a cafe. 'Or that one.'

One candid shot after another appears. My jaw drops. Lola is clearly oblivious of the camera in *all* these later shots, most of them taken well after her holiday job at HOPP ended. They show her at all times of the day; getting on a bus, leaving school and then on various pavements with Brendan, kissing, getting into his car, standing outside restaurants.

A chill runs down my spine.

Hamish has been stalking Lola for months.

'Did you get any sense from Hamish that… that he had done… that he was *capable* of doing this?' Michael asks.

'No, of course not.' I stare across the line of photos. A close-up of Lola gazing at her mobile catches my eye. The strap of her dress hangs off one shoulder and her lips are pressed together in concentration as she peers at the screen. How dare nosey, efficient, camp Hamish see my daughter as sexual prey? 'There's no way Lola knows anything about this.'

Michael makes a face. 'We can't know that for sure. Those early pics suggest he might have tried it on back in August, and she was too embarrassed to say. Like she didn't with Brendan.' He hesitates. 'Exactly how old is this creep, anyway?'

'Thirty-five, I think,' I say.

Michael lets out a low growl. 'You know she was still seventeen in most of these pictures.'

Another picture catches my eye. I gasp. 'Look.' The photo shows Lola, dressed in her custard yellow coat, standing in the porch light outside Brendan's house.

'Look at the date,' I whisper. 'And the time.'

Michael peers more closely. 'Bloody hell.'

'I know.'

Our eyes meet for a second, then I let out a long, shaky sigh.

This picture was taken just before Brendan was murdered.

THIRTY-TWO

I stare at the picture of Lola in her yellow coat, standing outside Brendan's front door. Michael looks up from the screen of Hamish's computer. The colour has drained from his cheeks.

'Do you see what this means?' he asks, his voice hoarse.

I nod. 'Hamish was there, outside Brendan's house the evening Brendan died. He saw Lola going inside.' I gasp. 'Which means he must have seen the murderer going in after her.'

'Ali, it was *him*.' Michael stares at me. '*Hamish* killed Brendan. It *must* have been him. It's too big a coincidence otherwise.'

'But…' I frown, it's hard enough accepting Hamish has been stalking Lola for months. Could he really be capable of murder, too? 'You think Hamish was that jealous? That he saw Lola going into Brendan's and flipped out?'

'What else?' Michael asks. 'It all fits. These pictures more or less prove it. And what about the knife in your bag? If it wasn't Pepper who put it there, it *must* have been Hamish. He was the only other person in the room.'

I glance over at Pol. He still has headphones on and appears entirely absorbed in his video game. Even so, I lower my voice.

'We should show all this to the police. Get them to investigate Hamish.'

'You don't think we should confront him ourselves?' Michael rubs at his forehead.

I stare at him. *How is that even a question?*

'No,' I say. 'Think about it. If Hamish is really a killer there's no way we should approach him on our own. We *have* to go to DI Barnbury.'

'Okay, then.' Michael lets out an impatient sigh. 'But we should talk to Lola first. Find out if she had any inkling Hamish was stalking her. Then the three of us can go to the police station together.'

It's a good idea. Once the police see this new evidence against Hamish they are bound to want to question Lola again anyway. I check the time; quarter to three. 'She should be back at yours by now.'

'Let's go.' Michael scoops up the laptop, then walks over to Pol and holds out his hand. 'Thanks, mate.'

Pol scowls, ignoring the hand. 'Like I said, don't call me again.' He turns back to his video game.

–

Outside in the car, I hold Hamish's computer on my lap, while Michael drives. His whole body is tensed. Usually a laidback driver, he's hunched over the steering wheel, clearly deep in thought.

'I'll call Lola,' I say, 'let her know we're on our way to pick her up.'

'No,' Michael says, shooting me a fierce look. 'She'll only ask what's up and then you'll have to explain on the phone. Or else you won't and she'll worry until we get there.'

'Okay.' I agree reluctantly. I don't want to wait, but Michael is right. It will be better to have this conversation in person.

'Maybe I should call Pepper,' I muse. 'Let her know what we've found out about Hamish…'

'I wouldn't do that either,' Michael says, glancing across at me again. 'If you tell her she might tell Hamish, which would give him time to—'

'Pepper wouldn't do that.'

'Then she'd have to pretend to Hamish's face that she doesn't know anything about his missing laptop, which he's going to notice is missing as soon as he gets back to the office. It's not fair to put her in that position.'

He's right again. I wriggle in my seat, feeling uncomfortable.

'Now I'm thinking about it,' Michael says tersely, pulling up at a set of traffic lights. 'It's probably best if I drop you at yours, then talk to Lola on my own before we all go to the cops.'

'Why?' I frown.

Michael shrugs. 'It's not a big deal, just, well, you know, sometimes it's easier for me and her to talk, with big, emotional stuff like this.'

I think back to the first couple of days after Brendan died, how Lola clung to her father.

'I guess that's true,' I say, nodding, though inside I can't help but resent him for it, just a little bit. 'What about Josh? What will you say to him?'

'Josh said he was going to Anil's after school,' Michael says, his hands gripping the steering wheel. 'Something about a *Call of Duty* marathon. And he's seeing Nadia later too, so I'm not expecting him home 'til late evening.' He clears his throat. 'Okay? I'll get Lola and we'll come straight over to pick you up.'

'Okay,' I say. 'Just don't be too long.'

The traffic lights turn green and we set off. Michael immediately hunches over the wheel again. I've never seen him look so stressed.

'Are you all right?' I ask, staring at him with concern.

'Not really,' Michael mutters. His lips are pressed tightly together, his knuckles white on the steering wheel. 'I'm just so angry about Hamish. I mean, on top of Brendan manipulating her, Lola has to deal with some bastard at her work pestering her, then setting her up for *murder* – not to mention the impact of all of it on you.' He hesitates. 'Plus, if I'm honest, I'm furious that I didn't see any of it. Not Brendan. Not Hamish. I've been blind.' His voice cracks.

'Hey, I didn't see any of that stuff either, and I've been working with Hamish every day for two years.' I glance at him. 'This isn't your fault, Michael.'

He clenches his jaw, clearly unconvinced.

'We're really getting somewhere now,' I point out. 'One step at a time. We get Lola and take everything to the police and trust that DI Barnbury will get to the bottom of it. Right?'

'Right.' Michael glances at me and heaves a sigh, then fixes his eyes back on the road ahead.

We fall silent. A few minutes later, Michael pulls up outside my house. As I reach for the door handle, he takes the laptop.

'I'll be back for you soon,' he says.

–

The house is dark and silent as I wander through the hall and into the kitchen.

I stare at the kettle. I easily have enough time to make a cup of tea. Except I don't want tea. I just want to get to the police and show DI Barnbury the photo of Lola outside Brendan's house on the night he died. That surely proves Hamish was not only at the scene but, along with all the other pictures, shows he had a motive – jealousy – for killing Brendan. I call Pepper and leave a voicemail saying that I've just got home and that I need to talk to her about Hamish urgently. I can't sit still so I drift through each of the downstairs rooms in turn, then absently open the post – almost all junk mail. I can't focus on anything except the need to take what Michael and I have found out about Hamish to the police.

Five minutes pass. Ten. Twenty. Thirty.

The doorbell rings. Surely that's Michael and Lola? I fling open the front door.

To my horror, Hamish is standing on the doorstep. I push the door to close it, but Hamish jams his foot in the gap. He lunges forward. He's too strong, my arms can't hold the door. I stumble back as he lurches inside. A whiff of his herby cologne overwhelms me.

'What are you doing here?' I back away, fear rising.

Hamish shuts the front door behind him then turns to face me. 'Hello, boss.' He gives me a tight, thin-lipped smile that doesn't reach his eyes. God, why didn't I see before what a total psycho he is?

'What do you want?' I take a step away from him.

Hamish keeps his gaze fixed on mine. The top of a neatly creased handkerchief peeks out of his jacket pocket as he spreads wide his arms, a look of fake bewilderment on his face.

'I'm hoping you can help with something,' he says lightly. 'My laptop appears to have vanished from the office and yet—' he pauses '—*and yet*, there wasn't a break-in. Now, I was out most of the day, but Pepper says she only left for twenty minutes or so. Which, I'm guessing, means that whoever came in and took my laptop had access to both our keys and our schedule.' He raises his eyebrows. 'Would you know anything about that?'

I shake my head, heart pounding. 'Of course not.'

'Interesting,' he says, in the same tone he might ask me to repeat something complicated at work. He tilts his head to one side. 'But clearly untrue.'

We stare at each other.

'Thief.' Hamish swallows up the space between us.

I hold my ground. There's no point pretending. No need to hold back. Michael will be here any moment. I take a deep breath. 'Murderer!'

'*Murderer?*' He shakes his head. 'Is *that* what you think? Jesus, you're even more unhinged than I—'

'You were there outside the house just before Brendan was killed.' My voice trembles. 'You... you were jealous over Lola and you stalked her and took her picture—'

'Whoa, whoa, whoa.' Hamish frowns. 'Back up there. I think *stalk* is a little excessive. I took a few photos of her, that's all. And if you've seen *them*, you've definitely got my laptop, so—'

'You took pictures of her for *months*,' I spit. 'Almost all of them without her knowing you were doing it. What's that if not stalking?'

Hamish purses his lips. 'She led me on, Alison,' he says, curtly. 'From the start.'

'She wasn't even eighteen when she came to the office last summer.' My voice rises.

'So what?' Hamish counters. 'She was still a massive prick tease.'

My jaw clenches tight. 'How dare you.'

'You don't believe she's a slut?' Hamish asks, contempt now creeping into his voice.

'Don't talk about her like that.'

'For God's sake.' He waves my anger away with an impatient flourish. 'You need to hear the truth. Lola acted like she was on heat around me the entire time she was working at HOPP. Certainly every moment you and Pepper were out of the office.'

'No.' I stare at him, feeling sick. 'No *way* is that true.'

'Oh really?' Hamish says waspishly. 'She flirted and flirted until I didn't know which way was up and, then, when I asked her out, she *laughed* at me. Said I was too old for her. What a joke. Brendan was *way* older than me.'

Fury rises inside me. I can't believe Lola had to deal with *another* older guy hitting on her. Especially one I thought I could trust.

'You asked out a teenager?' My voice fills with contempt.

'She wasn't acting like a teenager; she was coming on to me like nobody's business. If I ended up a bit obsessed with her it's only because that's exactly what she wanted.' Hamish sniffs. 'She's a manipulative bitch.'

I clench my fists. 'She's *friendly*,' I snap. 'Which you are so arrogant you misinterpreted. But even if she *had* shown an interest, you should have kept your distance. She's not just a lot younger than you, you were in a position of responsibility over her. You—'

'You don't see her,' Hamish interrupts. 'You don't get her at all. And you're treating *me* like a villain when the truth is that *I'm* the main reason Lola wasn't arrested weeks ago.'

'Because you held back from telling the police you saw her entering Brendan's house?' I shake my head. 'They knew she did that anyway, from the video cam.'

'Oh, I saw a *lot* more than that.' Hamish's voice takes on a chilling edge. 'I saw what Lola was wearing. I saw her coat. That entry cam cut her off at the neck.'

'So what?' I demand. 'The police already examined her coat.'

'No. They examined the coat she *told* them she was wearing,' Hamish says with a sly smile. 'But this was the coat she was *actually* wearing. That bright yellow vintage Gucci of hers. The one Pepper gave her.' He raises his eyebrows. 'If you've really seen the picture of Lola outside Brendan's house, you'll know I'm telling the truth.'

My memory skitters back, over the photos. Hamish is right. Lola *was* wearing her yellow coat outside Brendan's house, not the black one the police took and examined. My insides fall away. Why would Lola have lied about which coat she wore?

'A mistake about a coat doesn't prove *anything*,' I snap.

'It proves what I already knew – Lola's a liar who manipulates people *all the time*.' He rolls his eyes. 'You really don't get it, do you? Lola did it. *She* killed Brendan. It was *her*.'

THIRTY-THREE

The atmosphere in the hall grows tense.

'That's ridiculous,' I splutter. 'Lola isn't capable of killing *anyone*. It was *you*. Out of jealousy. You watched her go inside Brendan's house, waited until she left, then destroyed the video camera and talked your way inside in order to kill Brendan.'

'Puh–lease.' Hamish frowns. 'Why would I do any of that? I mean I was as appalled as you that she was dating that old has-been and yeah, I'll grant you, I did experience the occasional flash of jealousy over it, but that doesn't mean I *killed* him.'

'So what were you doing outside Brendan's house that night?' I demand. 'If you *were* innocent, if you'd seen someone *else* go in to murder him, you'd have come forward as a witness. It doesn't make sense.'

'Actually, it makes perfect sense,' Hamish says lightly. 'Let me tell you exactly what happened.' He clears his throat. 'I didn't just see Lola *before* she went into Brendan's house. I saw her *afterwards* too. She must have come out of the garden door, which I couldn't see from where I was standing, then walked up to the main road where I spotted her.' He pauses. 'I checked the time, so I remember – it was 7:55 p.m., much later than she told the police.'

'You're lying— Oh!' I gasp, a fresh realisation dawning on me. '*You're* the anonymous witness, aren't you?'

Hamish purses his lips, a silent acknowledgement.

'Oh my God.' I clutch my forehead. 'It was *all* you! You lied to the police that Lola left Brendan's place later than she did, so they'd be more likely to think she was the murderer. You set her up.'

'For God's sake, I've been trying to *protect* her.' Hamish's voice rises. 'Don't you understand? I could tell straight away something was wrong from the way she was hurrying along the road, all hunched over, not wearing her coat even though it was cold. I assumed she and that ancient boyfriend of hers had had a row, so I followed her, waiting for the right moment to go up to her, offer some consolation, you know?' He winks at me and I clench my fists. 'However, just as I was about to approach her, she did something strange.' He pauses. 'She'd been carrying a plastic bag since the house, which I assumed had her stuff in it as she'd passed several bins and not put it in. But then, after a few more streets, she dumped the bag in a bin after all. I mean, if it was just rubbish, why didn't she get rid of it earlier? I waited till she'd gone around the corner, then went to see what she was throwing away. Guess what I found?'

'I don't want to listen to any more of your lies.' I check the time. Where the hell is Michael? He and Lola should have been here by now.

'Inside the bag, I found Lola's yellow coat,' Hamish says, as if I hadn't spoken. 'It had a thick smear of blood down the front. Made me gag, actually.'

'You're making this up.'

'And that wasn't all,' Hamish says. 'Wrapped up in the coat—' he pauses for effect '—was that knife you found. The murder weapon.'

I stare at him. '*You* had the knife?' The pieces fall into place with horrifying elegance. Of course Hamish had the knife; he was the killer.

Hamish nods, modestly. For a bizarre moment, he looks pleased with himself, as if he's shown me a draft press release that he's particularly proud of.

'I realised immediately that Lola was getting rid of her bloodstained coat, along with the murder weapon,' he explains, 'so I decided to hang onto them myself. I thought she'd be grateful when I told her I had them; maybe so grateful that she'd even see the light about us getting together.' He chuckles.

'You're disgusting,' I snarl.

'No, your daughter is the disgusting one. Instead of being straight with me when I told her about the coat and the knife, she strung me along like before, making out she was interested in me and simply waiting for the right time for us to be together. Of course, in reality, she was buying time and never had any intention of—'

'For God's sake,' I snap. 'The poor girl was trying to deal with you *blackmailing* her!'

'She manipulated me,' Hamish protests. 'After a few days I realised I needed to raise the stakes.'

My eyes widen, as I realise what he's referring to. 'So you decided to plant the knife in my handbag, where Pepper would find it and call the police – to intensify the heat on Lola. Your plan was to remind Lola you still had her coat, which you'd covered in Brendan's blood, in the—'

'Which got covered in Brendan's blood when she killed him.'

'In the hope that she'd be prepared to sleep with you in order to get her coat back.'

Hamish stares impassively at me.

'What I don't understand,' I go on, 'is why you went to the trouble of planting the knife in my bag. Why didn't you just take it to the police station? Or make an anonymous call to let them know where it was?'

'Well, I was trying to kill two birds with one stone at that point,' Hamish says waspishly. 'I thought it might be to my advantage if the Brendan murder enquiry came a little bit closer to the office, so I was planning to "discover" the knife in your bag in front of Pepper – then, of course, she beat me to it. Not to put too fine a point on it, but after your slack showing at work over the past few weeks – I was confident that if I told Pepper how upset I was about the whole incident, and that I, the person who'd been holding the office together, was thinking of leaving, she'd let you go instead.'

My jaw drops. Hamish has manipulated us as effectively as Brendan ever did.

'You're unbelievable,' I say, my voice hoarse.

'Just looking for ways to move on with my career,' Hamish says lightly. 'I'm well due a promotion and you know it.'

I shake my head. 'Well, there won't be a promotion now,' I snarl. 'When I tell DI Barnbury what you just told me, he'll realise *you* killed Brendan.'

Hamish gives me a pitying look. 'What makes you think he'll believe you? He already knows you'd say anything to protect Lola. And, like Pepper's always saying, what sells is the story, and my story fits far better with the narrative your DI has come up with so far.'

'Then I'll make him rethink it.' I swallow hard. 'I'll explain how you've been stalking Lola for months, how you saw her enter Brendan's house, then destroyed the security camera and went in yourself to—'

'I didn't touch the camera,' Hamish says quickly. 'That was Lola. I saw her do it. That was what first made me think she and Brendan were having some sort of row.'

'That's ridiculous,' I scoff. '*You* destroyed the camera, then you went inside *after* Lola had left and killed Brendan out of jealousy.'

Hamish rolls his eyes. 'Wrong, wrong and *wrong*.'

'You're delusional,' I say. 'You'll pay for what you've done.'

'I'm afraid you're the delusional one.' Hamish offers me a wry smile. 'Like I said before, Alison. You don't know your daughter as well as you think you do.'

I look away, a terrible desolation sweeping over me. Hamish is clearly lying. But Lola has lied too. Why didn't she tell me that Hamish was so predatory? I can't bear to think of her alone, dealing with his abusive pestering all summer. And why didn't she tell me – or the police – that he was blackmailing her over the coat she wore the night Brendan died? My stomach churns. How did Hamish get hold of that coat anyway? Did Lola leave it behind at Brendan's house? Where is it now?

'What did you do with Lola's yellow coat?' I demand. 'You found a way to get the knife to the police. Why haven't you given them the coat as well?'

'The coat is an insurance policy, to protect myself,' Hamish says briskly. 'So long as Lola knows I have it, and that it's got Brendan's blood all over—'

'Blood you put there,' I interrupt.

Hamish shakes his head. 'Lola's not stupid. She's not going to start throwing accusations about me around if I'm in possession of such a key piece of evidence.'

'Maybe not,' I acknowledge, 'but once the police see the photos on your laptop, it will put any evidence against Lola in a different light.'

'It'll still be my word against hers.' A slight shake creeps through Hamish's defensive snarl.

I leap on it. 'And who's to say your word will carry more weight than hers?' I draw myself up. 'Your stalker photos of Lola demonstrate you were still obsessed with her even though she'd rejected you, while the picture taken the night of Brendan's murder actually places you at the scene. You're bigger and stronger than she is, far more likely to have overcome Brendan in a struggle.' I pause. 'That's motive, opportunity and means. I wouldn't be so sure about the police believing you rather than her.'

For the first time since he arrived, Hamish looks uncertain.

Energy surges through me. 'How about we do a deal?' I suggest. 'It's in both our interests that the picture of Lola wearing her yellow coat outside Brendan's house doesn't come to light. I don't have the laptop here, but I'm prepared to get it and give it back to you – with *all* the incriminating pictures deleted – provided you give me Lola's coat. Agreed?'

Hamish considers this for a long minute.

'Okay,' he says at last. 'But don't even think about double crossing me on this or I'll make things ten times worse for Lola.' He pauses. 'I'll need a bit of time to get the coat. It's hidden somewhere safe.' He frowns. 'I'll text you where to meet me and we'll do the exchange. Give me half an hour.'

I nod. He fixes me with a fierce look, then stalks away. As he leaves the house, I sink against the wall, my legs suddenly shaky. I fumble for my mobile. Outside, the light is starting to fade from the day. I call Michael. He doesn't pick up. I call Lola. No reply.

Why aren't they answering? Why aren't they *here*?

I pace up and down. For a moment, I catch sight of my reflection in the hall mirror. My face is pale, my unbrushed hair frizzing out in wisps. Then I snatch up my phone and call Michael again and leave a voicemail: 'Where are you?' I can hear the fear as well as the anger in my voice as I speak. 'I've just—' I stop. After the police took all our devices the other day, I'm aware that leaving a long voicemail explanation about everything I've just learned – or directly asking for Hamish's laptop – is a very bad idea. I take a breath. 'Listen. Change of plan. I *really* need, er, that device we were looking at earlier. Call me as soon as you get this.'

I end the call and try Lola's mobile, but just get a message saying the phone is unavailable and to try again later.

I wait a few minutes, then try them both again. Nothing. A text pings through from Hamish with an address in Wood Green. He wants me to meet him there in twenty minutes. There's something vaguely familiar about the address, but I can't place it. I try Michael yet again, almost shrieking down the phone that he needs to call me.

My thoughts run in panicky circles. What will happen if I turn up to meet Hamish without the laptop to trade? Surely he'll be furious. Possibly angry enough to take Lola's coat to the police.

I'll have to find some way to stop him. As I get in my car, it strikes me that going to a meeting with a murderer with no backup and no leverage is possibly the most stupid thing I've ever done. And yet what choice do I have?

If Hamish has really covered Lola's coat with Brendan's blood, it's the most damning piece of evidence against her so far.

Not only that, but it's evidence she has already lied about.

I have to get the coat back. This may be my only chance.

I leave the house and drive off, my heart in my mouth. I arrive at the address Hamish gave me a few minutes early. It's the upstairs flat B of a small, terraced house conversion. Rain starts to fall as I get out of the car, but I'm only vaguely aware of it as I hurry across the road and along the path to the front door. As I draw closer, I realise that the door is ajar – just a fraction. I push it open, revealing a dark narrow corridor with stairs at the end. Flat A is to my right, on the ground floor.

Footsteps sound upstairs in what must be flat B.

Is Hamish here already?

My pulse quickens as I creep up the stairs.

THIRTY-FOUR

I reach the top of the stairs. The tiny landing is dark and gloomy; the door to flat B yawns open. More bangs and crashes echo from inside.

I suddenly realise why the address seemed vaguely familiar to me before. This is Hamish's place; I've seen the details on his HOPP contract. Fear grips my throat, squeezing tight. Why would Hamish lure me to his own home? It can't be for any good reason. *Shit.* Why didn't I insist that we met somewhere more public?

I creep to the flat's front door and peer inside. The large, open-plan living room is a mess: all the squashy, taupe sofa cushions are on the floor, while an array of glasses, plates and colourful vases, presumably from the open, empty sideboard, are scattered between them. Knowing Hamish as I do, I can't believe he lives in such disarray. But why would he have turned his own flat upside down?

There's a door in the far corner of the room. A series of loud thuds comes from inside it; the sound of boxes being dropped on a wooden floor.

'Hamish?' My voice quavers as I call out.

The thuds stop. Silence.

'*Hamish?*' I call out again, my guts churning.

The corner door opens. Michael appears.

My jaw drops. 'What are you doing here?'

'Good, you're here, Ali. You can help us.' Ignoring my question, Michael turns back, into the room.

I pick my way across the floor towards him. 'What are you talking about? And who is "us"? Oh!'

I stop in my tracks, as Lola materialises in the doorway. 'Mum!' Her face is panic-stricken. 'Please help!'

I hurry towards her. 'What on earth is going on?' I demand.

I reach Lola. Over her shoulder I catch a glimpse of what must be Hamish's bedroom. Clothes have been torn out of the wardrobe and dumped in piles. Michael is just visible, lifting the mattress off the bed and peering underneath it.

'We had to break in,' Lola pleads, wringing her hands. 'There's no more time. We had to find it.'

I stare at her, uncomprehending.

'It's Lola's yellow coat – from the photo outside Brendan's house,' Michael says, from the other side of the bed. 'It's here, at least I think it is. We've got to get it back.' He stands up, letting the mattress fall back onto the bed with a thud.

'I've been calling you to—' I start.

'I haven't checked my mobile for over an hour,' Michael says, turning to the bedside table and pulling it away from the wall to peer behind it. 'There isn't time.'

'Listen—'

'Hamish put Brendan's blood on my coat, Mum.' Lola is close to tears, fidgeting from foot to foot in front of me. 'We have to find it. If the police get it, it'll—'

'Stop!' I yell. '*Listen!*'

Lola blinks, staring at me. Michael straightens up. They both stare at me.

'I've just seen Hamish. He's bringing the coat here,' I say, as evenly as I can.

Michael's eyes widen. 'How did you get him to agree to that?'

'I promised him his laptop in exchange,' I say. 'Where is it?'

Lola indicates the coffee table in front of the sofa. I walk towards it and shift the sofa cushion blocking my view. There, on the glass, is Hamish's MacBook. I turn towards the others.

'We need to delete the picture of Lola in the yellow coat,' I say. 'All the others too. And any backups. I know they show Hamish stalked her, but I don't want him to have them back.'

'Already done. It took everything I had, but I persuaded Pol to do me one last favour and he ensures me it's like they never existed.' Michael smiles, his face filling with relief.

Beside him, Lola still looks trepidatious.

'Hey, Babycakes, this is a good trade,' Michael says, putting his arm around her shoulder. 'We'll get the coat back, remember? Without that the police have no physical evidence against you.'

Lola nods, leaning against her dad. She's as pale as the wall behind her.

'When will Hamish be here?' Michael demands.

'Any minute.' I fix my gaze on Lola, my voice filling with concern. 'Why didn't you tell me about him, darling?' I ask. 'Why didn't you say that he's been harassing you since the summer?'

Lola's face reddens as she meets my gaze. 'It... it was too embarrassing,' she mumbles. 'It started so long ago, at work... whenever you and Pepper weren't around.'

'Oh, Lola.' My stomach twists into a knot.

'Hamish kept pestering me,' she explains, her lip wobbling. 'He invited me round here loads of times, even when I kept saying no.' She draws in a shaky breath. 'I wanted to tell you, Mum, but Hamish made it sound like if I said anything, I was the one who'd get in trouble.'

My head reels. *How did I not see what was going on?* I glance at Michael. He doesn't seem surprised at what Lola is saying. Does he know already about Hamish's abusive behaviour? My mind fills with confusion. Something doesn't add up here.

'What about your yellow coat?' I ask, my voice growing firmer. 'Why didn't you say that Hamish was blackmailing you over that, threatening to frame you for Brendan's murder? God, why did you lie to the police that first night and say you weren't wearing it?'

'I left my yellow coat at Brendan's the night he died,' Lola mutters. 'I was so upset I just ran outside without it. It was stupid to lie to the police, but I didn't have a choice. Hamish had already messaged me to say he had it before the police even turned up at our house that first night.'

I stare at her. 'Wait. *What?*'

Lola drops her gaze again.

My head spins. 'But – but that means you *knew* Hamish was the killer? Right from the start?'

Lola exchanges a look with Michael. He gives her a nod of encouragement.

'Hamish never admitted anything,' she says. 'He kept saying he'd just found my coat covered in blood, but yes, I guess I did know...' She swallows, tears bubbling in her eyes. 'I just didn't want to face it. Hamish made it sound like if I said anything about him, he'd find a way to hand over the coat, that all the evidence would point at me.

He… he said that if I did what he wanted then he'd keep the coat a secret.'

'What he wanted?' I feel sick.

Lola's cheeks flame scarlet. 'I said no. I'd been saying "no" for months, first while I was working at HOPP over the summer then later, when I started dating Brendan and Hamish got really jealous about it.' She lowers her head. 'You asked why I didn't tell you everything. Well, mostly I was just too ashamed to talk about it. I felt like I was letting you down, that I should have dealt with Hamish better…'

'Oh sweetheart.' I walk over and squeeze her hand.

Lola glances at her dad, anguish on her face.

Michael clears his throat and I suddenly realise he hasn't reacted with surprise to a single thing Lola has just said.

'How long have you known about this, Michael?' I demand. My mind goes back to his endless hushed chats with Lola during those first few agonising days after Brendan's death. Tears prick at my eyes. Surely he can't have known from the beginning?

Michael hesitates. 'Lola told me everything after her first police interview.'

It's like a blow to the stomach. 'So why didn't you do something?' I demand. 'Stop Hamish? Protect Lola? Why didn't you tell me?'

'I was trying to keep you out of it, I'm sorry.' Michael frowns, his eyes intense. 'Lola explained that Hamish was blackmailing her over her coat and we decided together that it wasn't a good idea to tell you or the police or anyone.'

'Why?' I glare at him, my fury rising.

'Well, for one thing, we knew Hamish would just deny blackmailing her. He'd come up with some story about happening to see her getting rid of the coat and—'

'Which is exactly what he did,' Lola interjects.

'Quite.' Michael sighs. 'I knew that a bloodstained coat which Lola had already lied about wearing would count as strong, physical evidence against her,' Michael goes on. 'That first evening, the police had already caught her saying she wasn't at Brendan's house when she was. I figured that her admitting to yet another lie the very next day would be the last straw. Especially when there was so much evidence against her. Better that we tried by ourselves to get the coat off Hamish.' He folds his arms, a grim, angry frown on his face. 'I was never going to let Lola anywhere near the man. She was always safe from his revolting attempts to… to pressure her into anything.'

The anger inside me subsides a little. Michael may have got it completely wrong over not confiding in me, but when it comes to Lola his heart has always, undeniably, been in the right place.

'The trouble was that Hamish had hidden the coat and wouldn't say where,' Lola adds. 'I tried to bluff him for a bit, then to trick him into making threats so I could record him, but he was always too clever.' She sighs. 'After a few days, he realised I wasn't going to give in to his blackmail and, you know, give him what he wanted…' She looks down, her cheeks flaring red again. 'At that point he got cross. Lost patience with me. That's why he made the anonymous witness call, to put pressure on me.'

'Oh, sweetheart.' I shake my head. 'You still should have told me. Both of you.'

'We wanted to protect you,' Michael protests. 'Which was working until Hamish put that knife in your bag.'

I gasp. 'Oh my God, you both knew that was him too?'

Lola nods. 'Hamish came to the conclusion I wasn't going to give him what he wanted, so he decided to use the knife in the same way that he'd threatened to use the coat: to make me look guilty.'

'While hanging onto the coat so he'd still have something to hold over Lola,' Michael adds.

'As you know,' Lola says. 'It worked.'

'When Lola was charged it was the final straw,' Michael says. 'That's when I knew I had to find proof against Hamish – something that would make Lola's story look more convincing; something that would explain why he'd hung on to her coat.'

I clap my hand over my mouth. 'Oh my God, *that's* why you wanted to go to HOPP earlier?' I gasp. 'You didn't think Pepper was guilty at all, it was just a cover to take Hamish's laptop.'

Michael frowns. 'I'm sorry I didn't explain, but I was getting desperate. I needed to get inside that laptop; see if I could prove Hamish was at Brendan's house the night he died, or maybe work out from his messages where he might have put Lola's coat. I didn't know about all the pictures he'd taken of her.'

'Neither of us knew about that,' Lola says with a grimace.

'After I left you, I went through the laptop again with Lola,' Michael says. 'Our best guess was that Hamish was hiding the coat here, at his home. That's why we broke in.' He pauses, offering me a crooked smile. 'And surely you can see why I didn't want you to know we were doing *that*? Like I said, I've only kept things from you to protect you.'

'*Protect* me?' My voice rises. 'You *lied* to me. You were happy to let me suspect all those other people I was close to, Seb – even Pepper. God, you even made out you—' I stop, not wanting to refer to the sexual charge between the two of us, in front of our daughter.

'I'm sorry,' Michael glances at Lola. Again, I have the sensation that something doesn't add up. He's trying to tell Lola something with his eyes.

'What are you hiding?' I demand. 'What else aren't you telling me?'

'Dad...?' Lola starts. But before she can finish, footsteps sound on the stairs.

I spin around as Hamish appears in the doorway, with the last person I expected to see standing at his side.

THIRTY-FIVE

Pepper stands beside Hamish at the front door, then follows him into his flat.

What the hell is she doing here?

The pair of them survey the room, taking in the mess. Hamish's eyes widen in horror, but Pepper's gaze quickly shifts to the three of us across the room; to Michael and Lola standing on either side of me. She frowns.

'Why are you—?'

'Where's my laptop?' Hamish pushes past her, his voice terse with rage. Lola shrinks closer to her dad.

I frown. Hamish isn't carrying anything. 'Where's the coat?' I demand.

'*I* took it from him,' Pepper says coldly. She brings a grubby tartan holdall out from behind her back and holds it up to me.

I frown. Is Lola's coat in there? What is Pepper doing with it? As we stare at each other, Hamish spots his laptop on the coffee table. Before any of us can stop him, he darts over and snatches it up. 'This is criminal damage,' he snaps, indicating his broken front door and the mess of his flat. 'You need to get out, now.'

I exchange a look with Michael, my eyebrows raised. If Pepper has the coat, then I'm sure I can explain to her outside why we need it. We can let Hamish keep his laptop.

Michael nods, then grabs Lola's hand. 'Let's go.' He leads her past Hamish and down the stairs. Pepper and I follow them. Hamish shuts the door smartly behind us.

As we emerge into the dull chill of the overcast afternoon I glance at Pepper. Her face is pale and strained.

'What happened with Hamish?' I ask.

'How did you get the coat?' Michael urges, turning on her.

Lola chews at her fingernails, huddled beside her dad.

'Let's talk through there,' Pepper mutters, indicating the park entrance along the street.

The four of us walk in silence to the park. The area just past the entrance is deserted, lined with heavy-boughed trees that sway in the wind.

Pepper stands in front of the three of us, the holdall still in her hand. I imagine Lola's bright yellow coat inside, a streak of rust-coloured blood matting the wool.

'I was just coming back from another interview with that awful detective – Bangberry, or whatever his name is,' she says.

'Barnbury,' I say.

'Yes,' says Pepper. 'Him. He started questioning me about the @AvengingAngel post; somebody had apparently convinced him that *I* was behind it.' She glares at me.

I stare back at her.

'But you *were* behind it,' Lola says. 'You wrote it because of Brendan, because of him raping Mum when they were younger.'

My breath catches in my throat. I shoot a glance at Michael. He's looking at me, but not with the expression of shock I'm expecting. Instead, he almost seems ashamed. I realise with a jolt that he already knows Brendan raped

307

me. Who told him, I wonder. Was it Lola, recently, or – something dies instead me at the thought – has he known for ages, years maybe, courtesy of Pepper's big mouth?

Pepper gives a self-conscious cough. 'Barnbury kept insisting that the fact I threatened Brendan in the post and went to huge lengths to cover up my real identity, makes me a suspect in his murder. Then he started accusing me over the knife, claiming that I planted it in your bag, Alison. He was pushing me to tell him everything I know and going on and on about how close he was to arresting me. *Me!*' Her voice rises hysterically. 'Can you imagine? *Me* arrested? A court case? My business would collapse within a week.'

'I'm sure the detective was just fishing,' Michael says calmly.

'Yes,' I add. 'He's convinced Lola is guilty, not you. He was just trying to build his case against her.'

'Well, it didn't sound like that,' Pepper snaps.

'What's this got to do with my coat?' Lola demands. She reaches for the bag in Pepper's hand, but Pepper whisks it out of the way behind her back.

'I got back to the office a few hours ago, feeling really upset,' she explains. 'I took a walk out the back, that patch of wasteland, just to try and calm down.' She pauses. 'And there was Hamish, digging this bag out from under a bush.' Pepper's voice fills with indignation as she holds up the bag again. 'I grabbed it and demanded to know what the hell he was doing and when I saw the coat inside, I recognised it as Lola's. The one I gave her for her birthday.' She hesitates. 'I saw the blood on the coat and Hamish started babbling about how he'd been trying to protect Lola by not handing it in to the police. Naturally, I told him not to be so stupid. That a bloodstained coat by itself doesn't prove anything. That it couldn't possibly be Brendan's blood.' She fixes Lola with a piercing look. Lola looks away, along the tarmac path. 'But Hamish said that it *was* Brendan's blood, that he'd followed Lola out of Brendan's house and watched her dump the coat – and the knife that killed Brendan – in a nearby rubbish bin.'

'He's lying,' I jump in. '*Hamish* killed Brendan. He made up a whole load of—'

Pepper holds up her hand and I stop talking.

'Hamish kept babbling about a deal he'd made with you Alison, that he needed to get to his house and give you the coat.' Pepper purses her lips. 'I said that if he didn't give the coat to me, I'd tell the police he was withholding evidence.' She pauses. 'He handed it over.'

My heart thuds painfully. Lola reaches for the bag again, this time swiping it out of Pepper's hands. 'Let me see it.' She wrenches the bag open. 'Oh!'

I follow her gaze. The bag is empty.

THIRTY-SIX

A car drives past, whooshing along the damp road outside the park.

'Where's the coat? What did you do with it?' Michael demands, his eyes intent on Pepper's face.

She stares back at him. '*Obviously*, I took it to the police station and left it there for the Detective Inspector along with a note about how it came into my possession.' She pauses. 'It was the right thing to do; I'm not risking my business. If Lola's innocent then that will come out.'

I stare at her in shocked silence. For a moment, the only sound comes from the wind, gusting through the bare branches of the tree over our heads.

Then Lola lets out a deep, despairing groan. 'Oh, no.' She drops the empty holdall. Pepper picks it up with a defiant swoop.

'Bloody hell, Peps.' Michael's voice is flat, all his energy of the moment past seeping away.

'I would have stayed at the police station to give a full statement,' Pepper goes on. 'I'm sure I shall have to go back and do just that, in fact, but I had Hamish waiting in my car and – as he said he was supposed to be meeting you here Alison—' she meets my gaze '—I thought I'd come here too and find out what the hell is going on. Why, in particular, the three of you are trying to conceal the existence of Lola's coat?'

'Because it makes Lola look guilty when she *isn't*!' I grab Pepper's arm; I *have* to make her understand. '*Hamish* is the one who killed Brendan. He kept the knife and planted it in my tote bag and he smeared some of the blood from it on Lola's coat.'

'And how did he get Lola's coat?' Pepper asks icily.

'She left it behind at Brendan's the night he died,' I explain, my breath coming hard and fast. 'Hamish watched her go into Brendan's house, then, after she left, he went inside, killed Brendan and put Brendan's blood on Lola's coat so he could blackmail her with it.'

I glance at Lola – she covers her face with her hands – then at Michael, who turns away. A queasy feeling churns in my stomach.

'Hang on.' Pepper gives me a sceptical look. 'You're saying that Hamish not only killed Brendan in his kitchen, but had the presence of mind to spot the coat Lola happened to have left behind and smear it with Brendan's blood, in order to frame and blackmail her? All in the space of, what, twenty minutes?' Pepper asks, her voice threaded through with disbelief. 'That man takes a week to write a press release. How on earth did he manage to coordinate a murder and plan a blackmail in less than half an hour?'

'He *did*.' I look at Lola again. She stares miserably back at me.

Michael is still turned away, his shoulders hunched over and his hands dug deep into his pockets. A terrible sense of foreboding washes over me.

'Michael?' I raise my eyebrows as he looks up.

'Yes, Michael?' Pepper says acerbically. 'What do you say?'

Lola clings to her dad's arm, her expression panic-stricken. Michael looks from me to Pepper.

'It seems obvious to me,' he says, 'that Hamish was obsessed with Lola and couldn't come to terms with her rejecting him. When she started dating Brendan it span him into a jealous frenzy. He made a plan to murder Brendan, then followed Lola, waiting for the right moment. When he saw Lola go into Brendan's house, he decided that moment had come. He was lucky over the coat, which Lola had left in the house by mistake, but his basic plan was always the same: to kill his rival and get Lola to sleep with him by blackmailing her with fake evidence that suggested she was the murderer.'

'That's right,' Lola says quickly.

Too quickly.

I frown, feeling uneasy. Is she still concealing something? I shake the thought off. She's surely just exhausted and wrung out and desperate for Pepper to believe her.

Pepper wrinkles her nose. 'I've worked with Hamish for two years. I can't believe he'd be capable of any of this.'

'He *was*,' Lola protests. 'He *is*.'

'He'd been stalking Lola for months,' Michael says. 'Ali and I found months' worth of photos of Lola on his laptop. They prove Hamish followed her everywhere.'

'It's true,' I add.

A look of shock crosses Pepper's face.

'That's why I went to his house just now,' I explain. 'Hamish agreed to give us the coat on condition he got his laptop back. Why would he have done that if there wasn't something incriminating on his computer?'

'So… you didn't go to the police with the photos, because Hamish had the coat?' Pepper says slowly.

'Because the photos make Hamish look like a predatory creep, but the coat makes Lola look guilty of murder?'

'Exactly,' I say.

'Don't you get it, Peps?' Michael asks. 'Hamish was right there that night, *and* he had a motive. *He's* Brendan's killer.'

Pepper looks at me. 'You really think so, Alison?'

I nod.

'Then we need to tell the police what we know,' Pepper says, starting to move away. 'Give them the context for that coat.'

'There's no point,' Lola says, her voice breaking on the words. 'It won't make any difference now. The coat you handed in to the police is that last bit of evidence DI Barnbury said he needed.' She holds up her fingers and counts off each point as she makes it. 'He's got one witness who supposedly heard me yelling at Brendan that I wanted to kill him, and another who claims he saw me leaving. And it doesn't matter that the second witness is anonymous and that the four of us know it was really Hamish, we don't have any proof of that, just as we don't have any proof he was stalking me.' Lola pauses. 'Worst of all, DI Barnbury has the murder knife from Mum's handbag – which he thinks I put there – and the coat I was wearing to Brendan's house the night he died, covered in Brendan's blood, which he's going to realise I lied about.' She looks up, her mouth trembling. 'I'm going to jail.'

'No.' Michael turns to her, his face grey and weary. 'It's not proof. None of it. We just need to hold our nerve and make sure the police understand how Hamish is responsible. How he targeted you from the start.'

'They'll just ask why I didn't tell them all that before,' Lola wails.

'We'll explain that he was blackmailing you.' Michael takes her hand. 'Remember, the only way he could have seen you at Brendan's was if he was there too. The only way he could have got your coat was if he arrived at Brendan's after you did, broke the video on the entry cam and made Brendan let him in. The only way he could have planted the knife was if he was the killer.'

Once again, I have the feeling that Michael is leaving out some big piece of the puzzle. 'Hamish has other explanations for those things,' I say. 'Lola's right. It will be her word against his.'

'We can still try,' Pepper urges. 'Come on, let's drive to the station right now.' She walks off, out of the park.

The three of us follow her. Lola is crying, trying to hide it. I take her hand and hold it as we walk. My mind cartwheels between questions: How could I have been so focused on what Brendan was doing to Lola that I completely failed to notice she was Hamish's victim too? How could a man I'd worked so closely with for two years be a stalker and an abuser and a killer? And how could the father of my children believe he was protecting me by keeping me in the dark about someone as evil as Hamish, especially when I saw him in our office every day?

Again, I get the strong sense that I'm missing something.

Pepper reaches her car first. She says she'll see us at the police station and then, with a final stern look, gets inside and drives off.

Michael, Lola and I walk on. My car is just up ahead. I don't know where Michael has parked. Lola's weeping turns into deep, chest-wracking sobs. I grip her hand more tightly. As we reach my car, Lola stops walking.

'It's no good,' she wails. 'I can't go to the police like Pepper wants. I can't do this anymore, it's too hard.'

I open my mouth to say, gently, that I don't think she has much of a choice. If she doesn't go to the police, they will almost certainly come for her. But before I can get out the words, Michael is speaking.

'You can do this, Lola.' His tone is soft, almost pleading. 'You just need to stick to our version of events.'

Our version of events?

That's a strange phrase to use. Why not say – *stick to what happened*? Or *stick to the truth*?

Because it *isn't* what happened. The realisation slams, hard, into my brain.

Their version isn't the truth.

THIRTY-SEVEN

I look up at Michael. He meets my gaze. I know he can see what I'm thinking. What I have suddenly understood.

He always could read me better than anyone.

Lola shrinks away from me, pulling her hand out of mine. The atmosphere between the three of us grows tense and tight.

'Ali.' Michael takes a deep breath. 'I'm so sorry.'

My mouth gapes as my mind runs over everything he has done since Brendan died; each separate action falling into place: the way he kindled my suspicions of Seb and Pepper; the way he manipulated me to steal Hamish's laptop; the way he has lied to me and hidden so much from me.

As the world shrinks to the guilt in his eyes, I realise the truth has been staring me in the face from the start.

'It was you?' I stammer at last. '*You* killed Brendan.'

There's a long silence, then Michael finally speaks.

'Yes.'

'Don't, Dad.' Lola's gasp is barely a whisper.

I focus on Michael. He has the strangest look in his eye. It's part embarrassment, part hopefulness, part anxiety. Bizarrely, it's almost the same look he had when he proposed.

I lean against the wall beside me, feeling weak. 'How?'

Michael draws himself up, lifting his chin very slightly. 'It... wasn't planned.'

I turn to Lola. 'Did you know about this?'

Lola nods, slowly. 'I was there.'

I draw my breath in sharply. '*What?*'

'Listen, Mum,' she says. 'That night, when I was on my way to Brendan's house, I called Dad. I don't know why, exactly, there was this bad feeling eating away at me. Part of me wanted to pull away from Brendan, like I told you, but when he stopped returning my calls and messages even though we were supposed to be going away together that weekend, I – I didn't know what to think. I couldn't focus on anything else, I was desperate.'

I shake my head. It's horrible how easily Brendan got under my confident Lola's skin. As easily as he got under mine, all those years ago.

'I couldn't call you, Mum,' Lola says, misinterpreting my gesture for disapproval. 'You're aways telling me how brilliant I am at everything, I didn't want to let you down by having you see how lost I'd got the minute I'd tried to do something for myself.'

Her words settle like stones in my stomach. Is this all my fault? Did I project too much positivity onto Lola? Did I set too high a bar for her to leap over? By keeping her close, while telling her how amazing she was, did I inadvertently limit her confidence instead of boosting it?

Lola steps back, letting Michael take over the story.

'As soon as Lola called, I set off for Brendan's straight away,' he explains. 'I avoided the front door – which I guess is why Hamish didn't spot me – because I didn't think Brendan would let me in. Instead, I climbed over the fence into his back garden and messaged Lola so she knew I was there. When she stumbled outside a few minutes later she was in tears. It – it was terrible, Ali. She was beside herself, one minute sobbing that she hated him for humiliating her, the next that she loved him and couldn't face the future without him.' He speaks faster, his voice jerky and full of emotion. 'Then Brendan appeared and saw me there and he made some comment about Lola being trash, which is when she shouted that she wanted to kill him. And I went over to him, told him to shut up and... and then he started laying into you as well.'

My throat tightens.

'Just ugly lies spilling out of him and then he said he had sex with you thirty years ago behind my back. That you were such a prick tease, leading him on. Something about a party, the bedroom with all the coats. Apparently I'd left already. And then how – this is how he put it – how you tried to "back out at the last minute" but he "knew" you didn't really mean it.'

'Oh, Michael.' Heat flushes my face.

'Lola had already told me you'd said he raped you.'

I stare at him. So he's known? All this time?

'Lola thought it was a ploy you'd invented to make her hate him and, though I was shocked you'd go that far, that's what I believed at first, too. But as I looked at Brendan in that moment, I knew without a shadow of doubt that what you'd said was true. I couldn't imagine the pain it had caused you.' Michael's face fills with hurt. 'I don't know what happened, it just all flared up inside me. How he'd lied to and abused you both. And there he was, just calmly turning away from me and sauntering back into his house. I saw red. I went into the kitchen and the knife block was there and before I knew what my hands were doing, I'd taken a knife and lashed out and I honestly didn't mean to kill him. It was just a random slash at his leg. But I knew as soon as the blood started flooding out of him that… that he couldn't survive losing so much, so fast.'

Horror fills me. I turn to Lola. 'Did you see all this?'

She nods.

'Lola wanted to call an ambulance, but Brendan was already almost gone,' Michael explains. 'I don't— I started thinking, fast. *Too* fast, maybe. I told Lola to destroy the entry cam, I thought that would make it look like someone else went into the house after her. She'd got blood on her coat and I was worried my DNA would be on the knife even though I'd wiped it, so I knew we needed to get rid of both of them and that we also needed to get ourselves out of there as fast as possible, but our footprints were in the garden, and my main priority was to get Lola away.'

'I took the coat and knife and put them in a bin bag,' Lola explains. 'I dumped them in a waste bin a few streets away – that's where Hamish found them, then I came home.'

'I got rid of our footprints by raking over the earth in the garden,' Michael says. 'Then I left too. The whole thing was stupid, but I was panicking.' He looks away, his face wreathed in shame.

'Oh my God,' I gasp. 'All the lies you told… How *could* you? Not just to me but what about Lola?' An angry heat rises from my chest, burning my throat. 'How could you put your own daughter through all those interrogations and the upset and stress of being a murder suspect?'

'No, Mum, no—' Lola tries to cut in.

'You *coward*, Michael!' The words burst out of me. 'You pathetic, lying *coward*.'

Michael hangs his head.

'You're not being fair, Mum,' Lola says sharply. '*I* asked Dad to keep quiet. The police already knew I was at Brendan's. I could have been done as an accessory anyway if… if the truth came out.'

Michael looks up, his face riven with shame. 'You're right, Ali,' he says heavily. 'Of course you are, but at the time I wasn't thinking straight and, once Lola and I had started telling lies, it was impossible to stop. I kept thinking the police would realise Lola was innocent and move on.'

'But they didn't, they *haven't*,' I spit. 'And still, instead of coming clean, you put all your energies into pretending to investigate Brendan's contacts and suggesting Seb might be the murderer and later going along with me over Pepper, and… and now with Hamish. Trying to convince everyone he's the murderer, when you know—'

'Listen, Ali.' Michael's voice is suddenly steely. 'I'm sorry for lying to you and, believe me, I'm very sorry for everything Lola has had to go through, but one thing I'm not sorry about is putting the blame on Hamish. He totally abused his position with Lola to manipulate her. He's been trying to blackmail her into sleeping with him for weeks. He's just as much of an evil bastard as Brendan ever was; he *deserves* to go down for murder.'

I slowly shake my head. This feels surreal. How can Michael have killed someone? How can so much have happened without me having a single clue about it? A deep sense of misery rolls darkly inside me. I'm as blind and stupid as Pepper and Hamish both said I was.

'We *couldn't* tell you,' Michael says, clearly sensing my thoughts. 'It wasn't fair to drag you into the mess I'd made. We had to keep it to just the two of us, or everything would have unravelled.'

I press my lips together, emotions swirling and tumbling inside me.

'Lola and I talked a lot,' Michael goes on. 'We went over and over what had happened that night, all through those first couple of days, making sure we had our stories straight.'

'I thought you were *comforting* her,' I say bitterly.

'I know it sounds terrible, but it honestly seemed like the only way to keep us both out of jail,' Michael says, his voice deep and pleading. 'You have to believe that if I'd thought Lola was ever in danger of spending a single night locked in a cell, I would have come clean in a heartbeat. That was a total red line for me.'

I look at him. He's telling the truth about that at least, I'm sure of it.

'We can make sure Hamish goes down for this, Ali.' Michael moves closer, swallowing up the ground between us. He looks deep into my eyes. 'So long as we keep our stories straight, we should be—'

'No.' I take a step away from him. 'No, Michael. No more lies. It's not right.' I glance at our daughter. 'It's not fair on Lola.'

She meets my gaze, her lip trembling. 'I don't want Dad to go to jail.'

'I know.' I take her hand. 'But Dad doesn't want *you* to go to jail and I think the risk of that is too high if you keep trying to pin this on Hamish.' I pause. 'I've heard his version of events and its plausible. *He's* plausible. What's more—' I turn to Michael, 'what's more, when the truth finally *does* come out, as I'm sure it will, Lola is highly likely to face prosecution for obstruction of justice, as well as accessory to murder. The only way to avoid that is to have you both come clean now.'

'You're saying…' His voice is hollow. 'You're suggesting I should hand myself in to the police?'

'Come *on*,' I say, my voice rising. '*You* did this, Michael, *you* killed Brendan. You forced Lola to cover it up.' I pause. 'Now you need to take responsibility for that. Admit you killed Brendan. Make it clear Lola had nothing to do with it, that she wanted to tell the police but you *bullied* her into keeping quiet.'

'Ah,' says Michael, his voice sinking with resignation. 'I see. Yes, that would work.'

'But you *didn't* bully me, it was what I wanted.' Lola lets out a deep sob. 'No, you can't, Daddy.'

I wait, watching Michael. There's a long pause, then he reaches out and takes Lola's free hand, so she is standing between us – like she used to when she was a child, holding onto our hands and urging us to swing her along the path.

'Mum's right,' he says at last, his voice full of feeling. 'This is the only way.'

My throat is dry, emotions tumbling through me.

'Are you sure, Daddy?' Lola asks, her voice tiny.

'Of course.' Michael's eyes glisten. 'Remember what I told you, Babycakes?' He squeezes her hand. 'I'd do anything for you.'

Lola nods.

I take a deep breath. 'Then it's decided,' I say. 'We tell the truth.'

THIRTY-EIGHT

ONE YEAR LATER

It's taken a long time, but life – at last – feels like it's back to normal. Well, a new normal.

Things are different at home: Lola is in her first term doing a Politics course at East Sussex university. She's come a long way in the past year, almost back to the happy, confident girl she was before she met Brendan. Not quite, though. There's still a darkness behind her eyes – a shadow that comes from his loss, from knowing that her father killed him, from keeping her dad's secret for so long. Even so, on an everyday level you'd never know how much sadness lurks under the surface. She calls me every few days, to let me know how well she's getting on with her course and about the new friends she's been making. We're closer than ever.

Josh and I are close too, on our own at home we rub along together with few tensions. I insist on us sharing an evening meal together, otherwise I let him be. He struggled, at first, to come to terms with what his father has done, but now he seems to understand and accept it; Brendan hurt Lola and Michael lashed out at Brendan. The death was an accident. I think Nadia, who he's still dating, has really helped him with that.

Anyway, so long as Josh keeps up with his schoolwork and lets me know where he is, I don't fuss around him too much. If there's one thing I learned with Lola, sometimes you keep your children closer when you let them roam.

I'm back to work at HOPP four days a week, which suits me perfectly. Pepper and I are as tight as we ever were. Pepper fired Hamish with no reference – both Michael and I testified to his stalking of Lola, which is now on police record, and Lola gave a statement about him blackmailing her. But, as there was no evidence to support the blackmail claim, a case was never made and, pretty soon, Hamish vanished from our lives. Pepper recently hired a new assistant – an eager graduate in her late twenties called Rosie who fits in well and – hilariously – has recently started asking me for dating advice. I haven't seen Seb since the day he picked up his things. Thanks to Brendan's mother and her solicitor, he has recently been recompensed for all the money I took – with interest, if you include the small payments I'd given him up to that point. I'm not dating anyone new.

There's been a police investigation into all the claims about Brendan's abusive behaviour – and I've spoken publicly about it at last. I wish I'd felt able to talk years ago; to share my story. What has helped the most is hearing the stories of the other women who came forward after his death. Somehow knowing that his abuse was part of a pattern, and that I wasn't the only person who suffered, has made it easier to bear.

I visit Michael in prison every couple of weeks. It took me a while to stop being angry with him, especially over making Lola an accomplice. But once it was clear the police had, at last, stopped investigating her, our lives settled down a bit and recently I've started to feel more sympathetic. Thankfully, Michael's clever lawyers managed to get the charges reduced so, despite his attempt to cover up his crime, we're hoping that, with good behaviour, he'll be out in five or six years. Josh and Lola visit him with me sometimes. Josh once a month or so and Lola whenever she's back from uni.

She's home right now, for the weekend, and her footsteps echo through the ground floor as she pads across the hall towards the kitchen where I'm sitting at our table, sipping at my tea and gazing out at the garden. It's freezing cold; a dull, grey day with frost still sprinkled over the tips of the grass. Upstairs Josh is still asleep. It's good to have both of them under my roof.

'Hey, sweetheart.' I smile as she walks in, tousled haired and still in her pyjamas, a warm jumper pulled on over the top and thick wool socks on her feet.

'Hey, Mum.' She makes for the kettle and is soon busy fixing a pot of coffee and a round of toast and almond butter.

She takes the chair opposite me, tucks her legs under her and gets out her phone. We sit in companionable silence for a minute or two, then I say:

'I'm going to see Dad later,' I say. 'Do you want to come?'

Lola grunts something indecipherable. She doesn't look up.

'Lola?'

She looks up slowly. 'I don't know Mum…' She makes a face. 'I've got loads of work to get through.'

I frown. 'It's only a couple of hours.'

Lola turns her head, gazing out through the window to our soggy back garden. 'Maybe…' she says, in a tone that is clearly an attempt to pacify me so we can move on.

I frown. 'Why don't you want to see him?'

'I do,' Lola says, setting down her phone. 'I just…' She hesitates. 'It just makes me feel guilty.'

I stare at her. 'Guilty about what?'

We look at each other for a long moment.

'Nothing,' Lola says. A strange look crosses her face. Part misery, part frustration, part shame.

Mostly guilt.

And then she looks me straight in the eye and says, 'Believe me, Mum, you don't want to know.' She spins around and hurries away.

Her words hang in the air. And even as part of me is asking myself what she means, part of me already knows. Perhaps, at some level, has always known. Because, as I sit in front of my cold tea, a memory I had forgotten flits across my mind's eye: Michael looking at Lola that day everything came out, then saying in a low, serious voice as he squeezed her hand:

Babycakes, I'd do anything for you.

What was he really talking about?

I push the question away. Lola's right, I don't want to know.

Instead, I go back into the kitchen and clear away the breakfast things – and, when the time comes for our visit to Michael in prison, I gather up Josh but leave Lola in her room, free.

Acknowledgements

Huge thanks to my editor Siân Heap and the entire team at Canelo, including Miles Poynton, Kate Shepherd, Nicola Piggott, Deirbhile Brennan, Thanhmai Bui-Van, Micaela Cavaletto and Felix Janosik. Also to my agent Eli Keren and the following writers whose feedback helped me shape this story in its early stages: Lou Kuenzler, Moira Young, Gaby Halberstam, Melanie Edge, Julie Mackenzie. A particular and heartfelt thanks to Eoin, who keeps me sane and cheerful while I'm writing. And to the various blended families of which I'm a part, for providing some of the inspiration for this book, especially to Joe, for whom I'd do (almost) anything.